Wayne Dundee's
THE BURNING SEASON

"Mike Hammer is alive and well, operating out of Rockford, Illinois." —Andrew H. Vachss, author of *Flood* and *Strega*

"Impressive . . . ambitious . . . blessed with a voice as clear and pure as a midwestern breeze. Joe Hannibal, Wayne Dundee's tough but human detective, brings a blue-collar sensibility to the genre that is as refreshing as it is real."
—Max Allan Collins, author of *Neon Mirage*

"If you're a fan of the private-eye genre, then Wayne Dundee's *The Burning Season* is for you. He takes the private eye Joe Hannibal through his hard-boiled paces with great verve and enthusiasm."
—Joe. R. Lansdale, author of *Act of Love*

"In Joe Hannibal, Wayne Dundee has created a tough, relentless, no-frills hero—a blue-collar private eye for the eighties and beyond. *The Burning Season* is fast, hard, explosive, and satisfying."
—Bill Pronzini, author of *Jackpot* and *Shackles*

Wayne D. Dundee

The Burning Season

A DELL BOOK

This is for Pam
and Michelle—
who else?

And in memory of my mother and her mother
before her, both of whom would have understood
Flo Odum.

Published by
Dell Publishing
a division of
Bantam Doubleday Dell Publishing Group, Inc.
666 Fifth Avenue
New York, New York 10103

ISBN: 0-440-20717-7

Reprinted by arrangement with St. Martin's Press

Printed in the United States of America

Published simultaneously in Canada

November 1990

10 9 8 7 6 5 4 3 2 1

OPM

ACKNOWLEDGMENTS

The path a writer travels is, ultimately, a lonely one. But if you're real lucky—as I have been—you may encounter along the way those who make the journey far easier than it might otherwise have been.

My thanks to the following, who, each in his own special way, helped and encouraged a big, plodding, stubborn farmboy to realize a dream:

Bob Randisi

Max Collins

Todd Moore

Ray Peekner

and, last but by no means least, Ed Gorman

While Hatchaloo County is, for the record, a mythical place, Williamson County is very real and the historical events mentioned in Chapter 14 were gleaned from two excellent books on the subject:

War in Illinois by Donald Bain © 1978, Prentice-Hall, Inc.

Bloody Williamson by Paul M. Angle © 1983, Alfred A. Knopf

"The melancholy days are come, the saddest of the year,
Of wailing winds, and naked woods, and meadows brown and sere."

—William Cullen Bryant,
Death of the Flowers

"When the house of your neighbor is on fire, your own is in danger."

—*a proverb*

1

When Junior Odum turned from his mother's grave, I stepped out of the shadow of the gnarled old cemetery oak and stood where he could plainly see me. The low-hanging full moon cast bluish highlights up and down the barrel of the .45 automatic I held leveled on him.

Odum's gaze went first to the gun, hung there a long moment, then lifted to my face. His expression remained impassive. He was a tall rawboned man of thirty, with unruly carrot-colored hair, pale deepset eyes, and freckles the size of kernels of corn sprinkled on either side of a blunt nose. A single, half-dried tear track ran crookedly down one cheek.

"So," he said at length, "you came for me."

I nodded. "That I did."

"Figured somebody might. You at the funeral this afternoon?"

"I was around."

"Figured that, too. Reason I waited to . . . say my good-byes. Thing I didn't figure, I guess, was that anybody'd be stubborn enough to hang around so long watchin' for me."

He had no way of knowing how close I'd been to relinquishing my vigil only moments before he finally showed.

Patience isn't generally my strong suit, but every now and then I can pull it off. I'd returned to the isolated rural cemetery shortly before dark, some three hours after the graveside service for Flo Odum had concluded. I parked my car in the weedy driveway of an abandoned farmhouse a couple hills away, then hiked across untended fields and through stands of timber in the fading sunlight, approaching the cemetery from the back side. I'm no Daniel Boone, but I hunted enough rabbits and squirrels as a kid to have learned something about how to move in the woods. And while a good share of my adult life has been spent hunting a different kind of game in largely urban settings, many of the same techniques apply.

I stayed inside the tree line at the edge of the graveyard for a long time, watching, waiting, moving up to tuck myself into the deep shadows at the base of the oak only after it was full dark. The man who had hired me was convinced that Junior Odum would hear of his mother's passing and would come out of hiding long enough to pay his last respects. After reviewing Odum's jacket, I tended to agree. Hence my willingness to travel the length of the state to cover that eventuality, and my client's willingness to pay the freight for same. The fact that the fugitive was a no-show at the funeral proved only that his grief hadn't overcome his survival instinct; I was still willing to bet a few uncomfortable hours that he'd put in an appearance as soon as he thought the coast was clear. When midnight came and went with no sign of him, however, I began to wonder if I was squatted there gathering dew for nothing. The fact that my pocket flask had run dry and I was suffering the pangs of a second- or third-stage nicotine fit hadn't helped my resolve any. It was down to a toss-up between which would arrive first, one A.M. or my decision to call it quits, when Odum came slipping through the moonlight.

"For what it's worth," I said now, "I'm sorry about your mother. Bracing a man at his parents' graveside is pretty low on my list of favorite things. But I've got a job to do, and you learn to take the shit with the sugar."

Odum grunted. "Boy, ain't that the truth." He regarded me closely for a minute, then gave a small nod, as if reaching a conclusion about something. "Decent of you, though, to stand by until after I had some time with her."

I shrugged, said nothing.

Odum eyed me some more. "You ain't no regular cop, are you?"

"Just the private kind," I answered. "Your bail bondsman brought me into this when he heard what happened. He had a hunch you'd show for the funeral."

"Hazelford. Cold-hearted old fucker. But I guess I can't blame him, can I? He played square with me and then I stuck it to him when I skipped. Felt kinda bad about that, I really did, but there was no way on God's green earth any judge or jury was gonna *not* put me behind bars. I decided I could handle a little remorse over skippin' my bail better than I could handle another hitch in the joint."

"If that was your plan, then you should have picked a different bondsman. Cyrus Hazelford has been on the scene too long. You don't last all the years he has by letting guys skip on you. He's got a long memory and a lot of contacts and a lot of favors owed."

"And he's got you, his top gun, his bounty hunter, huh?"

I shook my head. "I'm nobody's top gun. I'm a licensed private detective. I do bounty work for Hazelford and a few others as fill-in once in a while. Sorry to disillusion you, but that's all it amounts to."

"Some guys make a livin' at it, though, don't they? Bounty huntin', I mean."

"Pick a subject. Somebody, somewhere, sometime has figured out a way to make a living at it."

"You know, maybe there's somethin' I could have got behind—bounty huntin'. My biggest problem, see, has always been that I just could never hack the bullshit they dish out in the workaday world. Punch some silly-ass clock, have some cigar-breathed fuckin' foreman who ain't smart enough to blow his nose if brains was dynamite tell you when you can take a piss and when you can eat and when—"

"Save your breath, Junior," I cut in. "I'm sure you've got plenty of good reasons for robbing gas stations and liquor stores instead of working for a paycheck like everybody else, but I'm not interested in hearing them. Not right now anyway. We've got a long drive ahead of us, you can tell me all about it then. Speaking of which, my car is about a mile from here so—"

"*You* save *your* breath, Mr. Bounty Hunter. You ain't takin' nobody no damn where!"

The new voice—female, intense, coming from somewhere only a few yards in back of me—rocked me like a blindside punch. Cursing inwardly, I fought the instinctive urge to spin toward it. I'd relaxed my guard after getting the drop on my quarry, had allowed somebody to sneak up behind me! But the fact that my .45 was still trained on Odum left me a trump card—one I couldn't afford to throw away by diverting my attention.

Our eyes locked, Odum's and mine. Half of his mouth curved into a sly, cautious smile.

Clouds skitted across the face of the moon overhead, causing shadows to leap in and out among the tombstones around us.

After several beats, I said, "Looks like I'm the one who didn't have all the angles figured."

"What you got behind you," Odum replied, "is a cousin of mine named Reba. She's just a little bit of a thing but it happens she's packin' a powerful big ol' shotgun."

"And it's aimed square at the back of your fuckin' head," Reba herself added. "Anytime I take the notion, I can blow your pumpkin clean off."

In a voice I managed to keep a hell of a lot calmer than I

actually felt, I said, "That's a real unpleasant thought. Here's another: This .45 I'm holding has a hair trigger and the body jerk I'd make if hit by a shotgun blast would undoubtedly cause it to go off and cut your cousin in half. The only question would be which of us—or pieces of us—would hit the ground first. If you're anxious to find out the answer, go ahead and shoot."

Reba snorted derisively. "Talk about your sorry-ass bluffs."

Odum was still watching me intently, still wearing that cautious half smile. "I ain't so sure," he said. "I'm lookin' straight in this sucker's eyes, cuz, and I don't think he's bluffin' at all."

"So what are you sayin'? You expect me to just back off and let him haul you in? I came here to cover your ass, not stand by and whistle 'So Long It's Been Good to Know You.' "

"And I appreciate that. All I'm sayin' is that if it comes to gunplay I got a feeling this big mother *would* find a way to take one or both of us out with him."

"Looks like what we've got here," I said, "is your basic Mexican standoff."

"Fuck your Mexican standoff!" Reba hurled back. "I say I can blow you the fuck away anytime I want and there ain't a damn thing you can do about it."

Odum gave me one of those "What are you gonna do?" looks and said, "Ain't it a fright the way youngsters pick up the bad language these days and flat refuse to listen to advice from their elders?" Then his eyes hardened and his gaze shifted past me, toward the spot where the girl's voice was coming from. "Now you just back up a corn row or two, Reba June Dallas, and quit talkin' like you ain't got a lick of sense. This man's a professional, not some beer-brave redneck you can hoorah with a lot of big talk. His name's Joe Hannibal, he's a licensed P.I., and he's got hisself quite a reputation up north there where I was. His showin' up down here now might could turn out to be a good thing for us if you'll just hold your tongue and let me do the talking."

Nobody said anything for a while. The only sounds were the night noises—country night noises; the kind I hadn't heard much of since I was a boy growing up on my grandparents' farm in Wisconsin. Crickets chirruping in the tall grass of the pasture that bordered the cemetery, bullfrogs ratcheting over along the river, fat September mosquitoes thrumming through the air. The town of Cedarton was a smattering of silent lights off to the north and in between, on some obscured stretch of back road, teenaged drag racers were shouting and squealing tires. Somewhere a dog howled in response. It all seemed an incongruous setting for drawn guns and harsh threats.

But the itch at the base of my skull—the approximate spot where Reba's shotgun was aimed—wouldn't let me stay lost in reverie for very long.

"Sounds as if you know a little more about me than you let on, friend," I said to Junior Odum.

He shrugged noncommittally. "I didn't place you at first, not until you mentioned you were a private cop. Hate to spoil my illiterate hillbilly image, but I tend to follow the newspapers pretty close wherever I'm at. You grab your share of ink up there in and around Rockford."

"So did you for awhile," I reminded him. "The Good Ol' Boy Bandit himself."

But he didn't want to get into that. "How about it, Hannibal? You willin' to talk a deal?"

My turn to shrug. "Maybe. I'm not sure you've got anything to deal with, but I'm willing to listen."

"What I got to deal with is this: it's a hell of a ways from Hatchaloo County back to Rockford. We're at one end of the state, it's at the other, and Illinois is one long damn stretch of real estate. *If* you figure a way to get me out of here past Reba's shotgun, you still got near four hundred miles to haul me. And if I've a mind to, I guarantee I can make that a pain-in-the-ass, fight-you-every-inch-of-the-way trip you'll wish you'd never started."

"Uh-huh. And the alternative to that charming scenario?"

"You do a job of work for me while you're down here. It's somethin' I can't very well take care of myself on account of bein' a fugitive and all, and somethin' your snooper skills should make you better suited for anyway. You do that, then I go back peaceful as a lamb. Hell, I'll even drive the car, you can stick your feet out the window and nap in the back seat if you want."

"Sure. And I'll just take your word on all that, huh?"

His eyes hardened into the same look he'd given Reba before. "I may be a wanted man, Hannibal. I may have stuck up those liquor stores and gas stations and I may even have chunked a couple of those damn fools on the head when they gave me no choice—but I never in my life went back on my word. I stole when I couldn't find honest work but I never took from a place that couldn't afford the loss and when I did take I always looked somebody straight in the eye, stuck a gun in their belly, and told them what was what. I never took advantage of anybody by lyin' or cheatin' or skulkin' around behind their backs. Maybe it all comes under the same heading for you, but in my book there's a big difference."

Don't ask me to explain it. I'm a born-again skeptic who's laughed in the face of a hell of a lot slicker pitches than that one, but this time for some reason my reaction was different. And it had to do with more than the shotgun at my back. Something about the tall young man with his knocked-around Howdy Doody features and his earnest pale eyes reached me. Maybe it was helped along by the uneasiness I felt over having waylaid him at his parents' graveside in the first place. Or maybe the rural setting had stirred my boyhood memories deeply enough to unearth some still innocent, still naive part of me that hadn't yet been soured on mankind. Or maybe I just read too damn many Robin Hood stories when I was a kid. Like I said, don't ask me to explain it because I can't.

All I know is that fifteen minutes later, after I'd heard the rest of what he had to say, I walked away from that cemetery without Junior Odum in my custody. I went one way, Odum and Reba Dallas—a tomboyish replica of her cousin, with an ancient twelve gauge slung across one shoulder—went another. I'd agreed to spend forty-eight hours on Junior's "job of work." At the end of that time—whether I was successful or not—he'd given his word to return peaceably with me.

That's right, his word.

They were without question the most bizarre circumstances under which I had ever taken on a client.

When I got back to my car, before turning the key in the ignition, I frowned at my dome light illuminated reflection in the rearview mirror and said, "Have you gone soft in the goddamn head or what?"

2

Gus Wilt, the sheriff of Hatchaloo County, seemed to be cast from a mold made in direct contradiction to the big-bellied, saggy-jowled southern sheriff stereotype. He was a lean, sixtyish man of average height, with a deeply seamed face and a bristly white mustache that lent a subtle touch of flamboyance to his otherwise sober demeanor. He moved slow and talked slow in a soft southern accent, and only his eyes, dark and quick beneath a ledge of cottony brows, hinted that here could be a very dangerous individual to cross.

"Mr. Hannibal," he said as I entered his office for the second time in as many days and took a seat at his gesture. "Not to sound inhospitable, but I expected we'd seen the last of you yesterday when your man failed to show."

Following SOP for bounty work, I'd checked in with the local authorities upon my arrival in Hatchaloo County the previous day, displaying papers detailing Boyd Odum Junior's wanted status and stating my intent to try and bring him in under the auspices of the century-old Supreme Court ruling that made bail skips fair game to virtually anyone acting in the interest of the court. I'd paid enough similar visits to various police departments over the years to have learned that, Supreme Court ruling or no, bounty hunters are not generally welcomed with open arms. Nor are private detectives, for that matter; making me a sort of double pariah. So I've learned to approach such encounters expecting the worst.

My reception by Sheriff Wilt, however, had been courteous and respectful in a businesslike manner. After advising me that his men were also on the lookout for Odum and that my actions could in no way interfere with their performance of duty, he went on to say that in the event I got a line on the fugitive first, his department would be willing to render assistance if needed. This morning I'd test how sincere all of that apparent professional courtesy had been.

"Looks like I'll be around a while longer, Sheriff," I said. "Another day or two anyway."

Wilt leaned back in his spring-tilt chair, fingers laced across flat stomach. "You still figure Junior Odum's going to show?" His brows lifted to a height of mild curiosity, but beneath them his eyes showed sharper interest.

"I doubt it," I answered. "In order for it to mean anything, his presence here should have been at—or at least near—the time of the funeral. We both know he never made it to the church or graveside services, and I even went back and staked out the cemetery until midnight last night without a nibble."

It wasn't a lie. Not exactly. By midnight, Odum *hadn't* shown up at the cemetery.

Wilt rocked back and forth ever so slightly in his chair. "Reckon I agree with you. Can't see no reason for Junior to poke his head up out of whatever hideyhole he's dug for himself—not anymore now. He's too well known around these parts. And not particularly well liked. Most everybody's heard about him being wanted for those robberies up north and there are plenty of folks who'd be more than happy to turn him in if they ever caught sight of him. Which is probably what kept him away in the first place. And that, I'd say, brings us round about to just why *are* you staying in

Hatchaloo County, Mr. Hannibal?" He paused, smiled faintly. "Again, not to sound inhospitable."

"Well," I said. "I'm changing hats."

"Changing hats?"

"It's an expression. I'm taking off my bounty hunter hat, putting on my private eye one. You see, certain members of Flo Odum's family have approached me and asked me to look into the circumstances surrounding her death."

Wilt digested this. He blinked a couple times. Slowly. "Members of Flo's family, you say. That takes in a pretty sizable chunk of population hereabouts, Mr. Hannibal. There's Odums and Dallases—that was her maiden name— scattered all over this county and most of the ones bordering it. The Odums are all cut pretty much from the same cloth —hard drinkers, hell-raisers, not much on holding down regular jobs. Not really *bad* folks, I guess, but what my Aunt Beulah, the schoolmarm, might have called ne'er-do-wells. The Dallases, on the other hand, they cover a lot wider range. They got their share of hell-raisers, too, but they also got folks serving on a couple different city councils, some park boards, and over in Williamson County, young Leroy Dallas is even wearing a deputy sheriff's badge these days. So you see, when you tell me 'members of Flo Odum's family' you really ain't telling me a whole hell of a lot. Care to narrow it down some?"

I shook my head. "No, as a matter of fact I don't. Not right now, anyway. It comes under the heading of Client Confidentiality."

"Client Confidentiality." He repeated the two words, pronouncing the second in deliberately clipped syllables. "Got a real impressive ring to it, I'll say that. Does it hold water up north there where you usually operate?"

"Far as I'm concerned it holds water wherever I go. If it didn't, I wouldn't stay in business for very long."

Wilt abruptly let his chair snap level and leaned forward, bringing his palms and forearms to rest on the desktop. "I'm going to do you a favor, Mr. Hannibal. I'm going to make your job real simple. I'm going to do those confidential clients a favor, too, by saving them all the money they'd spend having you chase your tail. Here goes. The circumstances surrounding Flo Odum's death are these: she fell asleep in bed one night with a lit cigarette in her hand and burnt herself up. Period. You're welcome."

"Did you conduct a thorough arson investigation?"

"I conducted a thorough investigation, yes."

"That's not what I asked."

"Hatchaloo County does not have a full-fledged arson unit, if that's what you're driving at."

"But surely you must have access to one. From a neighboring county, or from Springfield?"

"Of course I have access to one—if and when it's warranted."

"You don't feel circumstances surrounding Mrs. Odum's death warranted an arson investigation?"

"I just *told* you all the circumstances of Flo Odum's death. Where the hell was the need for an arson unit? Flo smoked like a chimney, always had, and she was getting up in years. Here lately she'd developed the bad and dangerous habit of nodding off with a cigarette going. She'd do it while sitting and watching the TV, she'd do it while rocking on her front porch, she'd even do it while riding in the car when the Pettibones picked her up for church on Sunday mornings. Her family damn well knows all that. Everybody who knew her knew she didn't hardly have an apron or dress left that wasn't full of burn holes, and wasn't an easy chair in her living room that didn't have at least one scorched spot on the arm or seat cushion. It was a sad and tragic thing the way she died, but it was an accident. What makes it hard for some people to accept, I guess, is that it was the kind of accident you could see a-coming, but there wasn't a blessed thing you could do about it."

"What about the threats she received during the weeks

just prior to her death?" I persisted. "Do you dispute the
fact that her refusal to sell land to Cord Toys had an awful
lot of people around here angry and upset?"

"First off, all I know about are some *alleged* threats. Nobody saw fit to tell me about them when they supposedly
happened, didn't come up until after Flo was gone. As for
the other, well, yeah, when Flo refused to sell her property
and Clayton Cord started making noises about moving his
whole factory if he wasn't able to expand, plenty of folks
who depend on Cord Toys for their livelihood naturally got
upset. A lot of them cussed Flo Odum, but just as many
cussed Clayton Cord. After all, he was the one threatening
to take away the jobs. But his house is still standing just as
big and bright and shiny as ever, and last time I saw him he
looked fit as a fiddle. Christamighty, you sound like you
think some wild-eyed mob went out and torched Flo's place
with her in it."

"I just think the timing of her death was pretty damned
convenient for a lot of people, that's all. Who has control of
the land now?"

"Her daughter Pearl, as it turns out. After Boyd Senior
finally drank himself to death last month, Flo got in touch
with young Andy Gritmeier and drew herself up a will.
Didn't make no big deal out of it, nobody even knew about
it at the time she done it. Excepting Andy, of course. It was
another one of those things that only came out after Flo was
gone. But surely you ain't accusing Pearl of burning up her
own ma to get that piece of land?"

"I'm not accusing anybody of anything. But tell me this:
if Cord Toys makes Pearl the same offer they made her
mother, is she likely to turn it down?"

The sheriff shook his head without hesitation. "Not likely
at all. You got to remember now, this piece of land we're
talking about ain't exactly Southfork or the Ponderosa. It
ain't nothing but clay bottom with a bunch of scraggly jack
pines. The only thing that makes it worth looking at twice is

that it's turned out to be in a sort of strategic location because Clayton Cord wants to go bigger and that's the only direction he's got to go. Hell, Flo's own husband was more than willing to sell. Boyd Senior was what you might call the classic example of one of them ne'er-do-well Odums I mentioned before. Never had more than a handful of dollars in his pocket at any one time in his life; you can imagine how Cord's offer sounded to him. And Flo, being the kind of wife she was, never argued it none. Leastways not in public. But after Boyd Senior was gone—and when I say he drank himself to death, I mean that literally; the doc'd been warning him for years to cut back on his liquor but when the toy factory made its offer, Boyd just couldn't resist celebrating so hard it brought on the stroke that killed him— well, that's when Flo showed she had a mind of her own. No papers had been signed yet, see, and when Cord's lawyers went out to get that taken care of, Flo politely but firmly told them she wasn't interested. That land had been give to her and Boyd as a wedding present from her daddy and after spending so many years on it she said she reckoned she'd go ahead and live out the rest of her time there."

"Which didn't amount to very damn long."

"Not the way it turned out, no."

"And the timing—the coincidence of it all—doesn't strike you as the least bit suspicious?"

Wilt sighed heavily. "Mr. Hannibal, if I got worked up over everything in this life that made me suspicious, I'd be a real agitated man. Without a shred of hard evidence pointing toward any kind of foul play, I got no call to spend this county's time or money on any further investigation into Flo Odum's death."

"Is there any call to spend the county's time and money blocking me then?"

"Meaning what?"

"Meaning I'd like to do some poking around in this matter. You mind?"

"You've got a state-issued license, how could I stop you if I did mind?"

"Come on, Sheriff. We both know how things operate in the real world. In the city, I might be able to conduct an investigation without police sanction for days before anyone caught on. Down here, you're not only going to know every time I fart but you're going to know which way I was facing and what direction the wind was blowing when I did it. If you decide you don't want me stinking up the countryside, you'll be able to come up with a dozen different ways—all perfectly legal—to shut off my gas."

Again the faint smile, this time with perhaps a hint of smugness. "Appears you do know how things work in the real world."

He said nothing further for a full minute. We sat regarding each other across the desktop. Wilt lifted his right hand and smoothed the ends of his mustache with the ball of his thumb. When he placed his palm back down flat, he said, "It's to your credit, Mr. Hannibal, that you came to me each time you figured you had business in my county and told me face on what you were about. I like that. I appreciate it. It sticks in my craw some that I don't know who your client is, but I guess I can live with that. A few years back it probably would have been cause enough for me to send you packing. Seems I've mellowed with age. So go ahead and you do your poking around. But hear this: you start stepping on toes—especially the *wrong* toes—I might be forced to change my mind. Comes to that, you'll be the first to know and I'll expect my telling you to be the end of it."

3

It was ten A.M. when I quit the stubby white brick building that housed the sheriff's department, jail, and various Hatchaloo County public service agencies. The morning was sunny, unduly warm for late September, and downtown Cedarton seemed to be bustling. I paused against the retaining wall that girded the front lawn of the county building, lit a cigarette, and contemplated what my next move should be.

Gaining the sanction of Sheriff Wilt had been a vital first step in whatever progress I was going to be able to make on Junior Odum's behalf. I hadn't planned anything beyond that because without Wilt's cooperation, since I wasn't kidding when I said I know of no way to discreetly conduct an effective investigation in a rural or small-town setting, I would have gotten about as far as the proverbial snowball we've all heard of.

I decided now would be a good time to sit down and map out some course of action and I decided a good place to do that would be in the diner across the street, the one whose cooking aromas were already tugging my nose in that direction. I hadn't eaten any breakfast, having tossed and turned in my lumpy motel-room bed long after returning from the cemetery last night, and then, when I finally did get to sleep, snoring past my intended wake-up time this morning.

There were no other customers in the diner when I entered. I hoped that wasn't a bad sign. A plump but pretty blond waitress and a guy in a T-shirt and white apron whom I took to be the cook were seated at the far end of the counter, hunched over cigarettes and cups of coffee.

I slid into a booth and snapped open a menu encased in foggy plastic. I heard the waitress heave a weary sigh and after a couple minutes she came over.

"G'mornin'. What can I get you?"

"Too late to order breakfast?"

"Nope. We serve breakfast anytime."

"Okay, I'll have the number six special then. Eggs over easy, but tell your cook to fry the sausage until he thinks it's burnt, then fry it some more. And a side order of American fries." To hell with cholesterol, I figure lead poisoning or nuclear winter is going to get me before hardening of the arteries ever has a chance.

"Coffee?"

"A potful."

She jotted the necessary hieroglyphics onto a standard green pad, carried it over to the guy in the apron. He glanced at it, disappeared into the back, and in a little while I heard the snapping hiss of the sausage patties hitting the hot grill.

I waited until I had some coffee in front of me, then took the pen and spiral notebook from my shirt pocket and began scribbling some hieroglyphics of my own. I'd been bombarded by names, dates, facts, and allegations in the last ten hours—all revolving around the death of Flo Odum; if I was going to have any luck untangling it all in order to determine if her death was intentional rather than an accident, I figured the first thing I'd better do was get some of the data down on paper so I could keep straight in my head who was who and where they fit—or seemed to fit—in the overall picture.

Junior Odum and Gus Wilt had told me essentially the same story. The difference lay in their interpretation of the events; that, and in the personal demons Junior was admittedly hoping to exorcise through me.

"The woman layin' in that fresh dirt over there," he had said last night, "was about the kindest, gentlest, sweetest creature the good Lord ever put on this fucked-up earth. I know, I know, everybody—least every *normal* person—feels that way about their mother. But Ma was one of the greatest, she really was. Anybody around here'll tell you the same—leastways they would have before that land shit came up. Ma took care of their sick, delivered their babies, patched up their marriages and their petty-ass feuds, saw to it that those with nuthin' at least had shoes and blankets to keep from freezin' in the winter, even though she'd go barelegged herself in a dress so thin you could pract'ly see through it. Never put us kids or the ol' man out, mind you, just herself. She was *always* puttin' herself out for others.

"And you know what she got in return? She got to live forty-nine years in a clapboard shack with outdoor plumbin' and newspaper insulation and tar-paper patches that she put up herself all over on the outside to keep out the rain and snow. And she got a husband who never worked at any one job longer'n six weeks in all those forty-nine years; a husband who'd do any kind of short-term scut work you want to name, then piss away the cash on cheap booze before he ever made it home so's he could wake up the next day with a hangover, bitchin' cause there wasn't no food in the house; a husband who the best thing she could say about after he was dead was 'he never beat me none.' And she got a son who grew up with his ol' man's taste for liquor and allergy to steady employment, but who figured robbin' places with a gun was a better way to get his cash than doin' scut work. And she got a daughter who managed to let herself be knocked up four times before she was out of her teens and ended up marryin' some fella who couldn't manage to hold down a job or turn down a drink or keep his eyes off any woman he wasn't married to. *Those* were the kind of things my ma got in return for all her compassion and caring."

He had to pause before he could finish. I could see him squeezing his eyes shut in hard blinks in an attempt to hold back his tears; the same tears he'd denied during his solitary time at the grave, but now, as he talked it out, could no longer keep in check.

"Funny, ain't it," he went on in a somewhat thicker voice, "how a person can keep foolin' themselves, keep convincin' themselves that they always got more time? You know, time to take care of this, time to straighten out that . . . then all of a sudden time's up and all you got time for is to fret and carry on about what you didn't get done.

"I knew what a disappointment I was to Ma—a disappointment just like all the others in her life. I never planned it that way, sure never *wanted* it that way . . . it just seemed to happen. Not that Ma ever complained or failed to show her love, mind you, that wasn't her way. But the law-breakin', and the bein' on the run, and the neighbors yackin' and pointin' their fingers cause of things me or the ol' man or Pearl done . . . it took its toll. I could see it and it tore me up inside to know I was a big part of it. Only I had this fantasy, see: I was gonna get my shit together, get straight with the law, then come drivin' home someday in a big-ass ol' Cadillac with honest-earned money pourin' out my ears. I was gonna buy Ma a brand-new dress, take her somewhere to get her hair done up all fancy, and take her out to the finest restaurant in the county—a place where they'd wait on her and fetch her things every time she so much as twitched a finger. And then I'd drive her home and we'd go right past all the neighbors that'd been yackin' and pointin' over the years and Ma could stick up her nose and say, 'See how my boy takes care of me' . . . but time ran out on me,

Hannibal. Time ran out and now Ma's in the ground and I'm standin' here blubberin' and nuthin' else is changed, yet nuthin' is ever gonna be the same again. . . ."

Another pause. The wetness around his eyes glistened blue-silver in the moonlight.

"She deserved to live better than she did," he said when his voice worked again, "and she *damn* sure deserved to die better than she did. Ain't no goin' back for me now to do the things I shoulda done for her, or to *un*do the things I shouldn'ta done . . . But the way I see it, I got one more chance to do right by her. If her death wasn't no accident— and there's plenty besides me who don't believe it was—then the sonsabitches responsible need to be caught and punished. A part of me wants to have them between my hands, to see them nailed to a wall and skinned . . . but that's the wild part, the same part of me that done the things that caused Ma so much grief, the part of me I have to control this time. This time it needs to be done right. For her. That's where you come in, Hannibal. The sheriff claims he can't find no sign of wrongdoin'. Well, it's up to you to find some for him. Take him by the damn nose if you have to and point him at the bastards who killed my ma. Then it'll be in the hands of a judge and a jury. I already know I probably won't be satisfied with whatever their idea of 'justice' turns out to be, but I swear I'll abide by it. And Ma can look down from where she's at and maybe smile a little and finally—finally—for once she'll be able to say, 'That's my boy and he saw to it the proper thing was done.' "

I suppose it had been those last few sentences that ultimately hooked me into accepting Odum's "job of work." I remember thinking *If this fucker's acting, he's doing a hell of a job* and then immediately cursing my cynicism. I'd lost my own mother—and father—in a car wreck when I was nine and still recalled the terrible hole their sudden passing made in my world. Understood the frustration of things left undone, knew the anguish over words forever unspoken.

Maybe in helping Junior I was seeking to exorcise a few demons of my own. . . .

"Mister? Mister, your order is ready."

I was abruptly aware of the plump waitress standing beside me with a plate of steaming food. I had spiraled so deeply into my thoughts that I hadn't heard her approach. I looked up with a start, then countered her uncertain smile with a sheepish grin and swept aside the pen and notebook so she could serve me.

"Let me know if I can get you anything else," she said after she had deposited the plate in front of me. She drifted away still wearing the uncertain smile.

The meal she left in her wake was delicious. Farm-fresh eggs with dark yellow—almost orange—yolks; equally fresh sausage, coarse-ground and formed into patties as thick as the edge of my wrist; a mountain of fried potatoes; and toast dripping with real butter. Not gourmet fare, perhaps, but nobody ever accused me of being a gourmet; I just know what I like. I wolfed it down like a field hand at the end of a long day.

When the plate was empty, the coffee pot drained, I pushed the dishwasher's work away from me and lit a cigarette.

The waitress reappeared. "Can I get you anything else?"

I shook my head. "No way. I'm out of room. Tell the cook everything was great."

She giggled. "He'd faint if I told him one of the customers actually complimented his cooking. Nobody ever does that. But then, you're not from around here, are you?"

"My accent gave me away, huh?"

"Well, mostly I just know everybody from around here. I saw you writing in that notebook thing before—you a reporter or something?"

Out of habit, I began considering what sort of line to feed her. But I ended up deciding there was no need for deception. As a matter of fact, considering the much-vaunted expediency of small-town grapevines, a little advertising might be the best thing I could do at this point.

I said, "No, I'm not a reporter. Actually, what I am is a private detective."

"You're kidding!"

"Swear it on a stack of your best flapjacks. Want to see my license?"

She surprised me. "Yeah!"

My expression must have shown something because she quickly added, "I mean, not that I don't believe you or anything, I'd just like to *see* one. The detectives on TV are always whipping them out and stuff but you never really get a look. I'm just curious."

I shrugged. "Nothing wrong with that."

I took out the plastic-encased photostat of my license, handed it over. She took it by the bottom corners, gripping it between the thumb and forefinger of each hand, and held it about six inches from the end of her nose. Her pretty blue eyes bounced back and forth as she read.

"I'll be damned," she announced when finished, "a real-life private eye. Must be exciting, huh?"

I put the photostat away. "Only on very rare occasions," I answered. "I don't want to disillusion you, but what you see on TV isn't much like the real thing."

"It says there you're from up north. Rockford. We had one of our local boys get in quite a bit of trouble up that way awhile back. Boyd Odum Junior—ever hear of him?"

"Matter of fact I have."

"Something to do with him what brought you all the way down here?"

"Well—"

"Wait a minute! Are you the bounty hunter? I heard there was a guy in town yesterday looking to nab Junior Odum if he showed up for his ma's funeral."

Like I said, small-town grapevines.

"Hoping to catch up with Junior was my original business

here," I conceded. "Turns out I'll be sticking around a couple more days on another matter."

Her eyes widened to near comic proportions and her voice took on a conspiratorial tone. "Is it something you can talk about?"

"Well, up to a point. It seems some of Flo Odum's relatives aren't entirely satisfied that her death was an accident."

"Oh, yeah. Lots of folks been talking about that. You know, the timing and all."

"I guess a diner like this is a pretty good barometer for a town's mood. Waiting tables like you do, you must hear ideas and opinions on just about everything, huh?"

"You kidding? Everybody says hairdressers and bartenders hear so much gossip and stuff. You don't know what gossip is until you get a dozen or so farmers and such gathered over morning coffee and sweet rolls. And some of the things they talk about"—she rolled her eyes for emphasis—"if the hairdressers and bartenders are hearing juicier stuff than I do, they must really be getting an earful!"

"Did you know Flo Odum?"

"Oh, sure. Practically everybody did—or at least knew *of* her. A lot of times, see, Flo would get talked about sorta in passing. I mean, maybe her husband or son-in-law would be in here shooting their mouths off, or maybe they'd just pass by outside, then when they were gone somebody would make a remark about them and pretty soon it would work around to Flo and what a sweet old gal she seemed to be and how nobody could figure why she deserved such a sorry lot in life."

"Most everyone liked her, then?"

"Oh, heck yeah. Like I said, she was such a sweet thing. Poor as a church mouse, thanks to that no-account husband of hers, but a real prideful person, and always worrying after somebody else she figured was worse off than her."

"How about Junior? I get the impression he never won any popularity contests around here."

"Not hardly. Oh, there's a few I guess who see him as some sort of rebel hero—a cross between James Dean and Jesse James, or something like that. But mostly he's thought of as a horse's ass. Seems he's been in and out of trouble almost since he could walk and at one time or other he's done devilment to practically everybody in these parts."

"Did you know him?"

"Kinda, but not very well. He was a couple years ahead of me in high school, but he dropped out early and then was in reform school or jail so much of the time you hardly ever saw him around. He dated my older sister once or twice, but he was too wild for her—and if you knew Becky you'd know *that's* wild."

"Getting back to the death of Junior's mother . . . you said a lot of people have been talking about it, about the timing and all. You mean they're suspicious, too, that maybe it wasn't an accident?"

"Well . . . suspicious might be too strong a word. Most everybody has a lot of faith in Sheriff Wilt and when he says it was all just a tragic accident, well, who's to dispute him? But still, there's no denying the coincidence and the . . . what's the word I want? Irony, that's it. No denying the irony of it; of meek, gentle Flo finally getting shed of her worthless husband and taking a stand against Cord Toys— and then all of a sudden turning up dead herself."

"Plus there were some threats involved, weren't there?"

"Yeah, that's what I heard. A couple 'nonymous letters in her mailbox, some stuff spray-painted on her front door one morning. Hey, no getting around the fact that a lot of people were pretty upset when Flo refused to sell her land to Clay- ton Cord. It wasn't really that they were *mad* at Flo, but they were scared—scared the toy factory might move away. And scared people will lash out at anything or anybody. Let's face it, this town—this whole stinking county—doesn't have much going for it. There's coal and even some oil around us, but what little there ever was of either in Hatchaloo has been gone for a long time. Still a few farmers out there scratching, but with prices what they are and land hereabouts poor to begin with, they're fighting a losing battle. So Cord Toys is by far the biggest single employer and most of your shops and stores—places like this diner—they all depend on the money that Cord employees put into circulation. Shouldn't be hard to see that if Clayton Cord ever *did* decide to pull up stakes, you might be looking at a ghost town a whole county wide."

The cook sauntered out of the back, wiping his hands on his apron. He shook a cigarette from one of the packs on the end of the counter, lit it, frowned in our direction through the billowing smoke.

"Corrie?" he called to the waitress after he'd taken a couple hard drags. "Don't you think you ought to get those dishes on in here and get 'em done up 'fore the noon crowd starts comin' in?"

My waitress sighed, much in the same way she had when I'd come in. "Okay, Harve," she called over her shoulder. "Be right there." She began gathering up my plate, cup, utensils.

"Didn't mean to get you in trouble," I said.

"No problem. Harve's okay. And he's right about the lunch crowd, the first of them will be coming in before long and I've got stuff to do in order to be ready for them."

I took a business card from my wallet, wrote the name and room number of the motel where I was staying on the back, dropped it in the pouch of her apron. "Like I said, I'll be around for a couple more days. If you should happen to overhear anything—or think of anything—that might be of use to me, I'd sure appreciate a call."

"Hey, you bet," she replied, smiling. "And you be sure to stop back, you hear?"

"Count on it," I told her.

She carried away my dirty dishes and disappeared into the back. I stood up, plucked my bill from where she'd slipped it under the sugar bowl, replaced it with a generous tip, and took the slip over to the cash register where a dour-faced Harve stood waiting. I handed him the bill and a ten and he went to work ringing it up. He was a tall, bony sort with an Adam's apple that thrust out nearly as far as the half-smoked cigarette in his mouth. There was a penguin tattooed on his right forearm and the way his long, stringy muscles fluttered under the tight skin as he worked the register made the bird waddle very realistically.

"You're the cook, huh?" I said, making conversation.

"Yep."

"Did an excellent job on my breakfast."

"Pretty hard to fuck up sausage and eggs."

"Oh, I don't know. You'd be surprised."

He held out my change, squinting through the smoke that curled up from the butt balanced precariously on his lower lip. He said, "Not me. I ain't been surprised since 1956."

I decided I'd bite. "What surprised you in '56?" I asked.

He dropped the money into my palm, then grinned broadly, causing the cigarette stub to snap to attention and point straight up alongside his nose. "Why," he said, "that was the summer I found out Mary Louise Loomis had two nipples on her left tit."

4

I walked back to my twelve-year-old Plymouth, still parked in the lot of the county building. After long and faithful service, my ancient Mustang had finally sounded its death rattle and coughed its last cloud of pollutants into the atmosphere, leaving me no choice but to send it to that big scrap heap in the sky. The Plymouth was strictly a desperation purchase, made at a time when my usually sluggish cash flow was creeping along at a near standstill. Despite its rust holes and missing chrome and general abandoned-alongside-the-road appearance, however, it drove out smoothly enough so that I'd had no qualms about traveling the length of the state in it.

I sat behind the wheel for a time, completing the notes I'd started in the diner. That done, I took the maps from the glove compartment and scanned them again. They were detailed representations of Cedarton and Hatchaloo County that I'd photocopied from a state atlas at the public library before leaving Rockford. Using addresses and other information from the jacket bondsman Hazelford had put together on Junior Odum, I had highlighted certain points and added some notations around the border. While I'd had no intention of paying a prolonged visit to the area, I learned a long time ago that, when operating on strange turf, it is best to familiarize yourself with the lay of the land as thoroughly as possible before going in. I had once been chased for three hours up and down the sandy back roads of northern Wisconsin by a carload of angry locals who sought to make me permanently horizontal, a chase I could have ended in a tenth of the time if only I'd had some idea where the hell the roads I was burning up were taking me.

With my mental picture of the vicinity refreshed, I put away the maps, fired up the Plymouth, pointed it toward the home of Pearl Stroud, Junior Odum's sister.

Pearl and her four children and her husband, Vern, lived in a trailer park just south of town. A rusting, BB-pocked metal arch over the entrance to the park proclaimed its name to be Shady Willow and one glance at the rutted gravel drive, weedy patches of lawns, and peeling, lopsided trailers that lay beyond told me it was hardly the high-rent district. As I turned off the county blacktop I noticed a young woman sitting on the grass with her back against one of the red-brick pillars that supported the arch. A bicycle leaned against the back side of the pillar. I rolled several feet past her before recognition sunk in and I hit the brakes. I backed the Plymouth up, steering off onto the edge of the drive, cut the engine, and got out.

"Almost didn't recognize you without your shotgun," I said.

"It ain't far away," Reba Dallas replied.

She had on cut-off jeans, a white T-shirt, and a pair of cowboy boots. Sat with her bare legs drawn up, arms resting across the tops of her knees, casually smoking a cigarette. I had never gotten a good look at her last night and saw now that there was considerably more femininity mixed with the tomboyish toughness than I had first guessed. Her legs were long and well shaped, and the bottom she was resting upon appeared to be nicely rounded. Her face—with its light dusting of freckles and the same blunt nose as her cousin—might never be pretty, but with a bit more maturity and the proper makeup and a hairdo more stylish than the functional blunt cut she presently wore, it could be quite interesting.

"Figured you ought to be showin' up here sooner or later," she went on. "I was gonna give you 'til noon."

"And if I hadn't shown up by then?"

"Then I was gonna go tell Junior that he'd hired hisself a pretty lazy damn detective."

"The word 'hired' implies an amount of money has been —or will be—paid. I don't think that quite fits the circumstances."

"By the look of that car you're drivin', you must do a lot of jobs that don't involve money for payment."

I had to laugh. "Touché," I said.

"Too what?"

"Never mind. Did you come looking for me just to try and pick a fight, or was there something else?"

She glowered up at me for a moment, then couldn't hold back a small grin of her own. "Both, I guess," she admitted. She turned to rub out her cigarette against the pillar, then got to her feet. Her bottom was indeed nicely rounded, and the way her small breasts bobbled under the T-shirt indicated she wasn't wearing a bra. And I guess the fact that I noticed these things indicates something about me.

Reba dug a piece of folded paper from her hip pocket and handed it to me. "Junior wanted me to give this to you."

I took the paper, unfolded it. A name and an address had been printed on it: TOM WYKERT, 411 BELL STREET.

"Who's this?" I said.

"He's shop chairman of the union out at Cord Toys. He was heard to've done a lot of spoutin' off about Aunt Flo back when there was talk of the factory movin' away, called her a senile old fool for one thing and said somebody ought to bring her in line for the good of the whole community."

"And Junior thinks he bears checking out?"

She nodded. "He never bothered to mention Wykert last

night, but after thinkin' on it some more he says maybe it'd be a mistake for you to concentrate strictly on Clayton Cord."

"Yeah, I've been thinking the same thing. His is the name that keeps coming up, but it sounds to me as if there are plenty of others around who stand to lose a great deal more than Cord if the factory ever relocated. What do you know about this Wykert?"

She shrugged. "Used to be a big barroom brawler. Still shoves plenty of money across the bar at Murphy's, but since he got elected shop chairman you don't hear much about the fightin' anymore. Some say he's more of a company man than a union man, but he keeps gettin' voted in 'cause people are scared of him."

"Sounds like he should be a real fun fellow to chat with," I observed. I entered Wykert's name and address in my note pad, also the name of the bar, Murphy's. "Anything else?"

"Junior wants to meet with you. Tonight. Late. Round midnight."

"Where?"

"I'll come by your motel and get you. Tell you then."

"Real trusting souls, you and your cousin."

She shook her head. "Got nuthin' to do with trust. You're not the only one hereabouts who'd like to see Junior behind bars, you know. He has to keep out of sight and sometimes that means stayin' on the move. No tellin' where he'll be by tonight."

"Not a very glamorous way to live, is it?"

"Nobody ever said it was."

"You did. In a way."

"What's that s'posed to mean?"

"Whenever you mention his name you get a kind of hero-worship gleam in your eye."

"A body could do worse than to have my cousin for a hero. He never took no shit off nobody and he never sat around feelin' sorry for hisself and whinin' about his lot in life. Most of all, he got the hell away from Hatchaloo County."

"You figure even a prison cell is preferable to Hatchaloo County?"

"Maybe. Most everybody I know is spendin' their life in some kind of prison anyway. They just call it by different names."

I didn't know what to say to that. It made me feel awkward that I couldn't think of a good rebuttal, as if I owed her one. Maybe I understood too well what she meant.

Finally, I said, "Look, uh, I need to keep on the move, too. You coming in while I talk to Pearl?"

"No way. Not when that fuckhead she's married to is at home. That's why I waited out here in the first place."

"All right. See you later tonight then."

She said nothing in the way of good-bye.

I got back in the Plymouth, turned the key, swung out onto the washboard drive again. In my rearview mirror I saw Reba Dallas push her bicycle out from behind the pillar. But it was more than just a bicycle; a small engine that I recognized as a wash machine motor because I'd seen similarly rigged bikes—although none in years—had been attached to the frame. I watched as she gave the start cord a yank, heard the snarl of the motor when it caught. Then she swung a leg over the seat and tooled off in a spurt of dust.

Under my breath I said, "I'll be damned."

Pearl and Vern Stroud's trailer, number twenty-seven, was in no better or worse shape than most of the others I saw. The thing that set it apart was the gleaming red and black Pontiac GTO parked in front. The Goat was at least six years older than my Plymouth but had been carefully and lovingly refurbished, right down to chrome tailpipes and an illegal rake job to accommodate oversized chrome-rimmed tires. It sat there gleaming amidst the rust and dust of the shabby trailer park like the proverbial diamond in the rough.

I parked beside it and as I piled out of my own heap I felt a sudden and unexpected pang of envy—maybe even resentment—toward the owner of the shiny car. Back in my late teens, when possessing a certain kind of car was one of the biggest goals in a guy's life, I would have given my left nut for a GTO. The closest I ever came was a bullet-nosed old Studebaker with unpainted galvanized patches riveted over the rust spots. Maybe that was one of the reasons my passion for cars didn't last very long. Over the years, an automobile had come to mean little more to me than a convenient method of getting from one place to another— although I *did* have enough vanity left to wish for something a little classier than the Plymouth. Still, it had been a long time since any vehicle had stirred a reaction in me the way the Goat did.

I climbed the steps of the trailer, knocked on the front door, stood admiring the still unattainable prize until someone answered.

The someone was a little girl of about six with scads of blond curls spilling down around a chubby face and eyes as blue and bright as only a child can have. "Who're you?" she wanted to know.

I smiled. "My name's Joe. What's yours?"

"Tabitha Marie Stroud. I had a friend named Joe once, but he moved away. Are you his daddy?"

"I don't think so," I said. "Is your mommy or daddy at home?"

She nodded. And then, with perfectly innocent frankness, she added, "Daddy's drunk again. Him and Mommy are fighting."

I grinned in spite of the complications that situation might present. I remembered a line from an old John Wayne movie: "Too bad, ain't it," Duke had mused in one of his rare reflective moments, "that kids have tuh grow up tuh be people?" Yeah, I thought; it sure is, big guy.

Before I could say anything further to the little girl, a slightly twangy woman's voice came from inside. "Who's that at the—Goddammit, Vern, can't you even get up to answer the door? . . . Look out, Tabitha; step aside, honey, so Mommy can . . ."

Tabitha was replaced in the doorway by a tall, slat-thin woman with stringy reddish blond hair and tired eyes that might have been as blue as the little girl's once, only a long, long time ago. She had Junior Odum's corn-kernel-sized freckles and the same blunt nose and there was no doubt I was looking at his sister Pearl.

Before she could ask, I said, "My name is Joe Hannibal, Mrs. Stroud. Hopefully your brother has been in touch and told you to expect me."

She nodded as she absently pushed hair back from around her face. "You're the detective. Sure. Junior couldn't come himself because . . . well, you know, somebody might be watching the place. But he sent word. Come in, won't you?"

The inside of the trailer was narrow and cramped, smelling of fried foods, pissy diapers, body odor, and some sort of cloying room deodorizer that only made things worse. There were toys scattered everywhere. A little boy who looked to be about a year younger than Tabitha sat sucking his thumb on a threadbare couch, enthralled by the stock car races being shown on the television. A still younger child lay sleeping beside him. The fourth child—or maybe there were more by now—was nowhere in sight.

Also watching TV, sprawled in a maroon recliner speckled with gray duct-tape patches, was a beefy, red-faced man wearing a dingy undershirt and holding a can of beer. I guessed him to be in his early thirties. He had thick arms and broad shoulders, but his gut was already stretching the undershirt tight and in a couple years it would overwhelm everything else.

"You already met Tabitha," Pearl said, making birdlike gestures, talking loud to be heard above the drone of the cars on TV. "That's Andrew over there—get your thumb out of your mouth, Andrew!—with little Johnny beside him. I've got another one playing outdoors somewhere—thank God. And this here's my husband, Vern. Vern, this is Mr. Hannibal, the detective I was tellin' you about."

Stroud's eyes never left the television screen. With no emotion or inflection in his voice, he said, "Big fuckin' deal."

I'd started to extend my hand to him. I drew it back at his words and felt some heat crawling up my neck. I entertained thoughts of drawing the hand back all the way, balling it into a fist, and knocking the rude sonofabitch through a wall.

I don't know what showed on my face, but Pearl said rather hurriedly, "Why don't we step into the kitchen, Mr. Hannibal. We can talk better there."

The kitchen wasn't a separate room, just an area at one end of the trailer, sectioned off from the living room by a fake wood divider. We sat at the table. The latter was littered with dirty dishes, bowls, and three or four opened boxes of cereal. Pearl paused for a moment, as if she considered clearing it. But it was obvious there was no place to go with the stuff; the sink, countertop, and stove were all covered with their own piles of plates, pots and pans, mixing bowls, and various packages of quick-fix ingredients. Pearl sighed somewhat fatalistically and plopped down across from me.

"Housekeepin' ain't my strong suit," she said.

"Don't worry about it," I told her. "I'm a bachelor so it all looks pretty normal to me." That wasn't exactly true, but I wanted to put her at ease. While I *am* something of a slob, even I know when to draw the line between messy and filthy.

"Look," I went on, "I know it's probably painful for you

to talk about your mother right now, so I'll make this as brief as possible. First of all, I'd like to know if you share your brother's conviction that her death was something more than an accident?"

She nodded solemnly. "Yes, I do. I feel it—down deep, where you feel blood ties and where you know your child is cryin' in the night even though you're somewhere where you can't truly hear it. I been hearin' my mama cry like that every night since . . . she's been gone, Mr. Hannibal. Cryin' cause of the terrible way she died and cryin' cause those that done it to her are walkin' around free."

I licked my lips. "That's, uh, interesting, Mrs. Stroud. But is your belief based on anything more tangible than that?"

She frowned. "I . . . I don't understand those big words."

"Tangible," I said. "Something you can see, feel, hear. I know about the threats in the mailbox and the hard feelings because your mother wouldn't sell her land and Cord Toys claiming they'd have to move their factory—I know about all that, and I agree that in the face of it your mother's death looks pretty suspicious. But that's only what is known as circumstantial evidence. I'm looking for something more than that, something that can be followed up on and maybe proven. Like, did anyone directly threaten your mother in front of witnesses, or was anyone seen fleeing the vicinity of her house at or near the time of the fire—those are the kinds of things I'm after."

"That's what the sheriff kept askin' me. I told him no, just like I have to tell you. But, dammit, *everybody* knows there was talk about Mama through the whole county—what a stubborn old fool she was and how she was gonna ruin a whole bunch of lives if the toy factory moved and how *somebody* had better do *something* to stop that from happenin'. Well, they did—somebody killed her!"

She was tensing up on me and I was afraid she might

snap. I shifted to a little gentler area of questioning. "The notes that were left in the mailbox," I said. "Did you see any of them?"

"Uh-huh. Saw 'em all."

"You didn't happen to keep any?"

"Uh-uh. I don't even know if Mama kept any. Course it wouldn't make no difference, they'd be burnt up now anyway."

"How many were there?"

"Three altogether."

"Remember what any of them said?"

"Not exactly. One said somethin' like 'Quit standin' in the way of progress you old fool,' and another went 'Take the money and run before somebody runs you.' It got a little scary."

. "Why didn't your mother tell the sheriff about them?"

She gave me a look. "You don't find Odums runnin' to the cops about hardly nuthin'."

"How about the message spray-painted on the door?"

"Yeah, I remember that one all right. Every single word of it. It was the worst of all. It said 'Get out or die, old bitch.' "

"Did the door incident happen before or after the notes in the mailbox?"

"After. Couple days after the last note."

"Did you have any feeling that the messages might all be written by the same person?"

"I—I don't think so. I mean, how could I know?"

I made a catchall gesture. "By their tone, by the sentence structure—maybe they kept misspelling a certain word."

Pearl Stroud gave a nervous little laugh. "I'd be the last person to notice any misspellin', Mr. Hannibal. But I see what you mean. Only I can't say one way or the other, I mean, the messages where choppy-like, you know? Not the way a body would talk or write regular letters." She shrugged. "It coulda been the same person, it coulda not been. I can't say."

The growl of racing cars on the TV in the living room faded and was abruptly replaced by the bouncy music of a commercial. Vern heaved up out of his chair with a bearlike grunt and lumbered into the kitchen area. He fired his empty beer can at an already too-full wastebasket in the corner. The new can dislodged another from the heap and the two of them fell to the floor and rolled until they came to a stop against one side of the stove. Vern seemed not to notice. He yanked open the refrigerator door, took out a fresh can, popped the tab loudly. Stood there slurping the foam that bubbled over. He never once looked at Pearl or me.

"Vern," Pearl said in a voice that quivered with tension, "maybe Mr. Hannibal would like a can of beer."

Vern tipped his can, swallowed deeply several times, lowered it, belched. "Only got two left," he said. "The way this fuckin' day has started out I'm gonna need 'em both. And more."

"Yeah," said Pearl dryly, "you always need more, don't you?"

Stroud spun on her with surprising hostility in his eyes and for the first time I realized just how drunk he was. "You ever stop to think that maybe you're the fuckin' *reason* I need to keep drinkin'?" he snarled. "You and them whinin', pissin', bastard-born brats we got crawlin' all over the place every minute of the day?"

Pearl shot to her feet. "Don't you talk about my kids like that, damn you. Not in front of them, not in front of company!"

Stroud looked at me for the first time and his mouth twisted into a viciously sarcastic smile. "Him?" he said, pointing, sloshing beer from the can in his hand. "This motherfucker ain't *company,* you dumb cunt. He's a leech! You really think he gives a rat's ass how your ol' lady croaked? Sheeeiit. He's heard about you inheritin' her land and he's lookin' to cut himself a slice, that's all."

I stood up, too. Slowly. Any cop on any police force in the country will tell you that one of the most dangerous situations you can be faced with is to find yourself in the middle of a domestic quarrel. The tide can shift in a thousand different ways and the end results can range from high comedy to deep tragedy. I'm no psychic, but I couldn't see this scene turning into a laughing matter.

I said, "That's a lie, Stroud."

"Says you," he sneered.

"That's right. Says me." Real snappy dialogue on both our parts.

"Please," Pearl said to everyone, and to no one in particular.

Stroud pointed again, sloshing more beer. "Get out of my house, leech!" he said to me. "Get out and quit upsettin' my wife."

It didn't seem like an entirely bad idea, but I wondered how serious a situation I'd be leaving behind. I glanced at Pearl. "That the way you want it, Mrs. Stroud?"

She stood rubbing white-knuckled hands together. "I just don't want no trouble," she said meekly.

" 'I don't want no trouble,' " Stroud mimicked in a crazy squawk. "Shut the fuck up, cunt! I don't need your say-so to throw this cocksucker out!"

Suddenly, unexpectedly, he hurled his can of beer at her. She got her arms up and the can bounced off one of her elbows instead of her face, but at such short range the nearly full can still dealt a savage blow. Pearl fell against the wall with a whimper.

"Mommy!" Tabitha cried from the living room. One of the other kids began to wail.

I came around to the end of the table and banged a forearm against the hinge of Stroud's jaw. The impact knocked him back against the refrigerator and when I went after him he surprised me by firing back with a cocked elbow that caught me right between the eyes. When he tried the same thing again, I got under it, pressed in close, and began pounding his flabby gut. I kept pounding until he quit trying to punch back, then brought the edge of my wrist up, slammed it across his throat, pressed the back of his head hard against the broad face of the refrigerator. I held him pinned like that. He stared back at me, bug-eyed, not struggling. A lot of spit and a little blood dribbled down over his chin and dripped onto my arm.

Every kid in the house was bawling at the top of their lungs by now and I tried to think of something to say to comfort them.

I looked around for Pearl. I didn't have to look far. When I spotted her, she was about a foot away, rushing at me with fists upraised and legs churning. Her first punch smacked into the side of my face, then she leaped onto my back like a quadriplegic spider, kicking, gouging, biting, cursing.

"Let go of him, you sonofabitch! Let go of him! Let go, leave him be!"

Jesus Suffering H. Christ, what had I gotten into?

I let go of Stroud and backed away a couple steps, trying to dislodge the whirlwind from my back. Stroud slid down the front of the refrigerator like melted ice cream and I could see I didn't have to worry about him for awhile.

I backed up another step, then doubled forward and dumped Pearl as gently as possible onto the floor. She lay there kicking up at me, wild-eyed, still cursing.

I backed off some more. When I did, Pearl got to her hands and knees and scrambled over to her husband. She threw her arms around him and pulled him hard against her. All the while she glared at me with hate-filled eyes.

"Get out of here!" she screeched. "Get out of here and leave us alone!"

It was obvious there could be no reasoning with her.

I glanced heavenward in a kind of helpless gesture, but

found no sympathy on the fly-speckled ceiling. When I turned and started for the door, the three crying children huddled in the kitchen entranceway scattered away from me with their howls rising in volume. I wanted to grab one of them—or all of them—and explain that I wasn't really the villain in this thing. Fat chance. With both their parents sprawled on the kitchen floor in my wake, they weren't likely to ever buy that.

They'd be seeing my face in their nightmares for years.

5

I turned into the first tavern I came to, ordered a shot and a beer, slammed them down in record time.

While the bartender was setting up another round, I went to the men's room and scooped some cold water onto my face. I studied my dripping mug in the mirror. It looked like I'd be lucky enough not to get a black eye from the elbow shot Stroud had landed, but Pearl had chewed the hell out of my right ear and left a tic-tac-toe pattern of scratches over one side of my neck. I shook my head in wonderment. I'd heard of instances where a neighbor or a cop had stepped in when some asshole was slapping around his wife only to have the victim come unexpectedly and violently to the aid of her spouse, but I never thought I'd be sucker enough to get caught like that. Just shows how wrong you can be sometimes. And fuck you, Sir Galahad, wherever you are.

I returned to the bar, tossed down another bourbon, took my time over the second beer. Now what? What had been a screwy damn case right from the get-go had just taken a turn for the worse. I could imagine what kind of monster Pearl Stroud would make me out to be. Even if Junior wanted me to continue, how much cooperation was I likely to get from remaining relatives and friends?

On the other hand, maybe the Strouds wouldn't be paid much attention. It was obvious they were no big plus to the community and I had a feeling that domestic blow-ups like the one I'd gotten caught in the middle of weren't at all uncommon with them. Reba Dallas had called Vern Stroud a "fuckhead" and Junior himself had referred to him as someone who "couldn't hold down a job or turn down a drink or keep his eyes off any woman he wasn't married to."

Besides, I didn't need any more friends or relations to tell me what a peach of an old gal Flo Odum was and how suspicious the timing of her death seemed. What I needed, damn it, was some hard evidence.

Something I wasn't going to find sitting on a bar stool licking my wounds.

6

"*B*omb shelter."

"The hell you say."

"Joe. Back in town?"

" 'Fraid not, kid. Still down south amongst the hills 'n hollers."

" 'Hills 'n hollers'?"

"It's a colloquialism. Spend much time down here, you start talking like that."

"Maybe you'd better get out while the getting is good."

"Can't. Still got things to take care of."

"Get your man?"

"Well, yes and no."

"Mmm. I'd say that covers most of the possibilities."

"It's a long story, Liz, one I'll have to tell you another time. Right now I need to talk to Bomber. He around?"

"Yeah. Some wine cooler salesman has him cornered. From the expression on his face, I think he'll be glad for the interruption. Hang on."

The Bomb Shelter, I guess I should explain, is one of Rockford's most popular watering holes. I spend enough time there to consider it my unofficial office away from the office. It is named after—not to mention owned and operated by—my buddy Bomber Brannigan, a mountainous chunk of humanity who terrorized the ranks of both pro boxing and pro wrestling for a number of years before opting to settle behind the stick of his own bar. Liz is Liz Grimaldi, Bomber's gal Friday and another buddy of mine, a very special one.

Bomber came on the line. "Hey, Joe. What's up?"

"I'll be out of town a couple more days," I said, "and I've developed this mad passion for lemonade wine coolers while I was away. I wanted to call and ask you to be sure and stock up on plenty for when I get back."

"Very funny. If I wanted to sell soda pop I would have bought a damn refreshment stand, not a bar. Now what's really on your mind?"

"I need you to get in touch with The Bug for me."

"The Bug? What in hell for?"

"I've got a job for him."

"You're kidding. I've known you to *knock* down a few things—not to mention a few people—but since when are you into *burning* down stuff?"

"What I'm interested in has already been burned down. I have a pretty good idea why, I need a more expert opinion on the how."

"That'll be a switch—for The Bug, I mean. You want me to have him give you a call?"

"No, just tell him to get his butt down here. He can catch a bus later tonight that will put him in Marieville—that's the next town north from where I am—at five-thirty tomorrow morning. I'll be waiting at the station."

"Uh, what if he's not interested. You want I should persuade him a little?"

"Tell him if he's not on that stinking bus I might have to suddenly remember what I know about where he *really* was the night Arnie Gunderson's fur barn burned down. That should be persuasion enough."

"Got it. Anything else?"

"Let him bellyache and squirm for awhile, then tell him

I'll reimburse him for the bus fare and throw in a few bucks for his time."

The subject of this particular line of conversation was one Franklin Kreeber—commonly known as Frankie The Firebug or, for short, just The Bug. He allegedly has torched more real estate in his forty-odd years than all the napalm ever dropped in Nam. While he hasn't been convicted of anything in over a decade, he has a quirky, furtive manner about him that leaves most everyone convinced he damn well hasn't quit the game but has just been lucky about not getting caught.

"What does any of this have to do with the bail skip you went after?" Bomber wanted to know.

"Long story. Tell you about it some other time."

"Right. Meanwhile, watch out you don't get your ass scorched while you're down there. You know what they say about playing with fire."

"Yes, Daddy. Say bye to Liz for me."

We broke the connection.

I was seated on the edge of the motel room bed in my undershorts. After leaving the tavern where I'd stopped to get my shit together following the episode with the Strouds, I had driven out to what was left of the Odum house. I don't know exactly what it was I was looking for, but whatever it was I didn't find it. One pile of burnt-out rubble looks pretty much like another to me. I had poked around long enough to get all sooty and dusty—necessitating a shower and a change of clothes upon returning to the motel—before I hit on the idea of sending for Frankie The Firebug. I reasoned that anyone who'd spent so many years rigging "accidents" ought to be able to spot the handiwork of somebody else attempting the same. If Sheriff Wilt wouldn't call in an arson unit, I'd call in one of my own.

I balanced the phone on one knee while I shook a cigarette out of the pack on the nightstand, hung it from a corner of my mouth, snapped a lighter to it. After I'd sent a couple clouds of smoke rolling across the room, I picked up the receiver again and punched out a second Rockford number.

Cyrus Hazelford answered after the third ring.

"Hannibal here," I told him.

"Joe. Yeah. Where you at?"

"Still right where you sent me—down here at the ass end of the state."

"Nuts. I was hoping you were calling to tell me you were back in town. With Odum."

"Not yet. But that's still on my agenda."

"Oh? Then he did show up down there, uh?"

"Yeah, he's around. I've seen him, just haven't put my net over him yet."

"Why not? There a problem?"

"Umm, 'problem' is too strong a word. I think 'complication' is a better choice."

"What's that supposed to mean?"

"It means something has come up—another matter I need to take care of before I can bring Odum back."

It was quiet on his end for a minute. Then: "This other matter—it involve Odum in some way?"

"You could say that."

"I could say a lot of things. I could say, for instance, that I don't like this worth a damn, Joe. You agree to go down there and do a job for me, and now all of a sudden here you are telling me you've decided to take care of something else *first*. That's bullshit. What if Odum is long gone by the time you finish with this 'other matter'?"

"He won't be. Just cool your jets, Cy, and trust me on this. For Christ's sake, you act like I'm some greenhorn out after his first skip. Have I ever failed to bring back anybody you sent me after?"

"You really want me to answer that?"

"Now who's talking bullshit?"

He sighed. "Yeah, yeah. Okay. You're a good bounty

man, Joe, but, Jesus, sometimes I think you give me more gray hairs than the skips do."

"See? That's what I get for trying to be a nice guy. This was supposed to be a courtesy call, to let you know I'd be gone a couple more days than we figured, so you wouldn't worry. And all you do is badmouth me for giving you gray hair."

Another sigh from his end. "Just do whatever the hell you have to do down there and then get your ass back here—with Junior Odum."

"Good plan. Why didn't I think of it? Tell you what; you can deduct the cost of a bottle of Grecian Formula from my . . ."

I didn't bother finishing it because I would have been talking to myself. He'd hung up on me.

7

The town of Cedarton, boasting a population of 4,500, was an orderly gridwork of streets laid out in the crook of an elbowlike bend made by the Hatchaloo River. The latter, moderate in width and relatively unpolluted, served as a natural boundary both to the north and west. As I drove from my southside motel toward Cord Toys, located at the opposite edge of town, I caught occasional glimpses of the river off to my left. Its gentle current and the way the sunlight played on the dimpled blue water cast an aura of tranquility over the community that made any idea of murder seem far away and preposterous.

I was absently noting the names on various business and street signs that slid by the windows, the way you sometimes do in a strange town. Abruptly, one of the street names registered something more than passing interest. Bell Street. And then I remembered the name and address Reba Dallas had given me that morning. Tom Wykert, 411 Bell Street, the union shop chairman who had been heard to make some pretty strong statements against Flo Odum and her refusal to sell her land.

I turned at the next intersection, looped around the block. I double-checked my notes to make sure I recalled the address correctly, then turned onto Bell and started watching the house numbers. Most likely, a union officer would be working the day shift, but you never know. Maybe I'd luck out and catch Wykert at home—or at least somebody I could leave my name with to let him know I was interested in talking to him.

Four-eleven was a simple but well-kept cottage, white with green trim, with a neatly clipped front lawn and a one-car garage squatting off to the side like a loyal pet. The garage door was open and I could see a fairly new compact parked inside. It appeared promising that someone was at home.

I parked my rattletrap at the curb, walked across the lawn, which smelled freshly mowed, thumbed the front doorbell. I could hear voices inside. Only after there was a titter of audience laughter did I realize it was a radio or TV talk show playing.

I was reaching to punch the bell button a second time when the door swung open and I was confronted by a tall, thick-bodied woman with ICBM breasts, gun-metal gray hair, and piercing eyes glaring out from beneath coarse black brows. When she spoke, I expected a window-rattling boom, but instead her voice was amazingly soft, almost lilting.

"Yes?"

"Is this the Wykert residence?" I asked.

"Yes it is."

"I'm looking for Tom Wykert."

"I'm sorry, but he's at work now. I'm his wife. Can I help you with something?"

I couldn't get over the contrast between her druidess appearance and her voice and pleasant manner. It was so striking that I wanted to make some comment on it. Instead, I decided I'd better stick to business. "My name is Joe Hannibal," I explained. "I'm representing the family of the late Florence Odum and I'll be in town for the next couple of days looking into some things for them. I'm hoping your husband will spare me a few minutes for some questions I have. Could you tell me when might be the best time to catch him?"

"What on earth would Tom know about old Flo's accident?"

I cleared my throat. "Well, probably nothing. It's just that, as shop chairman of the local union, I expect he's privy to a pretty wide variety of opinions and observations. You see, there are certain factions who suspect Mrs. Odum's death might have been something other than an accident. I'm hoping your husband can shed some light on the likelihood of that, based on the general mood of the cross-section of people he comes in contact with every day."

"Good lord, you mean Flo might have been murdered?"

I held up my hand. "I didn't use that word, Mrs. Wykert. Your county sheriff, who I'm sure I don't have to tell you is a very capable man, is convinced it was an accident. Nor do I have any reason to believe otherwise at this point. I'm just taking a sort of second look to try and satisfy everybody that all the possibilities have been explored. Now, do you think it would be okay if I stopped by later and talked with your husband?"

The Wykert woman chewed her bottom lip. "I'm not sure. . . . What I mean is, I'm never sure exactly when Tom will be home. He gets off at four, but often as not one of the second shift stewards will have a problem and he has to stay over for that. And when he finally does get away, well, he usually likes to stop and have a few beers somewhere. He's good about calling when he knows for sure what time he'll be home—so I can have supper ready and all —but until then I never know when to expect him."

Nice arrangement, I thought. "How about if I do the same?" I suggested. "Call, I mean, before I come over?"

"Well . . . I guess that would be all right." She worried the lip some more. "I have to be honest with you, Mr. Hannibal, my husband is what you'd call a real moody person. If he has a bad day at work or something, he can be a grouchy bear long after he gets home. And this Odum–Cord Toys thing has had him on edge for a real long time—you know, the threat of all those people losing their jobs and all. I don't know how he's going to take to the idea of somebody showing up now with the notion that Flo maybe didn't die an accidental death after all."

I said, "I'm not out to cause anybody any trouble, Mrs. Wykert. Unless, of course, there *is* a murderer running loose. I think your husband may be able to help me get a handle on that. That's why, sooner or later, one way or another, I intend to talk to him." I handed her one of my business cards. "Please tell him I stopped by. I'm staying at the Lincolnway Motel. I'll be in and out, but he can leave a message if he wants to get in touch with me."

Cord toys sprawled across the top end of town, jammed tightly into the crook of the river's bend. It fronted on a scattering of boxlike prefab houses, a small shopping center, a bowling alley, and a pair of bars. To the east, stretching just outside the city limits, lay the choppy, jack-pine-covered hills of the Odum property. From where I parked—in a section marked VISITORS ONLY—if you looked real close you could see the top of the house's blackened, but still standing, stone chimney, poking stubbornly above the ragged pine points.

The factory's parking lot was an open expanse of dusty crushed limestone. At the moment it was filled with row after row of cars and pickups in every size, shape, and color imaginable. The factory grounds proper, however, with a dozen or more various-sized buildings, were surrounded by a high chain-link fence. As far as I could see, there were only three points of ingress: two turnstile gates for pedestrians entering from—or exiting to—the parking lot and, down near the river, a wide swing gate for semi traffic to pass in and out of. All three were monitored by guard stations.

The guard in the kiosk at the turnstile I chose appeared as ancient and faded as the limestone crunching beneath my feet. He looked up as I approached, seemingly barely able to lift his head under the weight of the badged cap he had on.

"Afternoon," he greeted from behind his slotted glass panel.

"Afternoon," I returned. Then, brusquely, businesslike, I said, "I'm here to see Clayton Cord."

His rheumy eyes slid up and down, taking in the way my untrimmed hair curled around the backs of my ears, the off-the-rack-at-Kmart jacket and slacks I wore, the Farm and Fleet boots still with traces of soot on them, and he knew damn well I wasn't somebody the company president was expecting. The old bird wasn't so far over the hill he couldn't spot that. For a second I could see him getting ready to challenge me, but then something shifted behind the eyes and I watched him change his mind and decide: "Fuck it, for three-forty an hour let somebody else argue with this clown." The battle cry of the American work ethic.

"Here," he said, shoving a ledger book through the slot. "Sign in, be sure to enter the date and time. On the way back, you'll have to mark your time out."

After I'd scribbled the necessary information, he gave me directions, pointing out a weathered boardwalk, telling me to follow that until I saw signs marking the main office building and reception area.

As I proceeded along the boardwalk, I surveyed the factory layout some more. But even at closer range, without actually going inside any of the various buildings, there wasn't much to see. Faintly, I could hear the high-pitched whir of pneumatic tools, the groan of hydraulic rams reaching their limit, intermittent bursts of compressed air; once or twice I caught a whiff of what smelled like wood varnish. Most of this seemed to emanate from three barnlike structures that ran perpendicular to the boardwalk. It was a sure bet the sounds and smells weren't escaping through their thick brick walls, but rather trickling from the rows of high, smudged windows, many of which were slanted open in deference to the day's heat. The other buildings scattered about —service shops and maintenance sheds, I guessed—seemed to be waiting in patient silence. The only visible activity was a swarm of fork trucks scuttling back and forth, blaring their horns whenever they'd plunge in through an open doorway.

The main office buildings, three stories of chrome and tinted glass, stood like a gold filling among decaying molars. Its cornerstone identified it as being less than a year old, while the other structures I'd seen I guessed to be circa 1940. Cord Toys was obviously a company with priorities.

One look at the receptionist and I knew it was going to be a lot tougher getting past her than it had been the old security guard. Bluish gray hair piled moderately high and sprayed until it was as rigid as her posture, flinty eyes unblinking behind bifocal lenses, lips so thin her mouth looked like a razor slash just before the blood starts to seep out.

"Good afternoon. How may I help you?"

The words were pleasant enough but the voice was hard and flat, brittle-sounding.

"My name is Joe Hannibal," I told her. "I'm here to see Clayton Cord."

"Hannibal?" She tasted the name and seemed to find it lacking. "I don't recall. . . . What firm do you represent, please?"

"My own."

She considered that, then finally condescended to check her appointment pad. "I'm sorry, but I don't seem to show anything—"

I said, "You won't find my name in there because I don't have an appointment."

She looked up, one brow arched sharply. "Oh? And you

expected to just march in here and be able to see Mr. Cord? That seems rather brash, don't you think?"

I tried a disarming grin. "I'm a real spontaneous guy. I was hoping Cord might be the same."

"I assure you he is not."

I shrugged. "So I'll wait until he has a few minutes he can spare me."

"That may take some time. Mr. Cord is a very busy man."

"I can appreciate that. I'm a pretty busy guy myself, Ms. ahh"—I checked the name plate on her desk—"Ms. Arnold. The thing I'm busy with right now is a matter that I happen to know is also of major importance to your Mr. Cord. If you were to inform him as to the nature of my business, I think it might surprise you how fast he'd *un*busy himself."

"At the earliest opportunity, I shall explain—"

I cut her off, showing her a very different kind of grin than I had before. "Oh, you'll explain all right. When Cord *does* find out why I'm here and that you kept me cooling my heels just so you could play your silly I'll-show-you-who's-Queen-Shit-around-this-office ego game, I figure you'll have a lot of explaining to do."

Splotches of bright red exploded across each cheek and her nostrils flared so wide that her glasses rode up. She reached jerkily to rearrange the glasses, all the while pummeling me with a hard stare.

She wanted to tell me to go fuck myself. She wanted to rip my dick out by the roots and impale it on one of her high heels. She wanted my mother to have flushed me down a toilet or my father to have spilled the seed that spawned me into a dirty pillowcase. She wanted all that and more, it was in her eyes. But what she *didn't* want was to gamble with her job. Especially not over an insignificant slob like me (just in case I turned out to be not so insignificant after all). It was another example of the kind of creeping corporate insecurity that's rotting away the middle management level of industry all across the country. It breeds vicious infighting on the one hand and a "whatever you do, don't make a final decision" mentality on the other. A few learn how to exploit this insecurity and thrive upon it, some eventually gag and end up on skid row over it. You used to see it only in men, but ever since Women's Lib came along and tried to redistribute our balls equally between the sexes, you find it in more and more women. The only difference is that they seem to develop the symptoms much sooner and much more acutely.

"Perhaps," Ms. Arnold eventually said, in a voice so tight you could have bounced dimes off it, "if you gave me some idea of what it is you wish to see Mr. Cord about, I could better judge the expediency with which I should contact him."

"Tell him I represent the family of Flo Odum and I'm here about the land he's been trying to acquire."

Five minutes later, I was being ushered into the plushly cavernous office of Clayton Cord. After a flurry of hushed phone conversations, a stone-faced, slightly flushing Ms. Arnold had escorted me as far as the third floor, where Cord's personal secretary, a bubble-busted strawberry blonde who introduced herself as Miss Dahlquist met us at the elevator door and took over.

Cord himself proved to be a tall, slender, fair-haired man in his early to mid thirties, considerably younger than I expected. Wearing a three-piece suit and a gleaming, well-practiced smile, he came striding around one end of his desk with outstretched right hand.

"Mr. Hannibal, I'm Clayton Cord. Pleased to meet you." His handshake was firm and dry, as carefully calculated as his smile. I felt an immediate measure of dislike for the man and it had nothing to do with whether or not he might be behind Flo Odum's death; it was too early for me to have formed any opinion on that. What rankled me was the half-cocky, half-smarmy air he had about him that proclaimed in no uncertain terms, "I'm willing to kick ass or kiss ass—whichever it takes—to stay on top, and I don't care who knows it."

I resisted an urge to squeeze him to his knees, and even managed a brief smile of my own. "Sorry to sort of barge in like this," I said, "but I only recently became involved with the Odum matter, so I've been playing catch-up. That means having to cut corners wherever and whenever I can."

"Hey, I know how it is," Cord replied easily. "Why don't we have a seat, make ourselves more comfortable? Would you like something to drink? Me, I'm a bourbon man and I usually indulge myself about this time of day."

"Bourbon's fine."

"Sue, two bourbon rocks please," he said to his secretary. "Then you're excused. Hold any calls, I'll buzz if I need you."

The strawberry blonde moved to some cleverly constructed walnut panels and slid them back to reveal a small but well-stocked wet bar. While she busied herself there, Cord gestured me into an indirectly lighted alcove where a half-dozen comfortable chairs were arranged around a glossy oval coffee table. The layout was a far cry from my own office back in Rockford: a narrow second-floor walk-up with a high, cobweb-streaked ceiling, linoleum on the floor, a Mr. Coffee atop one of the file cabinets behind my desk, a minifridge in the closet, and a single client's chair augmented by a lopsided old couch over against one wall. I'd have to remember to extend an invitation for Cord to stop by if he was ever up that way. Show him how slick us big city dudes have it.

We sank into chairs, facing each other over a curved end of the table. A large portion of the alcove's back wall was taken up by an ornately framed painting of a somber-faced gent wearing a gray business suit and a red bow tie. He was posed seated on the corner of a desk. On the desktop next to his hip was a toy train made of brightly colored carved wood and behind that loomed an insidiously smiling jack-in-the-box.

Young Cord noticed me noticing. "That was my father, Malcolm Cord," he explained. "The painting was originally commissioned for a *Life* magazine cover back in the late fifties. In the accompanying article, they called him the Toy Wizard of the Midwest. There may have been more than a little hype there, but Pop was quite a guy all the same. He learned the art of woodcarving—or 'whittlin' ' as he called it —as a boy, and used it as a form of relaxation all his life. As a young man, he went into partnership with another fellow on a small grocery right here in Cedarton. When business was slow, Pop would whittle. One day a peddler who was making deliveries to the store noticed some of the stuff he had carved—little dogs, cats, ducks, things like that—and he offered to take some of them with him on his rounds and try to sell them for a small commission. Up until then the stuff Pop whittled had either piled up in a back room somewhere or been given away to anybody who showed an interest. So he figured what the heck, and let the peddler take a few things. When the peddler came around the next time, he not only had sold everything he'd taken but had *orders* for more. And that's how it went for the next several months, with the peddler returning each time with more and more orders until Pop could hardly keep up with the demand. Well, along about then is when a little thing called the Great Depression hit. It didn't take long for the grocery store to go belly up, but Pop's carved toys continued to sell. Not as well as before, naturally, but well enough for him to earn a considerably better living than most folks around here were able to. The tougher times are, you see, the more people depend on escapism and entertainment to take their minds off their troubles. Pop's toys were durable and inexpensive—just the ticket for somebody wanting to provide a little joy in their kids' lives when they could barely afford to put food on the table."

Providing an ironic counterpoint to those words, Miss Dahlquist arrived with our drinks. Up close she smelled of sandalwood, and as she leaned to place a coaster and glass in front of me I could hear the whisper of silky underthings beneath her simple skirt and blouse. The bourbon, I was sure, would be of top-shelf quality and Cord evidently used the same criteria when it came to choosing secretaries. Since he'd already admitted to indulging on a regular basis as far as the bourbon was concerned, I couldn't help wondering if he also indulged himself in other ways here within the privacy of his executive sanctum.

Lucky bastard probably did, I decided, my gaze enviously following the curve of Miss Dahlquist's hip as she turned to place Cord's drink in front of him. Try as I might, even though he'd been nothing but friendly and courteous so far, I just couldn't warm to the man. For a minute there, when he'd started to talk about his "Pop," I thought I was going to have to change my mind. But that didn't rest long. The more he talked, the more obvious it became he was reciting names and events as detachedly as a grade-schooler who has learned his history lesson well but has no genuine feeling for what he's memorized. Not only had there been an absence of love or pride in young Cord's voice, but I sensed in it instead a kind of sneering resentment for the man and accomplishments of which he spoke.

After Miss Dahlquist had withdrawn and we'd sampled our drinks, I made a gesture with my hand and said, "So your father's 'whittlin' ' eventually led to all this."

Cord lowered his glass, exhaled a loud, satisfied sound, nodded. "That's right," he said. "But the key word there is 'eventually.' You see, Pop never was what you'd call a real astute corporate businessman. Not enough drive for increased productivity and profits, very little marketing sense, absolutely no killer instinct when it came to dealing with the competition. He was an idealist, God help him, and he went to his grave believing in such archaic values as personal integrity and loyalty and fair play."

"Those are traits a lot of people wouldn't exactly call reprehensible."

"No, of course not. Hell, most people would *call* them admirable. But you and I both know, don't we, Mr. Hannibal, that what people say and what they practice are two very different things. Cord Toys grew and prospered in the boom years following World War II, during a time when there still *was* a certain amount of integrity and fair play in the world and people like my father weren't instantly ground to hamburger. Even so, it's a wonder he didn't end up on a pile of wood shavings with his pockets turned inside out and everything he owned signed over to some sharpie. But somehow that didn't happen; somehow Cord Toys continued to grow, albeit in my opinion at a maddeningly slow pace. And, also in my opinion, sometimes more in spite of my father than because of him. For instance, while the rest of the country was going nuts over things like coonskin caps and Hula Hoops and plastic action figures and video games —and every other toy company you can name was cashing in with their own version of each—what was Cord Toys producing? Why, wooden pull trains and cars and trucks and ducks that float in the bathtub—the same frigging things we've been turning out for fifty years. 'Toys should stimulate a child's imagination, not take the place of it,' Pop would say whenever I tried to convince him to branch out into other things. The jack-in-the-box in the painting? That's about as high tech as he ever got."

"But now that you're in charge, you can finally take the company in some new directions."

"You bet. Hey, if that makes me sound cold, I'm sorry. I loved the old man. He'll be gone two years in January and I miss hell out of him every minute of every day. That's one thing, that's father-son stuff. But strictly from a business standpoint, he'd outlived his time and, while he may not have been an actual detriment to the company, his short-sightedness and narrow-mindedness were very limiting. He sent me away to school, saw to it I was thoroughly educated in the mechanics of modern business, now I'm finally getting a chance to put some of that to use. Besides, it's not like I'm doing some kind of about-face on him. He knew exactly how I felt, knew the changes I was likely to make when he was gone. He must have accepted it or he wouldn't have left me in control, right? It may not have been right for him, but in his heart I think he knew the changes I advocated would be good for the company."

I wondered if, in his heart, Malcolm Cord also knew his son was an asshole. I took a long pull on my bourbon to keep from saying something I wouldn't necessarily regret but would almost certainly be counterproductive to my cause.

Cord took another hit of his drink, too. As he lowered his glass, I watched his eyes change subtly, turn shrewd and measuring. He said, "All of which brings us, in a round-about way, to why you're here, Mr. Hannibal. Naturally I'd intended to contact Pearl Odum, but I wanted to wait the proper amount of time in deference to her mother's passing. I'm glad she took the initiative via you. As you drove up to the plant, you no doubt saw the geographical position I'm in. In order to do the things I want to do with Cord Toys, I need to expand the size of our present facility. I obviously can't go north or west because of the river, and if I try to go south—even if I got around the current zoning laws—which, frankly, wouldn't be that big a deal—then I'm faced with having to buy up more than a dozen separate lots all with commercial and/or residential structures on them. The individual owners would gouge me until I bled on the initial sales, and I'd still have the expense of clearing the build-ings."

"That leaves east," I said. "The Odum property. No zoning laws to grease because it's outside the city limits, a single owner to deal with, only the rubble of a shack and a handful of jack pines to clear away."

He nodded. "Even if I have to pay an exorbitant amount up front, which I was—and am—willing to do, it still figures to work out a hell of a lot smoother that way."

"How about relocating Cord Toys entirely? Wasn't there talk of that?"

"It was an option considered, yes."

"Considered seriously?"

"When it comes to business—especially the business of running Cord Toys, Mr. Hannibal—I am entirely serious."

"Some folks hereabouts seem to think the talk of moving the plant away was just a scare tactic, a ploy to put added pressure on Flo Odum in order to get her to sell."

"Some folks hereabouts think you can cure warts by chanting over them in the middle of a crossroads under a full moon. So what?"

"So this is a desperate county. Cord Toys is about all it has going for it. When you started talking about possibly moving the plant—whether it was serious or just smoke— you scared the hell out of a lot of people. Flo's sudden demise and the subsequent widely held belief that her daughter won't be nearly so stubborn about hanging on to a worthless patch of clay bottom must have caused a collective sigh of relief you could've heard all over this end of the state."

The eyes changed again, the shrewdness crowded now by hard glints of suspicion. "Exactly what are you getting at? You represent Pearl Odum, right? She *is* willing to sell, right? Is all this innuendo some kind of half-assed attempt to drive the price up even higher?"

I shook my head. "I don't represent Pearl Odum. At least not in the way you think."

"What do you mean you don't represent her? You said you were her attorney, you said you were here about the land."

"I never said I was an attorney. I'm a private detective. I'm here about the land in the sense that I'm trying to determine if someone thought it was worth killing over."

Cord shot to his feet, the color draining from his face. "Jesus Christ!" he said. "I heard some clown had shown up, trying to sell a cock-and-bull story about the old woman's death not being an accident. Is that your game, Hannibal? Are you sitting here in my office—in *my* fucking plant—and accusing me of murder?"

I leaned back in the chair, laced my fingers across my stomach, looked up at him. I liked seeing him like this, agitated, his cocky demeanor knocked all askew. I said, "You keep reading things that aren't there into what I say. I never accused you of anything—I merely said I was trying to find out if 'someone' is a murderer."

"Well, I assure you my misinterpretation of your words won't be a problem any further. This conversation is finished." So saying, he spun and marched over to his desk, where he plunged down the lever of the intercom with a dramatic flair. When Miss Dahlquist responded, he said, "Sue, get Security up here immediately. We have a very unwelcome visitor I want escorted out!"

I covered the distance to the desk in long but unhurried strides. I reached out and clamped Cord's wrist in a hard grip just as he was releasing the intercom switch. I held it that way until the back of his hand turned approximately the color of skimmed milk. Pressing my face close to his, I said, "Call off the dogs, toy man. I was just leaving. If I wasn't, you wouldn't have enough kiddie cops in this whole fucking county to make me."

He tried to pull his hand away, but I held it fast. He tried to glare at me, but didn't like what he saw on my face and had to look away.

"Call off the dogs," I said again.

I shoved his hand closer to the intercom box. After a few

seconds, his index finger flicked out and depressed the lever again. He swallowed hard and, in a slightly strained voice, said, "Cancel that request for Security, Sue. Mr. Hannibal will be leaving on his own accord."

I released my grip and he pulled away. He backed off a couple steps, shooting his cuffs and straightening his suit. From a safer distance, he tried the glare again. "I don't know who the hell you think you are, mister, but if you think your lies and strong-arm tactics are going to work around here, you've got another think coming."

"I never lied to you. I stated my name and the nature of the business I wanted to discuss with you. It was your own greed that made you jump to the wrong conclusion."

"You know damn well I never would have agreed to meet with you if you'd said up front you were the private eye looking into the possibility of Flo Odum being murdered."

"Why not? If Flo's death *was* murder, I'd think that you, the county's most prominent citizen, would surely want to see the truth found out and justice done. Unless, of course, you have something to hide."

"I have nothing to hide!"

"Maybe you don't figure you could handle the guilt if it turns out she was fried by some Cord Toy employee over-reacting because he was scared silly of losing his job after he heard your idle threats to move the plant."

"The weren't idle threats, I told you. Moving the plant was a seriously considered option. If this kind of shit keeps up, I may *still* move the damn thing!"

I showed him my shark's grin, let it spread out slow and wide. "I almost hope you do that," I said. "If there *is* some-body out there who reacted murderously when it was only bullshit, maybe this time it'll be you they come after."

He went white around the lips and his mouth opened and closed a couple times before he got any words out. "That's insane. This whole conversation is insane! I said before that it was finished—this time I mean it."

He marched to the office door, yanked it open meaningfully. I took my time using it and managed not to flinch when he slammed it hard behind me.

8

*B*ack out in the parking lot, I sat in the Plymouth and smoked a cigarette.

There was little doubt that, in spite of Sheriff Wilt's warning, I had just stepped on the *wrongest* toes in Hatchaloo County. I'd let my instinctive dislike of Clayton Cord outweigh my better judgment and had pushed him harder than his ego would ever allow. Little prick was probably already on the phone to the sheriff, whining about being harassed and using lines like "Do I have to remind you whose taxes pay one hell of a chunk of your salary each year?" And while I read Gus Wilt as being a basically honest cop, I knew all too well that if you want to go through life with a little butter on your bread then you've got to pay attention to the man with the churn. I figured it wouldn't be long before the good sheriff was on his way to inform me I was no longer welcome to wear my private-eye hat on his turf.

Which meant I'd have to stay a couple steps ahead of him. At least until Frankie The Firebug got in tomorrow. I was anxious to find out what The Bug could discover at the fire site. And there was also my meeting with Junior Odum scheduled for later tonight. Even though he was somewhat hamstrung by his fugitive status, I was pretty sure Junior wouldn't be content to just lay low and let me do all the work. If either of my unlikely allies could help me turn up something I could use to convince Wilt that Flo Odum's death had been more than an accident, then I felt certain no amount of bluster from Clayton Cord could stonewall a more thorough investigation.

If.

But if we didn't turn up anything, then I'd be looking at the Hatchaloo County line in my rearview mirror. And if a murder *had* taken place, then the killer would remain on the loose.

I looked over once again at the soot-streaked chimney poking above the jack pines. The spot suddenly seemed to be taunting me, thrusting up the stony digit as if giving me the finger. What the hell had really gone on there the night of the fire? Would I ever know, or were all the answers buried with a stubborn, prideful old woman?

I flipped my spent butt out the window and dropped the Plymouth into gear. The tires sprayed limestone. I wasn't sure where I wanted to go, only that I had to keep on the move, keep stirring the pot.

As it turned out, my trip was a short one. When I started to swing from the lot, the name of one of the bars across the street—Murphy's—caught my eye. I remembered Reba Dallas saying that Tom Wykert "still shoves plenty of money across the bar at Murphy's." I checked my watch. Past three. Wykert's wife had said he got off at four and liked to stop for a few beers. I decided as good a course of action as any would be for me to kill an hour or so over a couple beers of my own in hopes the shop chairman wouldn't be delayed too long by second-shift problems before stopping in and maybe affording me a chance to have my talk with him.

The Plymouth made the journey across the street okay and I went inside.

Murphy's was a long, narrow, high-ceilinged room with the bar running along one side and a handful of booths along the other. The walls—where they weren't covered by liquor advertisements or gag signs that said things like OUR CREDIT MANAGER IS HELEN WAITE; IF YOU WANT CREDIT, GO TO HELEN WAITE FOR IT—were mustard yellow in color with wood trim stained dark by dozens of layers of paint and varnish. A juke box, a cigarette machine, and a cooler filled with take-out goods occupied spaces where additional booths had once stood. At the far end, the room flared out and became half again as wide. There was a pinball machine back there, all but hidden by stacks of cardboard beer cases; the obligatory pool table squatting stubbornly in the middle of the floor; and a pair of round-topped card tables for playing euchre or five-card pinochle crowded into opposite corners.

It was a blue-collar bar like thousands of others you can walk into in any state of the country. I know, I've been in enough of them to qualify as something of an expert.

The place smelled of furniture polish and glass cleaner and disinfectant and sweat and cigarette smoke and spilled booze and spilled blood. It was a hybrid scent I found at once exhilarating and depressing. There were other odors, too, less pungent, more subtle, but there nonetheless: the residue of high hopes and shattered dreams, of boastful proclamations and sobbed confessions, of little men feeling big and big men feeling small, of women made to feel like everything and nothing at all. In a certain frame of mind, you might come here and never want to leave. At another time, you couldn't run fast enough or far enough.

I dug a ten from my wallet, spread it out atop the bar, slid onto a stool in front of it.

The bartender was a short, husky guy in his late twenties. His hair was clipped in a tight crewcut and he had on a red-trimmed T-shirt that showed off his flat slab of stomach, sloping shoulders, and cantaloupe-sized biceps. It was obvious he lifted a lot more than just bottles of booze to pour drinks from.

He came over in the rolling gait of a perpetual jock. "Afternoon. What can I get you?"

"Big Bud," I told him.

While he was taking care of that, I pondered the menu posted above the cash register. It may not be generally acknowledged, but factory-district taverns tend to serve some of the best food around. My faith in this truism, combined with the fact that I hadn't eaten for nearly half a dozen hours, made it easy to decide to sample some of Murphy's fare. When the bartender returned with a glass and a bottle of Budweiser, I informed him I also felt up for a cheeseburger and a side order of potato salad.

He nodded. "Get right on it."

I put some of the Bud where it would do the most good, then topped off the glass and swiveled slightly on my stool for another look around. I imagined things would change drastically when the first shift let out across the street, but in the meantime business was hardly booming. Besides me, the place only boasted three other patrons: a pair of gangly young guys shooting pool (badly, from the look of it) and a dark-haired woman who shared the bar with me. The latter was seated several stools down, watching the pool players with a kind of bored disinterest, giving the impression she wasn't with either of them.

Dwight Yoakam was singing "Honky-Tonk Man" on the juke box, accompanied by the irregular click-clack of the pool balls.

I lit a cigarette. The smoke I exhaled swirled out into a shaft of sunlight that slanted in from the front window and collided with a thousand dust motes already dancing there.

I drank some more beer and when I lowered the glass, I began tapping it in time to the music: If I wasn't careful, this could turn into something it shouldn't. A few more beers in me, a few more quarters in the juke box, I'd be ready to make a night of it.

The bartender had disappeared through a pair of batwing

doors behind the bar into what I assumed was the kitchen. He came back out now carrying a heaping bowl of potato salad with a plastic fork stuck in it, a fistful of napkins, and salt and pepper shakers. "Burger be up in a minute," he said as he deposited his load in front of me.

I sampled some of the potato salad and found it needed only a sprinkle of salt to be damn near perfect. When the burger came, it was in the same category. Meat patty as thick as the head on a good glass of beer, charred on the outside and juicy pink in the middle, fat slab of cheese, generous layers of raw onion and pickles, sturdy bun all but dwarfed by what it was trying to contain.

By the time I got on the other side of the food, it was pushing four. I signaled for another beer. I wanted to try and pump the bartender a little before he got busy with the factory crowd. As he set up another Bud, I said, "I may be a stranger in town but I sure picked the right place to stop for a bite to eat. That was great."

He nodded. "Glad you liked it."

"Far as I'm concerned, you can't hardly beat a burger and a couple cold beers. Never could see throwing money away in one of those swanky restaurants just so you can be greeted at the door by some dork in a monkey suit and waste your time soaking up phony atmosphere instead of good, honest suds."

The bartender smiled noncommittally, said nothing.

I rambled on. "Speaking of atmosphere, I guess yours here will be changing pretty quick when that factory across the way lets out, uh?"

Another nod. "Usually works out that way."

He took my ten from the bar, carried it over to the register, and began ringing up my tab. Not exactly what you'd call the talkative type.

I shifted into a more direct gear. "Hey," I called, "take out enough to set yourself up with something."

He finished making change for the ten, turned back wearing the noncommittal smile again. "Thanks, but no thanks," he said. "I got a long night ahead of me. I start drinking now, I'd never see closing time." He scattered my change out in front of me.

"Besides, Reggie don't drink much at all no more. 'Less it's that shitty-tastin' Gatorade, or some kind of fruit juice or somethin'. But anything with nasty ol' alcohol in it ain't good for buildin' those pretty muscles, is it, Reggie?"

I hadn't noticed until she spoke, but the dark-haired woman had vacated her stool and moved down to lean against the bar at my left elbow. From a distance I would have guessed her to be in her mid-twenties, but up closer I saw that she was looking back on thirty. She was attractive in a coarse, blatant kind of way, with a foamy mane of hair and prominent breasts proudly displayed by a low-cut black sweater. There was a certain hardness around her eyes and mouth and a trace of too-much-booze puffiness in her face that indicated the miles covered in those thirty-odd years hadn't all been smooth ones.

In response to the woman's remark, the bartender, rather stiffly, as if reciting a lesson, said, "Alcohol is a depressant and it depletes your body of important fluids."

The woman showed him a bawdy, lopsided grin. "Ooo, I love it when you talk dirty. I been waitin' to deplete your body of some important fluids for a long time now, Reggie honey. When am I goin' to get my chance?"

The bartender—Reggie—actually blushed. He could feel himself doing it and it pissed him off, I could tell by the way the muscles bounced over the hinges of his jaw and the way he wouldn't look at me. "You want something, Meg," he said to the woman, "or did you come down here just to be embarrassing?"

"Aw, am I embarrassin' you, Reggie honey? You're the one who started with the sexy talk and all, so I naturally figured—"

"What do you *want,* Meg?" The look he gave her along with the question warned her not to push it any farther.

She heeded the warning, but couldn't resist a triumphant little smirk. "Okay, you ol' poophead, I need some change for the juke box is all. 'Scuse me for livin'."

She handed him a couple ones and he gave her back a handful of quarters. As she pushed away from the bar, she hesitated ever so slightly in her turn toward the juke box and gave me a smoldering once-over, her heavily mascaraed eyes filled with all sorts of challenges and possibilities. And I had just enough loneliness and beer in me to feel a responsive surge in my groin. I followed her progress toward the music machine, watching the sway of her ample bottom in a pair of jeans as tight as sausage skin. She knew I was watching and I knew she knew. It's a routine that's been around, in one version or another, ever since Eve purposely let a fig leaf slip in order to get a rise out of Adam. This particular variation had no doubt been played out hundreds of times right here in this room.

Even young Reggie recognized it for what it was. From behind the bar, he said, "You don't want to mess with that, man. She's a pig."

I turned slowly back to face him, rolling things over in my mind. I had *x* amount of time to kill before Tom Wykert showed up—if indeed he stopped in at all today. In the meantime, if I hoped to nudge loose any stray bits of information that might be laying about, were my chances better with the taciturn Reggie or the brash Meg? Again, it wasn't a real hard decision to make. I'd be a liar if I said the inviting waggle of her ass or the yard-and-a-half of cleavage she'd displayed while leaning against the bar didn't figure into it to some degree; but I'd like to think that, by and large, my reasoning was rooted more in logic than hormones.

I grinned at Reggie and said, "I'm not Jewish, son. I got nothing against a little pork now and then."

He looked at me for a minute like he was genuinely disappointed in me, then gave a fatalistic shrug and drifted away.

I slid from my bar stool, carried my glass of beer over to the juke box. A new song had begun to play and Meg's blue-jean-encased rear end was twitching rhythmically to the beat as she scanned the selection list, poised to punch another number. I moved up beside her and leaned against throbbing, pulsing neon.

"Bad thing about juke boxes," I said, "is that one person forks over the money while everybody else gets to listen for free."

"But the good thing," she countered, without looking up, "is that the one doin' the payin' gets to do the choosin'. You wouldn't believe some of the shit they got on here that people will go and play."

"So you keep feeding the box in order not to have to listen to somebody else's lousy picks, is that it?"

"Sometimes. Sometimes I feed it just to keep it playin'. For the company. Only thing worse'n sittin' alone in a bar listenin' to lousy music is sittin' alone in a bar listenin' to *no* music.

"Pretty thing like you shouldn't have to be alone unless that's the way you want it."

"You think anybody who really wanted to be alone'd come here to do it?"

"How about I take a shot at it then? Keeping you company, that is. Let me buy you a drink."

She showed me a smile. "Thought you'd never ask."

She named her poison and while she finished punching the rest of her selections I went to the bar and ordered a margarita for her and another beer for me. Reggie's expression remained carefully blank as he filled the order. When I turned back with the drinks, Meg had taken a seat in one of the booths.

I settled in across from her and we drank a toast to keeping company.

After we'd lowered our glasses, she said, "I heard you tell Reggie you were a stranger in town. You move here, or just passin' through?"

"Just passing through."

"Yeah. Dumb question. Who'd move *here* from anywhere, right?"

I shrugged. "It seems to have certain attractions." I was looking at her cleavage when I said it.

She smiled again, enjoying the crude flattery. "You got a name?" she wanted to know.

"Sure. Doesn't everybody?"

"Mine's Meg. What's yours?"

"Hannibal. Joe Hannibal." I could almost hear the theme music in the background; eat your heart out, Sean Connery. "I'm the private detective," I went on, "who came down from up north hoping to nab Junior Odum if he showed for his mother's funeral. Well, he didn't, but I hung around because members of the Odum family asked me to look into the circumstances surrounding Old Flo's death. And if you haven't already heard about all that by now, then you're practically the only one in Hatchaloo County who hasn't."

Her head was bobbing up and down by the time I finished. "Yeah. Yeah, sure, I heard about you. So you're the guy." Her eyes narrowed with a hint of suspicion. "Say, I'm goin' to be real disappointed if it turns out you only bought me this drink so's you could ask me a bunch of questions and stuff."

"Why should I want to ask you a bunch of questions? Do you know something that could help my investigation?"

"All I know is what I read in the funny papers."

"Okay. So I bought you the drink because I try never to pass up an opportunity to spend some time with a pretty lady."

"Boy, what a horse laugh you'd get from most of the folks in this town if they heard you call me a lady."

"That sounds like their problem. I spend a big chunk of every day not giving a rat's ass what other people think."

"Hey, I like your style, mister. Live and let live, right?"

"Something like that."

"So what brings you here to Murphy's in the middle of the afternoon?"

"Did you accept that drink just so you could ask me a bunch of questions and stuff?"

She giggled at my teasing. "Come on. I'm kinda glad you're not, but shouldn't you be out chasin' down clues or followin' up on leads or somethin' like that?"

"If I had any clues to chase down or leads to follow up on, I most likely would be doing just that. But I seem to be fresh out of those things at the moment. I guess you could say I'm here because I got no place better to be."

"Join the club."

Offhandedly, I said, "Oh, there's the chance I might run into a certain fella here—a fella who could maybe clear up a couple points for me."

"Yeah? Who'd that be?"

"Guy by the name of Tom Wykert. Know him?"

She rolled her eyes. "Yeah, I know him all right. Let me give you a word of advice on that one, mister: don't go crowdin' Tom Wykert with a bunch of questions."

"Why not?"

" 'Cause he's an ornery, hot-headed sonofabitch. You catch him in the wrong mood, he might give you the kind of answer you wouldn't want to hear—like a beer bottle alongside the head or a kick to the balls. I've seen him do exactly that kind of thing for hardly no reason at all. He's quick and he's mean and he's vicious. He's the type ain't satisfied with just puttin' a man down, he'll want to go ahead and stomp that man into the ground."

I frowned. "I heard he was some sort of union official over at the toy factory. Normally, a position like that would indicate somebody who's fairly levelheaded."

"Sure, he's shop chairman of the local there at Cord. But believe me, it ain't got nuthin' to do with his levelheadedness. I think the people voted him in 'cause they figured he'd intimidate the company; now they're afraid to vote him out 'cause he intimidates *them*."

It was a familiar tune. Reba Dallas had hummed a few bars of it when she first told me about Wykert. "But he does stop in here pretty regularly, is that right?" I asked of Meg.

"Most every day, yeah." She dug out a cigarette, lit it, exhaled smoke through her nostrils. She scowled at me. "Look, if you're here just to see Tom Wykert, then I'll thank you kindly for the drink and be movin' out. I thought maybe me and you could have some fun together. But waitin' around for you and Wykert to butt heads ain't my idea of fun."

I reached out and touched her arm. "Hey," I said with an easy grin, "calm down. Nobody said I was in a *hurry* to talk with Wykert."

"Uh-huh. But that's only 'cause he ain't here yet, right?"

I withdrew my hand, shrugged. "Have it your way."

We sat there eyeing each other through the curling cigarette smoke. After a while, she gave a shake of her head and accompanied it with a rueful smile. "Can you believe this?" she said. "I'm sittin' here talkin' tough to a for-real private eye. Jeez, you'd think I was Lauren Bacall or Veronica Lake or one of them babes from some old black-and-white detective movie."

"Nah, you're not the Bacall or Lake type," I told her. "They were slinky and scrawny. You're a Jane Russell all the way."

She frowned. "Did Jane Russell ever make any movies with Humphrey Bogart?"

"Not that I know of."

"Well, hell, that's okay 'cause you're not the Bogart type any more than I'm a Bacall. He was kinda scrawny, too, wasn't he? Let's see, you'd be more . . . a Bob Mitchum maybe, or a Burt Lancaster . . ."

I laughed. "Burt Lancaster with a boot heel nose job maybe."

"Did Jane and Burt make any movies together?"

"Who cares? We're Joe and Meg, not anybody else. We'll write our own script."

She took the middle finger of her right hand and ran it around the rim of her glass, wiping away some of the salt crystals Reggie had smeared there, then inserted the fingertip in her mouth and slowly drew it back out. It was a highly suggestive bit of business, made even more so by the smoky gaze she was aiming at me the whole time. "I like the sound of that," she said. "Writin' our own script. I already got a couple scenes in mind I think'd be real entertainin'."

The conversation seemed abruptly to have taken a turn toward something far removed from Tom Wykert or the expansion of Cord Toys or Flo Odum's death or Junior Odum's capture or any of the things I was supposed to be concerning myself with. What's more, I didn't find that eventuality particularly unappealing. The woman had obviously been around the block a few times, but what the hell. I was hardly a choirboy fresh for the plucking. What I was, was a skirmish-scarred veteran of a too often lonely profession a long way from home, with a reckless amount of booze in my gut, half a hard-on in my pants, and too much time to kill before my next clear move. All things considered, we very likely would have ended up acting out some of those scenes from Meg's script.

But it never came to that because the front door opened and somebody walked in.

"Hey, Reggie. Set me up a shot and a beer. Make the beer Stroh's, the whiskey Johnnie Walker Red. And don't go too far with the bottle."

I didn't recognize the voice of the new patron, but I had no trouble recognizing the expressions that fell across Meg's face. It wasn't fear exactly—but apprehension and concern, and plenty of both. It tore her gaze away from me and made her go tight around the mouth. I tensed a little myself, then twisted in my seat to have a look at the newcomer who'd caused such an adverse reaction in my companion.

Vern Stroud was just hiking a leg to climb onto a bar stool when our eyes met.

The leg froze in mid air. After several beats his mouth curved slowly into a mocking, nasty smile. "Well, looky, looky here," he drawled. "If it ain't the sucker-punchin' shamus hisself."

The foot returned to the floor with a soft plop and he pushed off on it, heading in our direction. He was more than a little unsteady on his feet. It was evident he hadn't stopped drinking after the incident in the trailer that morning. It was also evident, both from his remark and from the meanness dancing in his eyes, that he hadn't forgotten my wallop to the jaw.

It seemed like a bad idea to let him corner me in the tight confines of the booth. I slid out and stood to meet him, trying to make the act appear casual, nonaggressive, not wanting to fuel his belligerence. He hesitated as I came to my feet, then veered slightly to his right and moved parallel with the end of the booth for several steps. He stopped as his bloodshot eyes seemed to spot Meg for the first time.

"And you," he said thickly. "What the hell you doin' talkin' to this nosy bastard?"

"I'm free, white, and over twenty-one," Meg shot back. "Who I decide to talk to is nobody's business but mine."

"Fuck that! I want to know what kind of shit you're loadin' him up with."

"Hey," Reggie called from behind the bar. "You got some kind of problem over there, Vern?"

Stroud reeled at the bartender's question, turning to glower at him. "Yeah, I got a problem," he said. *"This* sumbitch—" he jerked a thumb in my direction—"is my problem. I tangled assholes with him once today and came off second best because he's a sucker-punch artist. Well, I mean to even the score right here and now."

Reggie's expression turned as hard as the polished wood of the bar top. "No," he said flatly. "Not in my place you're not. You know I don't allow that kind of shit in here."

"Then why'd you allow *this* piece of shit in here?" Stroud demanded. Again a thumb jerked in my direction.

The drunken slob was starting to get on my nerves. I said, "In the past two minutes, Stroud, you've called me a bastard, a sonofabitch, and a piece of shit. I think that's about enough."

"Joe . . ." Meg said cautioningly.

Stroud spun to face us once more. "I don't give a flyin' fuck at a rollin' doughnut *what* you think, buster," he sneered at me. Then his eyes swung to Meg. "And you, you whore, I'll be dealin' with you when I'm finished with him."

"That's it," Reggie said. "Out! Hit the fucking door, Vern. Right now. I've told you enough times about starting trouble in here."

Everything went quiet for a time. Even the juke box was between plays. The two gangly guys at the pool table stood motionless and bug-eyed, looking like they wanted to crawl into a couple of the pockets and hide.

Stroud stood motionless, too, except for a bit of drunken teetering. His eyes whipped back and forth between Meg and me. After several long seconds, he took a tentative step back. Then another. As if obeying Reggie's command. But suddenly, with surprising speed and coordination, he spun and snatched up one of the bar stools then whirled back, jabbing it at me like a lion tamer's chair.

"Come on, you cocksucker," he jeered. "Come on, let's get it done. Let's see how tough you are when you ain't comin' in behind a sucker punch."

Before I could respond in any way, Reggie did a one-hand vault over the top of the bar and came bounding between us, wielding a miniature Louisville Slugger. With the latter, he backhanded a ringing whack to one of the metal stool legs. Stroud recoiled, more from surprise than from the force of the blow.

"Goddamn you, Vern," Reggie said. "I'll split your skull with this if I have to. Then I'll have your sorry ass hauled to the county jail and I'll sign every complaint I can get my hands on. You know damn well the sheriff over there has no love for you."

Stroud looked suddenly betrayed and confused, like a child who's been punished for a reason he doesn't understand. "But I owe that sumbitch, Reggie," he said, almost whining.

"Fine. But settle with him somewhere else. Not here, not in my place."

Nobody said anything. The juke box had begun playing Springsteen's "Cover Me."

Stroud slowly lowered the bar stool. "Shit," he said, then let it drop. It rolled jerkily away from him.

Reggie lowered the Louisville Slugger as well. "Go home, Vern," he said, softer now. "You need to get some sleep and you need to stay away from the bottle for awhile. I don't want to see you back in here anymore today."

"Yeah," Stroud said dully, to no one in particular. Slowly, shufflingly, without even a glance in my or Meg's direction, he turned and walked out the door.

"What an asshole," Meg said when he was gone.

Reggie gave her a look that could have meant a lot of things, none of them very nice.

Before the two of them decided to get into it, I said to him, "Thanks for stepping in when you did. It could have gotten a little hairy with that stool."

The no-nonsense young bartender shrugged. "I don't allow that kind of shit in my place, that's all."

"Just for the record," I said, "that so-called sucker punch

was my reaction to Stroud's nearly braining his wife with a full can of beer."

"Yeah, he's real good at that kind of thing," Meg said bitterly.

Reggie paid her no attention this time. "Look," he said to me, "no offense, but I think it would be best if you finished your beer and then found someplace else to do any more drinking you might have in mind."

"What the hell for?" Meg exploded, coming to her feet. "He didn't start anything, why should he have to leave?"

Still ignoring her, still looking at me, Reggie said, "Because I don't want to go through this all over again if Tom Wykert shows up."

I smiled knowingly. "You're not exactly the friendliest character who ever poured me a drink, but you run a tight ship, I'll give you that. I understand where you're coming from. I'll be on my way."

"Well, *I* sure as hell don't understand where he's coming from," Meg said.

I shushed her. "It's okay. Really. I'd probably do the same thing in his place."

I leaned over and began picking up my change. Reggie retrieved the fallen bar stool and put it back where it belonged. One of the pool shooters began lining up his next shot.

Meg stood by looking uncertain.

Finally, she moved close and pressed herself against me. "I'm coming with you. Right? I mean, we're . . ."

I took her two hands in mine and held them between us, creating some distance. Her return grip was tentative. "Look," I said, "wherever we were headed a few minutes ago was probably never a good idea in the first place. And now . . . well, the moment's past. Burt and Jane never did make a movie together, I think maybe we ought to take our cue from them and leave it be."

Her eyes wouldn't meet mine. "Yeah. Sure."

"Besides," I went on, "I'm fast becoming the most unpopular guy in town and from the sound of it you've already got enough troubles of your own. You don't want to add to your problems by sticking too close to me."

She pulled her hands away and placed them on her hips. "Look, mister, if you want to leave, leave. But don't be tellin' me what *I* want, okay?"

I nodded. "Okay. But I would like to tell you one thing."

"And that is?"

"I don't know what's gone on between you and Vern Stroud, but he obviously felt he has some kind of claim on you. Whatever's done is done, but you can do better than him, kid. You really can."

"Yeah. Just look around. I got the cream of the crop hangin' all over me, don't I?"

"You've got to quit selling yourself short before anybody else will."

"Hey, I really appreciate all this swell advice, Hannibal, but I think I'd rather just have another drink, you know?"

I shrugged. "Yeah. Well, I'm persona non grata around here, so I can't buy it for you. See you around."

"Sure. I'll try to pick you out of the crowd."

She turned and headed for her original spot at the bar. This time the exaggerated switch of her ass sent a very different message than it had before.

9

It was a couple minutes past four when I emerged from Murphy's. Across the street, lines of Cord Toys employees were filing out through the turnstile gates and scurrying toward where they were parked. I fired up the old Plymouth and got rolling without wasting any time, hurrying away from there before the street began to fill with vehicles. There are few things on this earth more indiscriminately ruthless than a motorized stampede of factory workers at the end of their shift.

I drove west until I reached the river, then turned south and followed the winding water along the edge of the town. I lit a cigarette from the dashboard lighter and exhaled a stream of smoke through the open window into the clean, cooling late-afternoon air. A kind of weariness started to settle over me, the aftermath of the emotional roller coaster I'd been riding combined with the alcohol I'd consumed and the pressing weight of my growing frustration.

I was no closer now to finding any of the answers Junior Odum wanted than I had been yesterday at this time—before I even knew the questions. Hell, so far I hadn't even been able to convince *myself* that his mother was murdered. Sometimes you get a hunch or a feeling about a case, but this time there was nothing. I don't like coincidences any better than the next guy—maybe less than most—but they happen every day. That's why somebody gave them a name.

I took a hard drag on the Pall Mall, watching its tip flare cherry red in front of my face. And people die as a result of careless smoking habits every day, too, I told myself.

Yeah. You bet.

But a hell of a lot more get killed each day by somebody else.

Just ahead, the street curved away from the river in conjunction with a section of the bank that jutted out, clifflike, over the water. The area was fenced by stubby white posts marking a small wayside park complete with a pair of outhouses and a scattering of picnic tables.

I pulled in and parked, facing the river.

I had the place to myself.

I cut the engine and sat there, smoking, ruminating, trying to draw together in my mind all the things I'd seen and heard and thought in the past dozen and a half hours, trying to form it into a pattern that made some kind of sense or at least gave me some kind of *feeling* for what I was about.

I was vaguely aware of the intermittent flow of cars coming down the street behind me, some continuing on out of town, most turning off into one of the residential blocks. Cord employees going home for supper and an evening in front of the tube.

The cars became fewer and farther apart until they tapered off completely, gradually leaving me with the sensation of being all alone on the edge of a remote wilderness. As long as I didn't turn around and look at Cedarton directly behind me, there wasn't a house or a sign of civilization in sight. Across the river was nothing but choppy hills covered by stands of thick timber, with an occasional outcropping of bare rock. A steady breeze was building and the ruffled trees, from a distance, took on the same shimmering appearance as the water, only covering a broader range of shifting colors. The leaves had begun to turn early that year, creating a spectrum that ran from green to purple, hitting shades of gold, orange, and red in between. Awash in slanting sunlight, it was truly something to behold.

I stabbed out my cigarette, got out of the car. I walked a ways, making sure to keep the town at my back. I stopped and reached high with both hands, stretching as far as I could, held it a long moment, then bent forward and touched my toes. Twice. When I straightened up, the wind gusted, stirring my hair, pressing against my face. It felt good, smelled good.

Without warning, my mind flashed to an image of Flo Odum. I pictured her standing outside her patched-up shack on a day like this, the wind in her hair, the good, clean taste of it on her lips. And I understood perfectly why she hadn't wanted to give up her piece of this land.

But was the good-smelling, clean-tasting breeze hiding something? Was the stink of murder somewhere close by—covered over, festering, its stench building until somebody came along and tore the lid off, exposing it for the vile thing that it was?

Would that somebody be me?

Or was there nothing ill in the wind after all and was I merely chasing the wild geese of coincidence and Junior Odum's guilt-fed demons?

Right back to square one.

Shit.

I jammed my hands in my pockets and walked to the edge of the cliff. The crash landing of my short-lived exhilaration left me weary again, unmotivated, aimless. The water seemed to have lost its sparkle and the trees across the river were just trees across a river. I considered going back to my motel room and waiting there until Reba Dallas came to take me to the rendezvous with her cousin. There was still the chance that Junior—or Frankie The Firebug when he got in tomorrow—would be able to provide me with something, a handle, a toehold, a glimmer of light to lead me out this dead-end tunnel I was floundering in. At least I had enough resolve to hope for that.

But if Clayton Cord had indeed sicced the sheriff on me, then the motel would be the first place Wilt looked—and would keep coming back to. So if I hoped to stay clear of the law, I'd best also stay clear of the Lincolnway.

I kicked some stones loose at the edge of the grass, leaned to pick one up, straightened, and sailed it down at the river. I was trying to make it skip, but it disappeared with a single kick of water and a "ker-blurp!" of sound.

As a kid I'd spent hours skimming stones across the duck pond on my grandfather's farm. Skimming and dreaming my boyhood dreams, my body and throwing arm on auto pilot while my mind played out fantasies that fluctuated primarily between the game-winning heroics of a big-league baseball player and the clenched-teeth deeds of a big-city cop. Later, when I learned you had to balance your dreams with practicality, I began to concentrate on the latter. Ironically, this path was pursued because of—yet at the same time in spite of—my grandfather. Gramps had been a big-city (Chicago) cop, you see, and some of my earliest memories were of him regaling the family with tales of his exploits. It was one such exploit that left him with the bullet-damaged hip that forced his early retirement and led to his purchase of the southern Wisconsin dairy farm where I grew up after my folks were killed. I had no recollection of him actually being a police detective, only as a grinning, shovel-handed, bib-overall-clad bear of a man with a weather-reddened face and a band of pale white high on his forehead from the cap he always wore outdoors. It had been his fondest wish that I remain on the farm he'd grown to love so, to take it over one day. But the seeds of those early stories were rooted too deep and by the time I graduated from high school I knew, with certainty and with a kind of sadness, that the only footsteps of his I could ever follow in would be on a police beat somewhere, not across the fields and pastures of the farm. He was there when I graduated from the academy, him and Gram, beaming, decked out in their Sunday-go-to-meetin' best, but I was never sure if the tears I saw glistening in the corners of his eyes that day were from pride or from disappointment.

I felt a sudden determination to skip a stone across the Hatchaloo River. The angle was all wrong. I'd been throwing from too high and the river wasn't all that wide to begin with, but with the right stone and just the right technique . . . I squatted and began rummaging through the gravel on the lip of the cliff, selecting only the flattest, smoothest missiles. When I had a dozen or so gathered, I stood, planted my feet, cocked my shoulders, and whipped one down at the water.

Ker-blurp!

One by one, I went through the whole handful without producing a single skip. Obviously defective stones.

I gathered up another dozen and started in with them. Beads of sweat popped out on my forehead and across the nape of my neck. No auto pilot today, no letting the mind roam down paths of boyhood fantasy. I blocked out everything else and focused with a kind of mad intensity on the task of making one of those soulless damn chunks of rock bounce on water. It was serious work, hard work, but a job that needed doing and, by God, I was just the cookie to do her. Yeah. Get that flick of the wrist down pat and it would be all over but the shouting.

I'd taken off my jacket and was on my fourth or fifth handful of stones, sweating like a horse, when my concentration was broken by the whine of a powerful engine downshifting in the street behind me. I turned, scowling, irritated at the interruption.

The engine belonged to a late model silver Corvette convertible. I watched as it swung in and parked alongside my Plymouth. Talk about a cold example of your have and have-not society.

I couldn't make out anything or anybody behind the smoked glass of the 'Vette's windshield, but I didn't have much time to wonder about it. The driver's door popped open and a woman got out. She paused, regarding me over the top of the door, then pushed it closed and came toward me. She was tall and slender, as streamlined as the car, with long walnut-colored hair that trailed out in the wind like that of the heroine in the cover painting of a paperback romance novel. She wore a salmon-colored sweatshirt with the neck and sleeves cut away and snug, faded jeans tucked into burgundy cowboy boots. She walked in long, clean strides.

"Hi," she said.

"Hello," I returned.

"Am I interrupting anything?" She had the kind of smoky, slightly scratchy voice that causes invisible, multilegged little creatures to scurry back and forth low across a man's gut. From a distance she'd appeared pretty, up close she was striking. Lime-green eyes beneath bold, dark brows, the cheekbones and smooth complexion of a model. I guessed her to be somewhere between thirty and forty, and in anything but direct sunlight she could have passed for twenty-five.

"Uh, no," I said in response to the question. "Nothing important."

I felt a little silly standing there with sweat dripping off the end of my nose, clutching my dusty bits of gravel.

"It looked like you were throwing something away."

I cleared my throat. "What I was doing was throwing stones. Down at the river there. Trying to, uh, make them skip across the water."

She looked past me and down, frowning. "You can skip them from this angle?"

"Well, not every time," I conceded. Then added stubbornly: "But it can be done."

She stood with feet shoulder-width apart, fingers jammed

into hip pockets, thumbs hooked through belt loops. "Is that some sort of thought stimulation process?" she wanted to know. "I was under the impression you hard-boiled P.I. types always chugged rye whiskey or found some overly endowed bimbo to slap around when you were stymied on a case."

" 'Hard-boiled P.I. types'?" I said. " 'Stymied'?"

"You *are* the private eye, right? Hammond or Hamilton —something like that?"

"Try Hannibal. Joe Hannibal. And yeah, I'm a private eye. But if you didn't even have the name straight, how were you able to recognize me?"

She cocked one eyebrow smugly. "You and your car make a rather unique team. I heard you described as a big, rough-edged guy driving a puke-green Plymouth with enough missing chrome and rust holes to qualify for federal disaster relief. Quote, unquote. That's a description that tends to stick in one's mind."

"I could think of somewhere else to stick it in whoever said it."

"Mmm. I see you've got the tough, corner-of-the-mouth snarl down very well."

"Yeah, but I haven't stymied a bimbo in, oh, six, eight weeks now."

"You throw rocks at the water instead."

"Whatever works, works. I never acquired a taste for rye whiskey, and good bimbos are getting harder and harder to find these days. Especially when you're operating on strange turf. Back home, I try to keep two or three of them on tap. Never can tell when I might need one to slap around in order to stimulate the ol' thought process."

"It's comforting to hear that certain traditions are being carried on."

"Uh-huh. You know, traditionally speaking, whenever a P.I. encounters an attractive dame in the middle of a case, it usually means one of two things; either she turns out to be the killer, or she's on hand to provide a little gratuitous sex. Sometimes both. I don't suppose I'd be lucky enough to have your arrival on the scene mean you're here to carry on that particular tradition?"

"Wow, that's some slick investigative technique you've got there, Hannibal. Multiple choice. (A) Are you the killer; (B) will you hop in the sack with me; or (C) all of the above? You really get anywhere with that?"

"I manage."

"It's a wonder."

"I appreciate your concern and the constructive criticism and all. Really. But you think maybe somewhere in here you could tell me just who the hell you are?"

"The name is Courtney Cord." She threw it out challengingly, as if it should mean something to me.

I thought it did. I said, "Would that be as in *Mrs. Clayton Cord?*"

She barked a quick, derisive laugh. "God, no. I'm Clayton's sister, not his wife. Bad enough to be related to him through a misfortune of birth, please don't suggest I had any choice in the matter."

"You don't sound especially fond of the lad."

"My brother is a pompous little turd. If you don't already know that, I expect you'll be finding it out soon enough."

I grinned. "As a matter of fact, I *do* already know it."

"You do?"

"I met with him about an hour ago. He kicked me out of his office."

She returned my grin. "Good for you. I'd be suspicious of anyone who met with Clayton and came away with a positive impression. Although I must say you don't look as if you'd lend yourself very well to being kicked out of anywhere by anybody—least of all my wimp of a brother."

I shrugged. "Let's just say I'd decided it was time to leave anyway."

She accepted that with a small nod, then eyed me solemnly. "We need to talk, Hannibal. A bit more seriously than this singles-bar banter we've been exchanging so far. Can we perhaps have a seat at one of those picnic tables over there so we could do that?"

I was about to answer in the affirmative when I remembered the stones I was still holding in my left hand. I don't fully understand why it was so important for me to make one of the damn things skip in the first place, and I understand even less why I felt comfortable enough in the presence of Courtney Cord to be willing to attempt it with her standing there.

But it was, and I did.

"I'd be happy to sit and chat with you, Miss Cord," I told her. "But first I have some unfinished business to take care of."

I turned away from her perplexed expression, shrugged once more into my stance, dropped one of the stones from my left palm into my right fist, wound up, and threw.

Again the single kick of water, again the dreaded kerblurp! of the stone sinking instantly.

I had three stones left. Fresh sweat was already trickling down my temples. Twice more I threw—long, sweeping sidearms with a finishing wrist flick, an upward flip of the palm at precisely the point of release in an attempt to make the missile break and start to swoop just before it hit the water. Twice more my efforts nose-dived immediately out of sight.

My remaining stone was a lopsidedly round lump, nowhere near flat enough or smooth enough, a piss-poor selection I probably couldn't skip across a sheet of ice. But pride —or some such foolishness—dictated I play the cards I'd been dealt. I was dripping sweat again and my shoulder was starting to throb. I could feel Courtney watching me intently, but I wouldn't look at her.

It was the bottom of the ninth, the count was full, the bases were loaded, and Reggie Jackson was at the plate.

And at this stage of this particular game, there were no foul balls, walks, or mere base hits left. The pitch either made it across the plate or it went out of the park. This would be my final attempt. If I failed, I would lose a kind of battle with myself—a battle that might appear childish on the outside, but down deep was something more.

I cocked my shoulders, went into my windup, threw. The awkward lump sailed out and down, broke at the last possible instant, started its swoop, and—snick-snickity-snick! across the water it scampered, then disappeared into the high grass of the opposite bank.

I gave the air an excited punch, drove it home with a satisfied "Yeah!"

When I finally turned to look at Courtney—fighting to be nonchalant, to be cool—she was watching me with a bemused smile on her lips. But in her eyes there was something else, something that gave me the eerie feeling she understood better what had just happened than I did.

She said, "You look as if you're going to bust if you aren't able to give somebody the high five."

"Would you?" I asked.

She gave me a little shake of her head, as if to say "I can't believe I'm really doing this," but all the while she was raising her arms. I clapped my palms against hers and tiny clouds of gravel dust spurted out on impact.

"There," I said, lowering my hands. "Now we can go have that serious talk."

10

"*E*verybody knows why you're in town."

"So it would seem."

"You're here to prove Flo Odum was murdered."

"Well, something like that. Actually I'm here to try and find out *if* she was murdered. There's a difference. The way you put it makes it sound like I might be willing to stack the deck if need be in order to make my case. All I'm after is the truth."

"The bottom line is the same as far as I'm concerned. If it does turn out she was murdered, who would be the most likely suspect?"

"I guess a lot of people would lean toward your brother. Him or somebody acting in his interest."

"Precisely. Clayton may be all the tings I said he was, and more. But he is *not* a murderer. You can trot out the old saw about blood being thicker than water if you like, maybe it applies here. Clayton and I haven't gotten along since . . . well, practically since we were both old enough to talk. But it is entirely possible to dislike someone—to loathe ninety-nine percent of the things they say and do and stand for— yet, if that someone is a close relative, to still feel a bond, a kind of love I guess you'd have to call it, toward them. That's how it is with Clayton and me. Still, I think I'm able to be objective. If you were to tell me he swindled the old woman, or pressured her unfairly or lied or cheated—I could buy any of that in a minute. But not murder. That I can't accept."

"Why? Because you truly feel he's incapable of such a thing—or because you're not ready to accept being the sister of a killer?"

"That's a hell of a thing to say."

"No offense meant. It'd be natural enough if you felt that way. We all feel a certain amount of responsibility for the actions of our friends and loved ones. If they do good, we're proud; if they screw up, we immediately wonder if we failed them in some way, if some of the guilt might be ours. Too often, unfortunately, that is the only guilt that's ever felt."

"Gee, I didn't know they handed out pop psychology degrees along with P.I. licenses."

"Nuts to that. Degrees are for jerks who think you can learn all about something without grabbing hold of it, without getting your hands dirty. Me, I'm the hands-on type. I've dirtied these paws on all kinds of bad shit. Enough to know you have to be able to recognize it for what it is so you can deal with it, or run the risk of letting it suck you under and smother you."

"You have such a genteel way of putting things, Hannibal."

"Yeah, but I get my point across, don't I?"

"Oh, sure you do. That you do."

We were seated facing each other across one of the picnic tables. The sun was going fast, but the breeze was still strong and warm. I was watching the way it played with Courtney Cord's long hair and more than once I had an urge to reach out and help it.

"All right," she said after a minute or so of brooding silence. "Anyone is capable of murder under certain circumstances. I'll concede that much. God knows it's a point that's been made over and over and over by everything from newspaper headlines to TV docudramas. I still don't for one second believe that Clayton *is* a murderer, but I'm obviously biased for all the reasons that have already been mentioned. Now here's the other side of the coin: I also don't believe for one second that Flo Odum's death was an accident."

That knocked my eyebrows up several notches. This woman with the swirling hair and lime-green gaze was full of surprises.

"You don't?" I said somewhat incredulously.

She gave a firm shake of her head and repeated, "Not for one second."

I cleared my throat. "In other words, you can't buy your brother as the perpetrator but you *do* buy Flo Odum as a murder victim."

"Exactly. So you see the quandary that puts me in. On the one hand, I want very much to see the investigation into Flo's death reopened. On the other, I'm concerned about . . . well, the grief such an investigation might cause my brother."

"Why?"

She frowned at the question. "I just told you why. We may have our differences, but Clayton is nevertheless—"

"No, I mean what makes you think Flo was murdered? Why don't you accept the official accident version?"

"The timing stinks. It would be too much of a coincidence to believe such an 'accident' befell her right at a time when it was so damn convenient for so many people. You've probably heard about the threats and the loose talk and all, but you can't imagine how it *felt* around here in those days just before the fire. There was an ugliness in the air—a mixed mood of apprehension and resentment that pressed down so heavy on this whole county you could actually feel it every time you stepped out of doors. It was a bad feeling, like the deep queasiness you get when you know you're going to be sick and there isn't a damn thing you can do but wait for it to be over with."

"You had a premonition Flo Odum was going to be killed?"

"God, no. You think I would have just stood by and let it happen? I had a feeling *something* bad was building, but I never dreamed it would be anything as bad as that."

"When I talked with Sheriff Wilt earlier today he also spoke of a bad occurrence he seemed to think somebody should have seen coming. Only he was referring to Flo's careless smoking habits. He said she had a history of nodding off with lit cigarettes in her hand and more or less implied a serious accident was inevitable."

"That's a crock."

"She wasn't careless with her smoking?"

"Well, not—okay, yes, she was. But she didn't fall asleep in bed with a lit cigarette and cause her own death, dammit."

"How can you be sure?"

"Because she wasn't stupid. She knew the problem she had. There was an accident only a year or so ago when she woke up in the middle of the night and decided to have a cigarette and ended up catching the bedspread on fire. Her husband was still alive then and between the two of them they managed to smother the flames before there was any serious damage done. That was one of the very few times the worthless shit she married was there for her. Anyway, after that Flo never took her cigarettes into the bedroom. She didn't even keep any ashtrays in there. She wanted to make sure she wouldn't be tempted to light up again some night or early some morning."

"How do you know all this?"

"She told me."

"Flo Odum told you so herself?"

Something in the tone of my question annoyed her, and perhaps rightfully so. "Is that so hard to believe?" she demanded.

I held up my hands in a warding-off gesture. "I didn't

mean to sound as if I doubted your word. It's just that I'm all too familiar with the pecking order that exists in most small communities. It surprises me to hear that two people on such extreme ends of the social spectrum as you and Mrs. Odum would be acquainted."

"There are probably a number of things about me that would surprise you, Mr. Hannibal. You seem to have some preconceived notions based solely on the fact that my last name is Cord. Snobbery works both ways, you know. If you could overcome yours long enough to just listen to what I have to say and not try to second-guess what my motives might be, I think you'd find me a valuable ally. Ironically, I may be the only person in Hatchaloo County who has no real stake in whatever happens with Cord Toys. I *care* what happens with the company bearing my family name, naturally, but my future isn't dependent on it in any way. That gives me a certain objectivity you'd be hard put to find in practically anyone else around."

"How is it that you have no stake in Cord Toys? You mean you don't hold a seat on the board of directors or at least a vice-presidency title in some capacity?"

"Nothing like that. My father was a bluntly practical man. I never showed the slightest interest in company matters despite being given several opportunities to become involved. Clayton, on the other hand, as usual displayed tendencies directly opposite mine. When it came time to hand over the reins, Father no doubt found his choice very clear."

"You and Clayton the only children?"

"Yes."

"So he got the gold mine and you got the shaft."

"No, I don't see it that way. Really. My father was also a fair man. He provided for me adequately, especially considering I was already quite successful in my own right. I believe he even included a few shares of Cord stock in what he left me, but I honestly don't know how many or what they're worth. At any rate, they would be my only direct link to the company."

"What is this other field you're a success in?"

"Art. I'm a sculptress."

"A sculptress?"

"As in someone who forms images out of stones or clay or what have you."

"Yes, of course I know was sculpture is but . . . well, I guess I imagined people who did that sort of thing always lived in New York or Paris or someplace like that; you know, in some bare little apartment with a skylight and stuff."

"And I always imagined that private eyes prowled only rainy, neon-splashed streets deep within the bowels of a large city. Just goes to show, right? But if it's any consolation, I *do* have an apartment in New York City. It's not quite as bleak as what you described, however, and I'm afraid it has no skylight."

"Okay. And I've prowled my share of rainy, neon-splashed streets."

"So the generalizations we all profess to hate so much yet still can't seem to keep from making about certain things aren't always so far off the mark, are they?"

"I don't know. I'd hate to make very many generalizations concerning you, lady. I have a feeling you'd always find a way to cram them back down my throat."

She laughed at that, let it settle into a wide, half-teasing smile. "Why, Mr. Hannibal," she said, "could it be that I frighten you just a little?"

"You're a lovely, intelligent, successful woman," I replied. "Don't you know that's one of the scariest things on the face of the earth?"

She laughed again. "I think I'll take that as a compliment of sorts and leave it go at that."

"Fair enough," I said. "Getting back to the Flo Odum thing, how is it that a successful artist with a New York address spends enough time down here in the boonies to become acquainted with a feisty old gal who's thrown the whole area into a tizzy?"

Her expression turned sober again. "Well, don't forget this is my home town. I also maintain a residence here. At one point in my life I felt certain I would kick the dust from these 'boonies' off my shoes, leave and never look back. But I discovered a strange thing. I found out that the Midwest in general and southern Illinois in particular are, well, a sort of energy base for me. If I'm away too long, my ambition, my creative juices, start to dry up. I become restless and bitchy and depressed and turn into a general pain in the ass for myself and everybody around me. If you want to be a success at the level I'm aiming for, you have to play the game to some degree; you have to make the scene in New York and L.A. and Paris and Rome. You have to attend a certain amount of openings and shows and galas, you have to mingle—in other words, you have to be *seen*. Like some ditzy movie starlet. And I won't deny part of that has its appeal. After all, can you imagine any girl born and raised in Hatchaloo County *not* being impressed upon attending a formal ball overlooking the Seine?"

I shrugged. "Every profession—hell, practically every aspect of our lives—has a certain amount of b.s. that comes with it. You have to determine your own personal gag level and learn to operate somewhere short of that line." I wasn't sure what any of this had to do with the question I'd asked, but she seemed to be working her way toward something.

Courtney made a face. "Christ, Hannibal, do your analogies always deal with bodily excrement?"

I showed her a lopsided grin. "Shit if I know," I said. "I'll have to start keeping better track."

She made a gesture with her hand. "Never mind. The point I'm trying to make is that sooner or later you still have to be able to deliver. They expect you to play their silly games, but above all they expect you to contribute your share to what the games are all about. I arrived on that glitzy scene fresh out of college, with lots of raw talent, a number of impressive works already completed, and several more in various planning stages. Those carried me for a long time. I became very good at the social thing, doing my version of an art world jet-setter, and at the same time I managed to turn out some pretty good stuff, made some fantastic sales. But, in retrospect, I was basically only finishing or refining projects I'd started back in college. After a while, as I got into totally new pieces, it became evident—first to me, then to others—that something was missing. Oh, I had the mechanics down well enough, better than ever; but there was no heart, no emotion, in what I was doing. And pretty soon there were no more fantastic sales. So during that time I hit the social scene harder than ever. When in doubt, party; that was my motto. I did a lot of drugs, a lot of men, a lot of foolish and even dangerous things that I managed to convince myself were loads of fun. And all the while my work got flatter and flatter. I was turning out crap no better than the stuff you can expect from any halfway decent ceramics class. Then, about six years ago, my mother passed away and I came home for the funeral. It was the first time I'd returned to Cedarton since leaving after I completed college. I stayed in the big house with Father, in my old room. I stayed there with him for nearly three months, looking after him, helping him to try and readjust to life without Mother. I guess you could say I was being the daughter I hadn't been for a long time. I even managed to get along reasonably well with Clayton for those few weeks. And by the time I was ready to leave, I'd discovered something very important—I'd discovered the source of my creative power, the energy base I mentioned before. It was right here. Cedarton, Hatchaloo County, the Midwest. When I got back to New York I was brimming with new ideas and new enthusiasm, and the works that came out of that were some of the best I've ever done. Needless to say, ever since then

I've kept in touch with my roots, my energy base. I maintain the place here in Cedarton as well as the one in New York and I spend several months of each year here. I also travel extensively throughout the rest of the Midwest, making notes, taking tons of photographs. Not all of it ends up in my work, of course, but I like to think that, even when I do a commissioned piece that may be totally unrelated as far as subject matter, part of the spirit I pick up out here, the heart, the emotion, always shows through and adds something to whatever I'm working on."

She paused, gazing out across the river and the trees, not looking at me. I wasn't sure if she expected me to say something or not. If she did, I didn't know what it should be.

After several beats, her eyes swung to me and she emitted an abrupt, self-conscious little laugh. "God, talk about your rambling, long-winded monologues, eh? I don't know what came over me."

I smiled at her. "Don't worry about it. I like listening to you talk. Hell, I like *watching* you talk."

She shook her head. "I haven't opened up like that to anyone in . . . well, I don't know when. Maybe never." Her smile faded and her gaze became direct, appraising. "It occurs to me you may be a hell of a lot better at what you do than first impressions would indicate. You come across as a sort of big, plodding bulldog, but underneath that, I think there's more than a little bit of wily fox."

"Sure," I said. "And underneath the hood of that Plymouth over there is a high-performance chrome engine that could suck your Corvette right up its tailpipe in a drag race."

"Maybe that wouldn't surprise me either."

"Come on. I dig awhile, then I stop and listen awhile. Sometimes I tip a few things over, then do my listening. It's no great talent, no big mental thing. I'm not Sherlock Holmes or Columbo. Mostly I'm just tenacious. I keep stirring and stirring until the rotten potato rises to the top of the stew."

"Hooray. An analogy without shit in it."

"Well, sometimes it's a turd that rises to the top."

"You're reaching now."

"Besides, if I'm so damn clever, why can't I get you to answer my question? You still haven't told me how you became acquainted with Flo Odum."

She tossed her head, fighting the breeze to keep long fingers of hair out of her face. "It's simple enough, really. I wanted—and still intend—to make her the subject of a major piece of sculpture. When word got out about her refusing to sell her land, I was immediately intrigued. In all honesty, I suppose my first attraction to her may have been as someone who was being a thorn in the side of my brother. But when I went out there to talk to her, got to know her, I began to feel something much more. I began to admire her. Her spunk, her spirit. When her man was alive she'd been willing to abide by his decision to sell the land. But now, with him gone and no binding papers signed, she had to rely on her own convictions. And she by-God decided that she *didn't* want to let the land go. What's more, she knew right from the start what a commotion her refusal would cause, but she was prepared to stand toe-to-toe against everything and everybody once she'd made up her mind. Do you see the beauty in that, Hannibal? The purity of purpose, of standing up for what you believe in, what you hold dear?"

"It took guts," I agreed.

"You bet it did. The same kind of guts that women of the 1700s and 1800s showed when they were willing to accompany their men into the American wilderness. They were expected above all to be ladies, then to cook and mend and heal and herd cattle and everything else that might be required, even to fight and shoot at the side of—or in place of—their men. And they accepted it; they accepted it and all the hardships it entailed because they believed in something.

The pioneer spirit. That's what I saw in Flo Odum, what I wanted to try and capture. The American pioneer spirit still alive and well in this crazy 1980s mishmash of confused sexual identities, me-first attitudes, what's-in-it-for-me-itis, and all the rest. One person—a woman, not Buford Pusser or Clint Eastwood or Rambo—willing to stand up for what she believed in, what she felt was right. No matter what the consequences. And the sad irony of it—aside from the fact that it got her killed—is that only a short time before she'd been willing to stand *down* over the same issue . . . because that was the way her man wanted it."

Just as, I thought to myself, countless men over the ages have turned away from their true convictions for the love of a woman. I thought it, but I didn't say anything. There had been a bit of a challenge in some of her remarks, but not enough to get into a sexist hassle over. Besides, most of what she'd said had been true and fascinating and moving.

I said, "Beauty, purity, the American pioneer spirit, tragedy, iron—you can bring all of that out of a chunk of granite?"

Courtney smiled wistfully. "I can only try. But I intend to try my ass off."

11

Courtney Cord's Cedarton residence was a two-story brick building located on the south side of town, not far from my motel. I followed her there at her invitation, my dilapidated old sedan groaning along in the wake of her powerfully rumbling sports car.

The building had at one time housed an auto garage and repair shop in its lower half, with the upper divided into three cramped apartments. Courtney, she informed me, had had it redone into a serviceable studio below and a single spacious apartment above.

"Come on over," she'd said, "We can talk some more there and I'll show you the photographs I took of Flo while planning my piece on her. Perhaps they'll serve you in the same way they have me, give you a better sense of the woman whose death you're investigating."

It had sounded like a worthwhile way to pass some time and, truth to tell, I was in no particular hurry to part company with this intriguing woman.

It was full dusk by the time we parked around back of her building (which, just incidentally, served to tuck the Plymouth neatly out of sight in case the sheriff and his men were indeed on the lookout for it) and went inside.

The studio was a broad, well-lighted rectangle filled with

a kind of organized clutter. There were a number of canvas-draped shapes which I guessed to be partially completed sculptures standing about, and various wooden crates and cardboard boxes, some of them wrapped in plastic. I spotted a couple easels holding large, thick sketch pads. At the far end there was a huge roll-top desk and what appeared to be a walk-in closet. And on the walls were dozens—make that hundreds—of photographs, most of them 8 by 11s, a few smaller, a handful that had been blown up to poster size. The place had a faintly damp smell to it, overlaid with an even fainter odor of chemicals or perhaps some kind of paint.

"Ta-da!" Courtney said. "Ye merry old workshop—what do you think?"

I made a gesture with my hand. "Seems impressive," I said. "Although, in all honesty, I've got to say I don't have the slightest idea what I'm looking at. I mean, I don't know what an artist's studio is *supposed* to look like."

"Well, this one's a gem. Take my word for it. I won't bore you with the details of any of these works in progress. Down here is where I've got the shots of Flo."

She walked briskly to the desk, rolled back the cover, began rummaging through the various slots and piles of papers she'd uncovered. While she was doing that, I took the opportunity to peruse some of the pictures on the nearby wall. I know only slightly more about photography than I do about art, but in both cases I damn well know what appeals to me. Most of the shots I examined seemed quite good; bold, vivid representations of whatever she—assuming the photographer was Courtney—was shooting.

"You take all of these?" I asked.

"Mmm. Yes, I did. It's a way of capturing and preserving subject matter so I can go back to it at any time I choose and incorporate it into a piece of work. Obviously I take a hell of a lot more pictures than I turn out pieces of sculpture. But you never know. I see something I find of interest, I shoot it."

"They're very good."

"Thank you. In the past few years, the photography has been threatening to take on a life of its own. I became much more involved in it than I ever anticipated, even started doing my own developing and stuff. That's my darkroom over there, what looks like a closet. Anyway, several of my friends in New York, people who know photography and have no reason to blow smoke in my direction, keep telling me many of my shots are good enough to be exhibited. I haven't gone that route, but it's tempting. Christ, I have enough trouble maintaining my niche just as a sculptress, without branching out, spreading myself even thinner. Still, photography does have an undeniable appeal. It's become more and more accepted as an art form and it has an excitement, an immediacy, you can find in no other."

I said, "Behold the turtle, he makes no progress unless he is willing to stick out his neck."

Courtney stopped rummaging and gave me a strange look. "What?"

"It's a proverb," I told her. "Chinese, I think."

"Gee, that's swell. It really is. But what the hell does it mean, and what does it have to do with what we were talking about?"

"It means you seldom advance without taking some risk, and it has everything to do with what you were talking about. You're obviously excited about photography, by the prospect of achieving something through it. Right? But at the same time, you're scared of harming the reputation you've already established in the art world with your sculpture. I was simply pointing out that playing it safe is usually the most limiting, shortsighted route you can take."

She just looked at me for awhile. Then: "You know, Hannibal, beneath that pool-hall-bouncer exterior you're really very deep."

I shrugged. "Hey, what can I say?"

"You're also a little weird."

"Well, yeah, there's that, too."

She smiled. "But those are my favorite kind of people." She held up a large manila envelope. "Here are the pictures of Flo. Come on, we'll take them upstairs and look at them over a couple drinks."

Upstairs was arrived at by climbing a spiral staircase that wound around a massive silver column. Halfway up, I realized that the column was the hydraulic ram of a car lift, evidently left over from the days when the place had been a garage, locked in the "up" position and chrome-plated. When I questioned Courtney about it, she confirmed my suspicion and explained, "It was the brainchild of a decorator friend I had come down and help me plan the apartment. I find it a little ostentatious, but he was so in love with the idea I let him talk me into it."

"I think it's neat," I told her.

"I'll be sure and tell Pietro you said that. He'll undoubtedly be thrilled at such a glowing testimonial."

"Pietro?" I asked.

"Don't ask," she tossed back over her shoulder.

The apartment was indeed spacious, comfortably furnished with only the subtlest touches of femininity. Earth tones brightened by carefully selected paintings on the walls and, surprisingly, a rather limited array of sculpted pieces. Two glaring exceptions to the latter were a pair of lamps that stood atop glassy tables at either end of a long couch. The lamps were the kind of garishly painted, ceramic-based monstrosities you usually find hawked only in less discerning novelty shops. They were identical, each with the figure of a comic, red-nosed drunk positioned to take a pee in a garbage can. The copper pull chain that turned the lamp on and off dangled from the drunk's open fly.

"Some of your early work?" I said to Courtney.

"No, smarty. Those are very sentimental items. They

were gifts from the first great love of my life. His name was Charles Chaznanski and he attended the same college I did, on a football scholarship. We dated a few times and he bought me those for my birthday after he'd learned what I was majoring in, that I wanted to become a sculptress. Poor Charlie, to him they represented the epitome of fine art. I keep them prominently displayed as a reminder not to take myself too seriously, because to the average person there isn't a damn bit of difference between what I do and those lamps."

"Chaznanski, huh? What was it you were saying before about the generalizations we tend to make not always being so far off the mark?"

"Now, be nice. The little fellow on the right is Moe, by the way, and the one on the left is Boris. Why don't you say hello, pull their chains so we've got some more light in here. Then have a seat, make yourself comfortable, while I fix us something to drink."

I introduced myself to Boris and Moe in the manner suggested, settled onto the couch between them.

"I've got bourbon, vodka, wine, and beer," Courtney called from the kitchen. "What's your preference?"

I called back, telling her bourbon on the rocks would do the trick for me.

While she was making drink-mixing noises, I picked up the manila envelope she'd left lying on the coffee table and poured out its contents. It held scores of photos. I figured I might as well start sifting through them. I was hoping she'd included a shot or two of the Odum house, reasoning that when I returned there tomorrow morning with The Bug it might be of some value to know what the layout had been when it was whole.

The first photograph I turned over was a close-up of the woman herself. Flo Odum. As I gazed down at the glossy black-and-white image, a strange sensation gripped me. I had never met Flo Odum, nor, in spite of the fact that she'd been the focus of practically everything I'd said and done and heard in the past twenty hours, had anyone described her physically to me. Yet the face I saw before me now— narrow, weathered, framed by wisps of colorless hair, high- lighted by blazingly intense eyes—was exactly the face I had pictured when I stood on the cliff overlooking the Hatchaloo River and flashed to a scene of the widowed matriarch sa- voring her land! The realization—one of those eerie, déjà vu- like moments that crop up just frequently enough to remind us there may be more going on out there than our five puny senses can confirm—should have been somewhat unsettling. Instead, it had a distinctly opposite effect, a calming one. It was as if a circuit had been reconnected somewhere and a roughly running engine—mine—had suddenly smoothed out. All the disjointed emotions that had twisted inside me after being kicked out of Murphy's untangled. I felt whole again, purposeful. The tough old face of the photograph and of my vision drew me in in a combined gulp and instilled in me the same kind of blind faith conviction I'd been running into all day long. It gave me none of the tangibles I'd been searching for, but at least it left me with a *feeling.* And that feeling—so immediate, so strong it jolted me like a blast of icy air—was that I surely was not gazing into the eyes of someone who'd foolishly brought about her own death.

Call it mystical, call it crazy, call it whatever you want— but for the first time since accepting the case, I was con- vinced I was investigating a murder.

"What's the matter?" Courtney said as she re-entered the room carrying our drinks. "You look like you've seen a ghost."

"Maybe I have," I muttered.

"What's that?"

"Nothing. Never mind."

I reached to accept the tumbler of bourbon she held out for me. Balancing her own drink—white wine, by the look of it—she deposited a pair of coasters on the coffee table, then deposited herself on the couch beside me.

The whiskey went down as smooth as a grenade sliding on a greased track, exploded gently in the pit of my stomach. Courtney sipped her wine.

She lowered her glass and gestured with it, indicating the photograph I still held in one hand. "I'm glad you found that one. It's one of my favorites. All the things I was talking about are right there on her face. Strength, integrity—do you see them?"

"Yeah, I see some things," I conceded. "It's quite a face."

I put the close-up to one side and began flipping through the rest of the pictures in the pile. We made small talk as I did this, commenting on some of the shots, the desolate beauty of the land, the way black-and-white photography seems to bring out sharper contrasts, starker realism. We agreed that the practice of color tinting classic old black-and-white movies for TV replay was blasphemy. And so on and so forth.

Until we eventually got around to what—in retrospect—my hostess may have had on her mind all along.

"When you saw my brother earlier," she said, "did you get a chance to talk to him at all before he kicked you out?"

"Oh, sure, we had a swell chat. Before he figured out who I was and what I really wanted."

"And I suppose his actions at that point only served to strengthen his standing as your prime suspect?"

I shrugged. "Not necessarily. It didn't do anything to endear him to me personally, but that's another matter. Besides, I never said he was *my* prime suspect; I said most people would probably see him that way. Matter of fact, if I was to make a list based on what I've seen and heard so far, I expect I'd have to rank him closer to the bottom than the top."

"Oh? Why's that?"

"Well, I keep reminding myself that if push came to

shove, if the Odum property couldn't be purchased and Cord Toys actually did relocate, one of the few people from around here who'd still make out okay would be your brother. Sure, he'd have the inconvenience and the expense of moving his facility, but in the long run, especially if the expanded product lines paid off, he'd wind up ahead of the game."

"I guess I hadn't thought of it that way."

"No, but I'm sure Clayton did. He may be a jerk, but he's not a dumb one. That's why I can't see him risking the whole ball of wax by being involved with murder—at least not intentionally."

"What do you mean by that?"

"I mean that if Flo was, in fact, murdered, I think there's a good chance your brother may have inadvertently caused it."

"You're talking in riddles. First you say you think he's an unlikely suspect, then you say he's probably the one who caused her death."

"Christ, does everybody in your family only listen to *part* of what someone says and then jump to the wrong conclusion? I said I doubt if your brother *intentionally* had anything to do with Flo's death. But that doesn't necessarily make him an angel. I don't, for instance, think he's above applying pressure to try and get his own way. You conceded that much yourself. In other words, while the option to move the plant may have been feasible if it became absolutely necessary, I think Clayton purposely fueled those rumors prematurely in hopes everyone who had something to lose if the toy factory left—which amounts to damn near everybody in this county—would jump on Flo's case for not giving up her land. Well, in their desperation, I'm afraid somebody may have jumped a little too fast."

"You make it sound like the whole county is suspect."

"In my book, it is. That's all I've been hearing ever since I got here, how everybody in Hatchaloo County—either directly or indirectly—is dependent on Cord Toys. That means that Flo, by not selling her land and maybe forcing the factory to move away in order to expand, posed a threat to every single one of them."

"That's ridiculous! That dear old woman never posed a threat to anyone in her whole life."

"That's easy to say from your viewpoint. Or maybe even from mine. But what if you're John Doe living on Elm Street and you've got a wife and a couple kinds and twenty years left to pay on a thirty-year mortgage and twelve years seniority on the jack-in-the-box line down at the toy factory and all of a sudden you hear that the place is going to close and move away because some crazy old broad won't sell a few measly acres of land for ten times what it's worth? No need to bother even looking around because you already know there's no other jobs to be had, and there's no chance of unloading the house because everybody else on your block is in the same boat, and to top it all off you just ordered braces for your youngest kid and the old lady is telling you she might be pregnant again. Now, you think you're not going to look at Flo Odum as a threat?"

"Okay, I see your point. But, God, what a depressing picture that paints."

"There are a lot of John Does out there, lady, and not just in Hatchaloo County. They're like time bombs waiting to go off. You get too many of them together in one place, anything can happen. Remember that ugly mood you told me about, the one that hung so heavy in the air you could feel it? That was their anger and desperation, building, feeding on itself, their fuses getting shorter with each passing day as the possibility of the plant moving away loomed larger before them."

"And Flo's destruction by fire," Courtney concluded grimly, "was the bomb going off."

I nodded. "That's the way it could have gone down, yeah —*if* Flo was murdered."

"You keep saying that. *If.* Dammit, after everything we've talked about, how can you be stubborn enough to still maintain her death might have only been a convenient accident?"

"Because," I told her, "if this racket has taught me anything, it's that nothing is impossible. Not even the most damnable coincidences. But for whatever it's worth, I'm becoming more and more inclined to agree that Flo likely had some help in shuffling her mortal coil."

"Well, hallelujah. But now that leaves you with a whole countyful of suspects. How are you going to narrow it down?"

"Like I said, I just keep stirring the pot, hoping something rotten works its way round to the surface. Only trouble is, I think my pot-stirring in this particular case is about to be cut short."

"What makes you think that?"

I told her briefly about Gus Wilt's warning and how I figured her brother, following my visit, had probably howled loud enough to give the good sheriff all the cause he needed to hang a No Longer Welcome tag around my neck.

When I was finished, she made a face and said, "So we're back to Clayton again. And you're absolutely right in thinking that's something he'd do—holler at the top of his lungs, demand his rights as a taxpayer to be protected from harassment."

"How about Wilt? What's his story? Does he dance to your brother's tune?"

"Mmmm . . . that may be putting it a bit strongly. I mean, there's no denying the Cord name carries a certain amount of weight around here. Gus has been sheriff for . . . oh, golly . . . twenty years anyway, maybe more. And we've always supported him. If Clayton were to suddenly throw his money and the family name behind another candidate come election year . . . well, it would undoubtedly hurt Gus's chances for getting back in. I assume he must be aware of all that, and therefore duly appreciative. But basically I think he's a decent, honest man and a good sheriff. I can't picture him being manipulated very far off course over anything he felt strongly about."

"Yeah," I agreed, "that's pretty much the way I sized him up. The thing that puzzles me, though, is why—if he's such a good cop—was he so quick to buy Flo's death as an accident? This is his county, his turf; he surely was aware of the land conflict, and if he has any instincts at all he must have picked up on all that tension crackling in the air. Given that, you'd think he'd be going out of his way to make damn sure her death *wasn't* murder, rather than be in such hurry to chalk it up in the other column."

Courtney looked pensive. "I guess there's something else I hadn't thought of," she said. "But once again you're absolutely right. The Gus Wilt I've known over the years has been meticulous about keeping this county clean, running to ground even the wildest rumors in order to lay them to rest one way or another." Her expression changed abruptly, took on an almost stricken look. "God, you don't think he's behind it or in on it in some way, do you?"

I shook my head. "I doubt that. Not when he was willing to let me poke around in the first place. There's some other explanation."

She pondered the matter some more. I drained the bourbon I had left.

After a little while, Courtney said, "How about this then: the sheriff is nothing if not a stubborn man. Maybe he simply jumped to the wrong conclusion, labeled Flo's death as accidental, and now is being too bullheaded to admit he might have made a mistake."

I shrugged. "Still not the mark of a very good cop. But it sounds more plausible that way than the other. Hell, you know him better than I do."

"If only you could turn up something that would *make* him listen to reason."

"That's exactly what I was hoping to do. But like I said, thanks to your brother I doubt if I'm going to get the chance." I considered that last remark, then added somewhat ruefully, "Of course, my handling of Clayton probably left a little something to be desired in the tact department, so I guess maybe I have to shoulder a chunk of the blame, too."

Courtney drew her feet up underneath her and leaned forward slightly, her eyes taking on an eager glint. "How about making another stab at it?" she asked.

I wasn't sure I was following her. "Another stab at . . . ?"

"Talking to Clayton. Maybe handling him a little differently, a little better. Maybe getting him to call off the sheriff so you can continue your investigation."

I said, "I'm not about to kiss up to him, if that's what you mean. I want to get to the bottom of Flo's death, but not that bad."

"No one's saying kiss up to him. I wouldn't ask anybody to do that, especially not somebody like you. But you just admitted you might have been somewhat crude the first time around—would it kill you to try a little diplomacy? I'd be on hand to help smooth out any rough spots."

"I thought you and Clayton didn't get along."

"Oh, we get along. We just don't get along well. But that doesn't mean we square off and start exchanging blows at the mere sight of one another. I'm still his big sister; that warrants me at least a modicum of respect and influence over him."

I absently rattled the ice cubes in my glass, wishing she'd offer me some more bourbon and drop this foolish notion. "I don't know," I said. "I've butted heads with guys like your brother before. I think trying to talk to him again now would only make matters worse."

"How? You already figure he's getting you rousted from the county. What have you got to lose?" She paused, cocked one eyebrow deliberately, then: "Come on, Hannibal . . . behold the goddamn turtle, remember?"

12

*T*he night air, which had seemed to be cooling when we were at the wayside park, now felt as if it had turned a corner somewhere and was warming back up. The Corvette cut through it like a dagger on wheels.

Courtney drove with a kind of controlled recklessness, deftly shifting up and down through the gears but jack-rabbiting her starts and taking corners a little too wide and a lot too fast. I sat in the passenger seat, grateful for the greenish glow of the dashboard lights that masked my white-knuckled grip on the arm rest.

The drive from Courtney's digs was mercifully short. After boomeranging me into finally agreeing to try another talk with her brother (if there's anything worse than getting your own words rammed back up the pipe at you, I'd like to know what it is), she'd divulged that what she had in mind was for me to accompany her to a party being held at Clayton's place that evening. "He won't want to make a scene in front of his other guests," she'd explained, "so he'll *have* to talk to you."

The party aspect had triggered a whole new volley of protests from me, but she countered them one by one and the bottom line was that I'd said I would talk to Clayton once again and she was going to hold me to it.

Clayton's house, located about a mile out in the country, was a two-story pseudo-mansion complete with tall plantation pillars in front and a paved circular drive that looped around a spouting fountain. The whole works sat five or six hundred yards off the road and the lane that led back to it, also paved, tonight was lined with parked cars. I noted that several of these had Missouri license plates and none appeared to be more than a couple of years old. My old Plymouth would have stood out like a plastic fork at a thousand-dollar-a-plate Republican fund-raiser.

Courtney sent her 'Vette slicing between the rows of gleaming vehicles. We passed some couples walking toward the house from where they'd parked.

Three quarters of the way around the circle, Courtney veered off and braked to a stop in front of the broad, flat door of a massive garage.

"Family privilege," she announced. "We save ourselves a hike. I always knew that sooner or later I'd find *something* beneficial about being related to Clayton."

She cut the engine, took a final hit off the joint she'd lighted on the way over, ground it out in the ashtray. Upon first producing the jay, she had said, "You'll have to pardon me while I prepare to spend an evening in the company of my dear brother and a hundred or so of his most intimate friends."

As the sweet aroma of marijuana had filled the car, I said, "That's real encouraging. You're the one whose idea it was to drag me to this shindig, and now you're telling me you need to toke a few in order to face up to it yourself?"

"Hey," she replied, "I've got a whole lifetime of reasons for needing to mellow out before spending time with Clayton. You've only met him the once." Then, when I declined a hit of the grass, she'd asked, "What's the matter, don't approve of the heathen devil weed?"

"No skin off my nose," I told her. "But I've already picked alcohol as my drug of choice, thanks. Been abusing my system with it for so long now, I guess you could say I've developed a sense of loyalty toward it. Wouldn't want to risk ruining a beautiful friendship by flirting around with something new."

Climbing out of the 'Vette, I immediately picked up the sounds of conversation, laughter, and music wafting on the air. Party sounds. The knot of apprehension that had been winding around in my gut pulled a little tighter. I like parties only slightly better than I like tooth extraction. Don't get me wrong, I'm almost always up for a handful of barroom buddies getting together after closing hours or an impromptu beer blast following a hot afternoon's softball game —anything like that. But planned parties, even when not hosted by a jerk like Clayton Cord, leave me cold. Like making love or eating Mexican food, it's the kind of thing best done spontaneously.

Courtney came around the end of the car shaking out her windblown hair. Before leaving her apartment, she had changed into a cream-colored silk blouse and a pair of chocolate-brown leather slacks with matching boots. She wore nothing under the blouse. Her nipples were dark, sharp points threatening to pierce the shiny fabric.

We fell in step and began moving across a strip of lush lawn toward the front door. As we walked, Courtney said, "Clayton and LuBeth—that's his wife—put on at least four of these bashes every year. Spring, summer, fall, winter. LuBeth calls them her 'seasonals.' I suspect she got the idea from a Harlequin paperback, or some similar source of inspiration."

"What's LuBeth like?"

"Oh, about what you'd expect of someone who'd marry Clayton. Sort of your quintessential pampered debutante airhead. She's from St. Louis—Clayton met her one summer when he was attending a series of business seminars there. I don't recall her maiden name, but her father made his fortune in plastic just after World War Two and the one and

only time I ever met him he seemed incapable of discussing
any other subject for more than thirty seconds. Her mother
is one of those sour-faced, double-chinned, blue-haired society dames like the Marx brothers used to love to deflate in
their old movies. They had LuBeth—as they say—late in
life. I figure it must have been a miscalculation in the ol'
rhythm method."

Clayton's wife being from St. Louis explained all the Missouri license plates I'd seen as we drove in. I said, "Does
LuBeth usually invite a lot of her friends from the old neigh-
borhood to these soirees?"

"Absolutely. I'm not sure if she's trying to impress the
people around here with her high society friends from the
big city, or if she's trying to impress the latter with the way
her husband rules his little backwoods county fiefdom.
LuBeth is kind of sweet in her own way, I guess, but she's
such a ditz and she dotes so sickeningly on Clayton that I
usually can't take much more of her than I can him."

Yup, I thought wryly, this is getting better by the minute.
Me rubbing elbows with the hoi polloi. A fish stick amidst
lobster. Gonna be a memorable evening indeed.

We'd reached the front door by then. I thumbed the bell
button and it was answered in scant seconds by a horse-
faced, middle-aged woman wearing a maid's uniform.
Courtney and the maid exchanged greetings, calling one another by name. The maid informed us that the party was
being held out on the patio. Courtney assured her she knew
the way.

We proceeded down a tiled hall that opened onto a living
room wider than your average city park band shell. The hall
had been lined with highly polished, ornately carved
wooden stands and paintings in gilded frames. The living
room was more of the same: overstuffed divans and high-
backed easy chairs and couches, gleaming antique end tables
bearing lamps with brass bases that shone like gold, textured
wallpaper, ankle-deep carpeting. All that was missing were

the velvet ropes and Please Do Not Touch the Display plac-
ards.

A third of the back wall was taken up by French doors
draped in gauze-thin white curtains. These stood ajar and
the party was taking place just beyond, its volume increasing as we crossed the living room. A Barry Manilow record
was playing, backgrounding the murmur of voices. There
were occasional guffaws and titters of laughter, each sounding about as sincere as the music.

Courtney nonchalantly slipped her arm through mine and
we emerged onto the patio.

There were maybe seventy-five people out there, most of
them seated around white metal patio tables or matching
wrought-iron chairs. To the left, a bar had been set up and a
handful of men were standing near it, talking animatedly,
gesturing with their glasses. To the right, a disc jockey,
barely visible behind his speakers and turntables and stacks
of records, was providing the music. Straight ahead, the patio eventually gave way to a pool deck where a half-dozen
adventurous souls splashed about in an oval of turquoise
water. Rows of hanging Japanese lanterns cast everything in
a soft golden glow.

I only had time to give the scene a quick once-over before
a slender woman with cotton-candy blond hair wearing a
backless polka-dot dress rose from one of the tables and
made a beeline in our direction.

"Courtney—what a delightful, delightful surprise!"

The blond woman and Courtney embraced lightly, brush-
ing cheeks together with all the warmth of brand-new in-
laws at a shotgun wedding.

"Joe Hannibal," Courtney said as she stood back from the
embrace, "this is our hostess, LuBeth, my brother's wife."

"Mr. Hannibal, the pleasure is all mine," LuBeth said,
holding out her right hand. There was just a trace of southern syrup in her voice, drawling the hard "i" of "mine" so
that it came out "mahn." Her grip somehow managed to be

firm yet at the same time delicate. I always feel a little awkward shaking hands with a woman, and this was no exception. While the complete sincerity of her words might be debatable, I sensed no masked hostility in them or in her manner, which meant either her husband hadn't told her about me yet, or she was a damn sight better actress than I was willing to give her credit for.

"Now, Courtney," she went on, "you aren't going to disappoint me by telling me this fine, broad-shouldered specimen is merely your analyst or some stuffy old art dealer or something like that, are you?"

Courtney smiled. "No, LuBeth, I assure you he is neither my analyst nor some stuffy old art dealer."

"Marvelous!" LuBeth clapped her hands together like a happy child. Turning back to me, she said, "Perhaps you aren't aware of this, Mr.—may I call you Joe?"

"Please do."

"Your presence here, Joe, marks quite an auspicious occasion. You see, not only is this the first time in ages that Courtney has made it to one of my seasonals, but it is absolutely the first time *ever* that she has attended any function hereabouts accompanied by a beau. Lord knows there's been all sorts of speculation about the wild, jet-setter life she leads on the Coast and overseas, but here in Hatchaloo County she's remained as unattainable as some mythical ice goddess."

"Really, LuBeth," Courtney said.

"Well, that's what you've been called. Luckily you've demonstrated your interest in the opposite sex with three highly publicized marriages, else one shudders to think what other category some of the cretinous minds around here might have placed you in."

Courtney's smile dripped venom. "One also shudders to think, LuBeth dear, what extreme measure I will be forced to take if we do not change the subject very, very quickly."

LuBeth looked blank for a long moment, then emitted a

self-conscious little giggle which she cut short by patting the fingertips of one hand to her mouth. "My goodness, I *was* babbling on, wasn't I?"

"Babbling is a good word, yes," Courtney said agreeably.

"It's just that I'm so pleased you dropped by with your gentleman friend and all . . . I guess I got carried away. Lord, I even committed a good hostess's most unforgivable sin—I haven't offered you anything to drink yet. Come, let's remedy that situation and then find Clayton. He'll be equally delighted that you're here."

I caught Courtney's eye as LuBeth turned away and silently mouthed "Wanna bet?" But things were looking up to some degree, at least: we were headed toward the bar.

Unfortunately, our trip got sidetracked almost before it began. It turned out that Clayton Cord was among the group of men I'd noted standing near the bar when we first arrived. He peeled away at the sight of his wife approaching with new guests, a smile instantly ready, one as broad and practiced and empty as the one he'd been wearing when I was ushered into his office.

The smile faltered a bit at the sight of Courtney, shattered completely when he recognized me.

"Clayton, darling, look who's here!" LuBeth said, fairly gushing with innocent enthusiasm.

Cord's eyes were snapping back and forth between Courtney and me so fast it made my own eyes ache just to watch. When he spoke—his voice strained through clenched teeth —it was impossible to tell which one of us he was addressing. "What the hell's the meaning of this?" he demanded.

As our bar-bound procession had ground to a halt, Courtney had once again slipped an arm through mine. She kept it there, standing with one hip slightly cocked, pressing against me. Calmly, with no expression on her face, she said, "Good evening, Clayton. You're looking well."

In point of fact, Clayton was looking anything but well. His face was flushed to near purple and he seemed to be swelling up around the neck and jowls. Like a cobra getting ready to attack. "Do you realize who this . . . this person is?" he said, this time clearly addressing Courtney and just as clearly referring to me.

"As near as I can tell," Courtney replied evenly, "he's the only man around here willing to look for the truth."

"The truth! The only truth is that this slanderous sonofabitch is out to cause me trouble. And you've allied yourself with him, is that it?"

"I've allied myself with finding out how and why Flo Odum *really* died. Are you saying that's something that will cause you trouble?"

LuBeth's mouth had fallen open in a kind of slack-jawed astonishment at this exchange. Abruptly, as if realizing how unbecoming the pose was, she clapped her lips shut, then wailed a plaintive "Clayton? . . . Courtney? . . ."

Cord ignored her, but used the interruption to evade his sister's smoldering question. He swung his gaze to me. "You've got your nerve, coming into my very home with your groundless damned lies and smarmy innuendoes."

I shrugged. "Your sister invited me to accompany her to a party. Where I came from, it'd be rude—not to mention downright dumb, considering the attractiveness of the lady —to decline such an offer."

Back to Courtney went his glare. "I suppose you're proud. You've really outdone yourself this time, haven't you? All the antics over the years, the embarrassing newspaper accounts from all across the globe . . . now you're trying to bring the dirt right to our front door, is that your goal?"

In a voice that could have frozen stone, Courtney replied, "No, Clayton, I think maybe *you're* the one who's brought the dirt here. My goal is to see that it gets uncovered."

LuBeth edged forward a step. Her teeth were bared in a tight jack-o'-lantern smile, her eyes shifting anxiously beneath knitted brows. "Clayton," she said, this time her voice more insistent. "Please? People are starting to stare."

Cord looked somewhat startled, as if he'd forgotten our surroundings. His own eyes flicked anxiously about. I looked around, too, but except for a handful of nosy jerks who were craning their necks obviously in order to see what was going on, as far as I could tell most of the other party guests were either unaware of or uninterested in what was transpiring between the four of us. Those few, however, were enough to defuse Cord. The color remained high in his face, but the visible anger that had been bunching up there like a flexed muscle began to fall away.

He sighed heavily, cleared his throat. "My gut instinct," he said to Courtney and me, "is to throw you two out on your impertinent asses."

"You and me have already boogied to that beat," I reminded him.

"But in deference to my wife and our other guests," he continued, stepping on my words, "I want to avoid a scene. You may stay. Help yourselves to the food and drink that is available, enjoy the music, enjoy each other's company. I insist, however, that you make no attempt to try and turn this gathering into some sort of public forum for discussing your half-baked notions on the Odum tragedy."

"The only person we're interested in discussing our 'half-baked notions' with," Courtney told him, "is you. Legitimate questions have been raised that need to be answered—need to be faced up to by you, Clayton. You can't just turn your back on them. The more you try, the worse it makes you look. No matter what you think, I don't want to believe you had anything to do with that fire. I really don't. The best way you can reassure me otherwise is to be open with Hannibal here, sanction his investigation rather than throw roadblocks in front of it."

"There's nothing to investigate. It was a damned accident!"

"I don't buy that. Neither do a lot of people around here. Maybe they aren't being very vocal about it at this point, but sooner or later they will be. It's not the kind of thing you can keep swallowed down. There's a great deal of suspicion in the air, Clayton, and most of it is aimed at you, at Cord Toys."

LuBeth Cord clutched her husband's arm. "What is she talking about, Clayton? It sounds . . . frightening."

Cord put his hand over LuBeth's, pressing it comfortingly. "Nothing to be alarmed about, darling. Really." He kept his eyes on Courtney. He sighed heavily again, then lifted the hand that had been touching his wife and made a condescending gesture with it. "All right, I'll talk to your damned detective. But not right this minute, okay? Later. If you don't mind, I'd like to mingle, enjoy my own party a little."

Courtney nodded solemnly. "Fair enough."

Cord looked as if he wanted to say something more but couldn't decide what. He shot me a brief, meaningless glance before turning toward the bar and tossing over his shoulder to no one in particular, "I need a drink."

The three of us stood looking after him in a tensely awkward silence.

LuBeth turned to Courtney. "I'm really disappointed in you. I was so genuinely happy you'd come to my seasonal when all you wanted was another chance to dig into Clayton, to upset him with some more of your antics."

With surprising gentleness, Courtney replied, "This is no antic, LuBeth. And I'm truly sorry if I've disrupted your party to any degree. But Clayton needs to deal with this thing—for his own sake, if nothing else."

"He's perfectly capable of looking out for his own interests," LuBeth insisted. "Lord knows he's never been able to count on your concern in the past."

Courtney's gentleness turned brittle. "Have it your way. I

hope you'll eventually come to realize that my motives in this aren't as dark as you think."

"We'll see. You'll pardon me if I can't muster up a great deal of optimism for that possibility. You'll also pardon me while I tend to my other guests. I'm sure you and your gentleman friend can fend for yourselves in my absence."

So saying, our hostess spun smartly on her heel and marched away. She hadn't gone three steps before she was able to produce a dazzling smile, which she aimed at the tableful of thick-ankled old broads directly in her path.

I dug out a cigarette, lit it, exhaled some pollution into the fresh evening air.

"I don't know about you," I said to Courtney, "but I'm not having nearly as much fun as I'd hoped for. And a miserable time is all I ever counted on in the first place."

"We're not here to have a good time," she replied peevishly. "We're here because someone has to get to the bottom of Flo's death. If they succeed in running you off, God only knows how long it will be before anyone else has the balls to try. And the more time passes, the deeper the truth will be buried."

"Good point," I said, pressing her in the direction of the bar. "Let's drink to it."

13

"People around here," I said, "seem to be divided over this issue into two distinct camps. On the one hand there are the doubters, the cynics you might call them, who find the timing of Flo Odum's death highly suspicious; on the other hand there are those like you who are so dead-set positive it was an accident—without benefit of a very thorough investigation, I might add—you won't even consider any other possibility."

"So what's your point?" Clayton Cord wanted to know.

We were seated, he and I, in his book-lined, darkly paneled, richly appointed den. Courtney was present also, standing over by the open window, gazing out at the starry night, absently rolling a tall Tom Collins back and forth between her palms. By prearrangement, she was to remain quietly on the perimeter of the discussion and let me do my thing.

More than an hour had passed since our arrival at the party. After our initial brief clash with our hosts, we had indeed been left to "fend for" ourselves—a task that consisted primarily of sipping drinks from the well-stocked bar and munching goodies from the catered buffet table. We'd seated ourselves on the far side of the patio, making it convenient for Clayton and LuBeth to avoid us while circulating among the other guests. Except for a handful of old family friends who wandered over at sporadic intervals to say hi to Courtney, we had one of the postage-stamp-sized tables to ourselves. It could have been an opportunity to make intimate small talk, maybe get to know one another a little better; except Courtney had slipped into a pensive, pre-occupied mood that hardly lent itself to small talk. I couldn't tell if she regretted getting involved with my investigation, or if she was just apprehensive about the forthcoming bit with Clayton.

At any rate, our melancholy little twosome had eventually been broken up by the appearance of LuBeth, who stood over our table and announced rather stiffly that Clayton was ready to talk to us and was waiting inside. Her manner made me feel like a stable hand being summoned by the lord of the estate.

"The point is," I said to Clayton now, in response to his question, "from an objective standpoint I can see where the doubters are coming from, but I'm having a little tougher time understanding the position taken by those in your camp."

"Oh. And you're Mr. Objectivity, is that it?"

"I'm trying to be. You don't make it easy."

"Why should I make anything easy for you?"

"Because the more you fight me, the guiltier it makes you look."

"That sounds very much like an accusation, Hannibal. Perhaps a libelous one."

"Slanderous."

"What?"

"Never mind. It wasn't an accusation in the first place. But let me put it another way: if you *don't* have anything to hide, why are you so strongly opposed to my investigation?"

"Because it's totally unnecessary and can only have an agitating effect on things. There's been too much turmoil in this county of late. It needs a chance to settle down, to catch its breath—not be stirred up all over again by the kind of nonsense you represent."

"Things aren't likely to settle down as long as people suspect a murder is being covered up."

"Yeah, well I think you're making a mountain out of a molehill there. I don't believe most people around here find a single thing suspicious about the way the old woman died. For one thing, everybody who knew her knew she smoked and sprayed spark and ash like an old steam locomotive. For another thing, most people around here are law-abiding citizens who have complete faith in their good sheriff. If Gus Wilt tells them something's so, then they accept it as so. Naturally the Odum bunch who hired you are an exception —most of them have spent so much time on the *wrong* side of the law that they obviously have no respect for anyone from the *right* side."

"What about me, Clayton?" Courtney said from the window. "I find Flo's death *very* damned suspicious. Where do I fit into your little caste system?"

"God only knows where you fit in, Courtney," her brother replied wryly. "And I expect you frequently surprise the hell out of even Him."

They made this exchange without looking round at one another. Courtney took a long pull of her Tom Collins, continued to gaze out the window, said nothing further.

"You mentioned Sheriff Wilt," I said to Clayton. "I have a feeling you probably gave him a call after my visit to your office this afternoon. Am I right?"

"Quite."

"I'm surprised he hasn't looked me up."

Cord smiled coldly. "Yes, so am I."

"I suppose I've got that to look forward to."

"I'll do my best to see you aren't disappointed."

I changed gears, swerved to a different lane. "Do you know about a man named Tom Wykert?" I asked.

Cord accepted the change-up maneuver with no apparent

break in his composure. "Of course I know Wykert. He's shop chairman of the union at Cord Toys."

"He has a reputation for violence and he was a very outspoken critic of Flo Odum's refusal to sell her land. Do you think it's within the realm of possibility that he might have participated in—or at least advocated in some way—the torching of Flo's house?"

This time the composure crumbled a little. "Jesus Christ, man, that's a hell of a bold question to ask! Wykert may be prone to violence, it's true—in a barroom brawler, back-alley ruffian sort of way. But to suggest he might be capable of cold-bloodedly . . . no, I couldn't comment on that. It seems awfully extreme."

"Would you say he has much influence over others?"

"Because of the office he holds, you mean?" He pondered the thought. "Hard to say. I don't know that his effectiveness as a negotiator or representative of the workers has ever been put to any real test. Cord Toys has always enjoyed a good relationship with its union. Wykert is a large, physically intimidating man with, as you mentioned, a reputation for violence. He may have a certain amount of influence over others, I suppose, but in my opinion it would be due more to his bullying nature than anything else."

"He allegedly called Flo Odum a 'senile old fool'—among other things—and was heard to suggest that someone needed to 'bring her in line for the good of the whole community.' Do you see what I'm driving at? What if somebody wanted to get—or stay—on the good side of Wykert, and took what he said maybe too literally? What better way to prevent the old woman from stepping out of line than to simply do away with her? Or maybe torching the house was only supposed to be a scare tactic, and Flo was unfortunate enough to get fatally caught by it."

"In any event, would the responsibility be Wykert's? If he didn't specifically instruct someone to take those measures, I mean?"

"Not directly, no. All I'm trying to show is that there are a number of perfectly logical scenarios—aside from the 'accident' one you seem so homed in on—that could have brought about Flo Odum's death."

"As I recall from some of the remarks you made in my office this afternoon, another of your scenarios would have it that the burning of the Odum house was the work of a Cord employee desperately fearful of losing his job if I was forced to move the factory away."

I nodded. "Matter of fact, that's my favorite."

"That's preposterous."

"No, it's not. And you know it. Just a few minutes ago, you said Hatchaloo County has been in a state of turmoil lately. Wasn't that precisely what you were referring to—the growing fear, the tension, the near-panic on some people's part as the deadlock over the Odum property dragged on? It's the kind of atmosphere almost bound to produce a desperate act."

Something in Clayton's manner had begun to change. He continued to regard me with a brooding gaze, but the arrogance and aggression in his eyes seemed to be receding. His posture, his shifting facial muscles, his hands that could no longer stay still, all bore signs of a man struggling with some inner conflict.

Abruptly, he heaved to his feet, turned and strode deliberately to a wall of books. He stopped and stood there with his back to me, feet planted wide apart, fingers interlaced over his tailbone. I had the feeling he'd probably seen his father stand just that way during times of stress.

I looked over at Courtney. She had turned from the window and was watching her brother with an unreadable expression on her face. She glanced my way, gave a "damned if I know" shrug of one shoulder.

I dug for a Pall Mall, snapped fire to it, let the smoke trickle out thoughtfully. I wasn't sure what it was I'd said to bring out this reaction in Cord, but I sensed he was on the verge of divulging something—something that was eating away at him, something he figured might be important to my investigation. I wasn't naive enough to hope for an obligingly blurted confession—I don't hope for money under my pillow from the tooth fairy anymore, either—but I had a hunch that whatever he was struggling with could be significant. All I had to be careful of now was to not get over-eager, not press too hard and screw it up, cause him to slide back into his defensive shell and start bucking me again.

Courtney evidently sensed some of the same things I did. Only she didn't see any need for restraint.

"Come on, Clayton," she said, "if you know something—or think you even *might* know something—that can help get to the bottom of this, for God's sake spill it. We're not out to badger anybody or disrupt Hatchaloo County any more than it already has been; all we're after is the truth."

Cord remained motionless with his back to us. I guessed that was a good sign. Better, anyway, than if he'd spun about indignantly at his sister's words.

Outside, the party was still going on. Through the open window where Courtney stood, I could hear snatches of conversation and infrequent brays of laughter. The disc jockey had a lilting Mancini instrumental playing. Just before Courtney and I were summoned by LuBeth, a few couples had begun to dance. I imagined more had joined them by now, moving smoothly through the moonlight and lantern glow in time to the music. The contrast between that mental picture and the tension that filled this room was as hard and sharp as a knife edge.

When Cord spoke, his voice sounded soft and far away, like the music. He still didn't turn, didn't move. I had to strain to hear him.

"Three nights before the Odum house burned," he said, "I received a phone call. It was late. Around midnight. I don't think LuBeth even heard the phone ring, she never asked about it. The voice on the other end of the line was male . . ." He paused, worked his shoulders slightly, moved his head a little each way as if he had a stiff neck. Then he finished it. "He wanted to know what it was worth to me to have the old woman gotten rid of."

The words hung in the air as ominously as the first thunderclap of an approaching storm.

I dragged some smoke deep. It tasted hotter and harsher than it had before.

Somebody needed to say something. I gave it several beats, then asked, "What did you tell him?"

Cord did the thing with his shoulders again. "I was dumbfounded at first, having just been woken from a sound sleep and all. I finally got around to asking him if this was somebody's sick idea of a joke. He said it was no joke. He told me to think about it, that he'd get back to me. Then he hung up."

"I take it you didn't recognize the voice?"

"No. I didn't."

"Was it disguised in any way?"

"He spoke in a harsh, sort of exaggerated whisper—a stage whisper, I guess you'd call it. But that's all. There was no handkerchief over the mouthpiece or anything like that."

"Could it have been Tom Wykert?"

"I don't think so. I've dealt with Wykert often enough. No, it wasn't him."

Courtney got in the next question. "Were there any more calls?" she asked. I could see her knuckles whitening around the Tom Collins glass as she anticipated his answer.

Cord exhaled a ragged breath. "No, there haven't been any more calls. And that's been almost the worst part."

He finally turned to face us. Gone entirely now was the smugness, the self-assuredness. His eyes seemed to have sunken deep beneath a concerned brow, his expression sagged with uncertainty. "Don't you see," he said, "it's the not knowing. The wondering. The waiting. In the first day or so after that phone call I managed to convince myself it was just some crank, some sick bastard who'd gotten my home number somehow and wanted to jerk my chain. I think I was able to actually put it out of my mind. Needless to say it came roaring back with a vengeance when I heard about the fire and that Mrs. Odum had died in it. I wanted to rush and tell Gus Wilt about the call—as if I had any idea who the hell was on the other end of the line. But then, when I heard the sheriff was calling the fire an accident, well, once again I managed to convince myself it had all been just a crank. That the two incidents were unrelated. Coincidence. It took a little more doing the second time, but I managed it."

I said, "So Sheriff Wilt knows nothing about the phone call?"

"Not unless he's the one who did the dialing. Once I'd kept mum about it for so long—well, you can see how I put myself in a position where it got harder and harder to tell anybody."

"How about LuBeth?" Courtney asked.

Cord shook his head. "I told you she didn't even hear the phone that night. Why upset her? I've kept it strictly to myself, bottled up tight. . . . Well, maybe not so tight. One minute I'd feel convinced everything was all right, the next minute I'd be cringing at the thought of the phone ringing again some night and that whispery voice telling me I owed him money for the job well done." He paused, his right hand twitching in a couple meaningless gestures as he groped for words. When he found them, he fixed me with a baleful stare that had just a trace of the old fire in it. "I thought I had it under control, but I guess I never really did. Maybe the only thing I had bottled up was my good sense. You've raised some valid questions, Hannibal, like Courtney said, and you're certainly right about the tension that had built up in this county before the fire. The phone call I got is proof, if any were needed, that a murderous mentality existed to at least some degree. Even if it was just a crank, the thought was there. So I won't stand in the way of your investigation anymore. But I won't wish you luck with it, either. Not in proving murder. That's an added burden Hatchaloo County doesn't need. Even with all that we've said here, you know the old woman's death *could* have still been just an accident."

I nodded slowly. "I've recognized that fact all along, Cord," I said. "It's you who's finally admitted—to yourself as well as to us—that the reverse could also be true."

14

When we got back out to the car, Courtney tossed me the keys and motioned me behind the wheel. I didn't argue. Show me a red-blooded American male who'd pass up the chance to drive a 'Vette.

I couldn't remember the last time I'd driven a stick, but it proved to be a moot point; that sleek, snarling, beautiful bitch of a machine responded to my touch as smoothly as if I'd been born with one foot on its clutch pedal.

At the mouth of the lane, Courtney had me ride on idle while she put the top down. Warm breezes skimmed over us, spraying long tendrils of her hair against my cheek and shoulder, pressing the scent of her deep into my nostrils. I gunned the engine and listened to the dual exhausts rap away in the night.

"You in any hurry to get back?" Courtney asked.

"Not particularly," I told her.

She pointed to the left, away from town. "Turn that way then."

I swung out onto the road. The yellowish headlight beams stabbed ahead of us, almost unnecessary in the brightness of the clear night.

Courtney settled back deep in her seat with closed eyes,

heaved a tremendous sigh. "God," she said, "I feel like a five-hundred-pound weight has been lifted off my chest."

"Because the confrontation with Clayton is over, you mean?"

"Mmm. Yes. Because it's over, and because it went . . . well, satisfactorily. I may have appeared calm and self-assured while I was talking you into coming with me, but down deep I dreaded going there tonight as much as I've ever dreaded anything in my life."

"I got the impression you sort of relished those little clashes with your brother."

"Maybe I do. But if he'd turned out to be a murderer, it would hardly have been a 'little' clash, would it? That's the thing I dreaded—what we might find out. What *I* might find out. You see, I've always been able to tell when Clayton was lying. I'd barely talked to him since Flo's death, and certainly not *about* her death. I was afraid when you started asking your questions, I might pick up on something—an inflection in his voice, a look in his eye—that would indicate he was lying. And if he was lying, of course, that could only mean one thing."

"But you came away convinced he was leveling with us, right?"

Her eyes opened and she turned her head to look at me. "Yes. Didn't you?"

I smiled with half my mouth. "In my business, it's best to assume that nobody is ever leveling with you completely."

"Damned cynical business you're in."

"Yeah, maybe it is. All right, let's say on principle I don't entirely buy Clayton's bill of goods, but at the same time I don't actively *not* believe anything he said. I guess it's unlikely he would have told us about the phone call if he had something to hide. After all, that revelation could be considered a pretty prominent mark in the 'Means and Motive' column under his name."

"He promised to tell Sheriff Wilt all about it first thing in the morning. And he also promised to call off the sheriff where you're concerned, leaving you to continue your investigation unhindered."

"Uh-huh. Unhindered except for the fact I haven't a single damn clue to go on."

Courtney frowned. "I guess what worked out good in one way worked out bad in another, didn't it? I mean, I'm relieved as hell that for the first time in days I can feel confident—really confident—that Clayton had nothing to do with Flo's death. Yet establishing that leaves your search for her actual killer a lot worse off."

"Hey," I said. "He's your brother, for crying out loud. No need to feel bad about being glad he's not a killer."

She frowned some more. "You know, I can't remember ever seeing him like that before. The way he was back there in his den. Sort of humble. Without his swagger, without his cocky attitude. They've been a part of him . . . well, forever it seems. Ever since he could walk and talk. I think Flo's death actually bothered him. Maybe, in his own way, he admired her, too. And his concern for the county seemed genuine. Could it be that somewhere deep inside the little shit has a heart after all?"

I said, "Sure. And now that we've kindled a fire in it, the warmth will grow and grow and pretty soon his compassion and generosity for the downtrodden will turn Hatchaloo County into Happy Valley, U.S.A."

"Don't be an ass, Hannibal."

"I'm not. I'm just trying to keep you from setting yourself up for a big disillusionment, that's all. Clayton is still the pompous turd you labeled him before. What you saw this evening was just an unexpected reaction to an extreme situation. When the dust settles, I'd be real surprised if he emerges as anything but his charming old self. Of course you can be consoled with the thought that when a donkey flies you shouldn't be too disappointed if he doesn't stay up very long."

"Oh, Christ. Another Chinese proverb?"

"No. I think I heard that one on *Hee Haw.*."

She sighed. "At any rate, I suppose you're right. Party pooper."

The county blacktop I'd been eating up with the Corvette had wound around this way and that until I no longer had any idea which direction we were headed. On a rare stretch of straightaway it climbed and dipped over a series of short, choppy hills—the kind that make your stomach squirm like a roller coaster ride—then went into a long, sweeping curve down a slight incline. I touched the brakes when I spotted a STOP AHEAD diamond piggy-backed atop a highway inter-section marker. Courtney bade me hang another left at the Stop sign. I recognized the highway as the same one I'd traveled during the last leg of my drive down from Rock-ford, so I knew we were now going north.

After a ways, we came to a broad, chunky bridge span-ning a band of water glittering brilliantly in the moon- and starlight. I guessed the latter to be the Hatchaloo River and Courtney confirmed my suspicion a moment later when, in a tour-guidesy voice, she said, "You are now leaving rustic Hatchaloo County and entering historic Williamson. Turn left again just across the bridge."

I made the turn and once more we were on a winding, dipping, twisting ribbon of blacktop. The 'Vette handled like a dream and I had the feel of it well enough by now to hope for a long, relatively straight and flat stretch where I could really stand on it.

"Know much about the history of southern Illinois?" Courtney asked.

"Sure," I said. "It made statehood around the same time as we did up north."

"Gee, you're a regular history buff. I suppose you know, then, all about how Williamson County for a long time was referred to as Bloody Williamson?"

"Catchy. Must have done wonders for the tourist trade."

"It was back during Prohibition. Your city slickers up around Chicago didn't have all the fun, they just got better press. There was daylight gang warfare down here that made Capone's dark alley ambushes look about as rough as soccer matches by comparison. We're talking converted tanker trucks with reinforced steel plate and torched-out gun ports that cruised openly up and down the roads carrying small armies of machine gunners in back just itching for the sight of some rival gang members to open up on. During that time, Bloody Williamson also gained the distinction of becoming the site of the first and only aerial bombing of U.S. soil when the Shelton brothers hired a barn-storming pilot to drop a few bundles of dynamite on the headquarters of their rival, Charlie Birger."

"Should I be on the lookout for dive bombers?"

"I think we're safe, especially in a moving target. None of the dynamite hit Birger's house and none of it exploded even where it did land."

"Capone liked to work up close and personal with a base-ball bat. Not as showy, but a lot more accurate."

Courtney hitched forward in her seat. "Slow down," she said. "Before long, there'll be a little park on your side. Pull in there."

We'd been traveling parallel to the river. The road began to angle slightly away from the water and sloped upward. I downshifted and spotted a row of stubby white posts that marked the entrance to the park. I downshifted again, slowed, turned in.

The park was a wayside affair similar to the one back in Cedarton where Courtney had first found me. This one was somewhat larger and had a reflector-studded guardrail running along the back side, near the edge of the bluff that dropped away to the river. At midpoint down the length of the rail, one of those broad, flat, carved wood historical markers had been erected. I nosed the 'Vette up to the rail, down a ways from the marker so we had a clear view of the river, and cut the engine.

"Potter's Point," Courtney announced. "It was here that Zedediah Potter, the first white man to settle in these parts, supposedly looked out over the land and the river one day a couple centuries ago and liked what he saw well enough to make the decision to stay."

"That what it says on the marker over there?"

"More or less. The marker's fairly new, the legend is old, old. Up until a few years ago, the blacktop we came in on was just an old gravel lumber road and this wayside was only a dirt path worn through the trees by teenage couples who came up here to park."

"What are you, a walking, talking encyclopedia of local history?"

She shrugged. "I told you, the Midwest—this region in particular—is my energy base. Once I recognized that fact, I made a concentrated effort to learn everything I could about it. It's really quite fascinating."

"Uh-huh. That why you asked me to go for a drive? So you could dazzle me with your vast knowledge?"

She looked thoughtful, made no reply right away. The dappled moonlight filtering through the trees cast silvery highlights across her face and gently blowing hair that, as far as I was concerned, were a damn sight more fascinating than any history lesson could ever be.

"I'm not sure," she said at length, "why I asked you to go for this drive. I just knew we couldn't stay at Clayton's party, and I wasn't ready to go home yet." Abruptly, her mouth curved into an impish grin. She twisted around in her seat and reached into the back. I heard the click of glass against glass. "As long as we're here, though," she said as she twisted back, "maybe you could help me dispose of this?" She held out a sealed bottle of expensive-looking champagne. In her other hand she held two long-stemmed glasses.

My turn to grin. In truth, all champagne looks expensive to me. And tastes pretty much like vinegar. But I didn't want to spoil her fun. I said, "Even more impressive that a lady with brains is a lady who prepares for life's basic needs."

Courtney laughed. "I boosted these from Clayton's liquor cabinet and brought them out to the car on one of my trips to the little girls' room. I figured after our audience with the lord of the manor we'd either have something to celebrate or a need to drown our misery. It won't be very cold but it should be wet and tasty."

"Tasty," I said, popping the cork. It sailed out over the windshield and the car hood and the guard rail and disappeared into the shadows beyond the rim of the bluff. I held the bottle outside the car until it quit foaming, then brought it back in and poured. Holding my glass high, I toasted, "Here's to Ebeneezer Potter and his foresight in pausing here two hundred years ago so tonight we have this historic, secluded little wayside in which to drink our stolen champagne."

"Zedediah," Courtney laughingly corrected.

I toasted again. "Him too."

The champagne wasn't so bad after all. It wasn't Bud, it wasn't bourbon, and it wasn't cold. But it wasn't too bad. At least not when partaken of in the company of Courtney Cord.

We drank and I refilled our glasses. Courtney's mood shifted, became more somber. She turned in her seat so that she was leaning back against the door, facing me. Her expression was thoughtful once again.

"Back there," she said. "At the party. When LuBeth mentioned my marriages and Clayton made reference to my past scandalous antics—what were you thinking?"

I frowned at the question. "I'm not sure," I said. "I haven't had time to give it much thought, really. I suppose at some point later on I would have wondered about it. Not that it's any of my business."

"I've been married three times."

I nodded. "Agrees with the number LuBeth gave."

"Once to a count, once to a Grand Prix race driver. The latter—Henri—died in a terrible crash in the south of France only fifteen days after we were married. The count was assassinated, but our divorce had been final almost a year by then."

"You're not trying to tell me you're some sort of kiss-of-death Black Widow or something, are you?"

"No, that's one thing I haven't been accused of. My second husband recently celebrated his seventieth birthday, as a matter of fact. He's a disgustingly wealthy banker from Boston. He likes crisp new bills and fresh young women. When the bills become worn, showing even the slightest hint of a wrinkle, he no longer cares to handle them. Being a banker, he still treats them with respect but they no longer stimulate him the way new ones do. Unfortunately, that is also true of him with women. You'd think he would have learned his lesson from the fantastic amounts of alimony he's paid out over the years, but he's a hopeless romantic who keeps convincing himself that each new bride—I was his sixth or seventh—is somehow going to sustain his interest."

"All of that while you were away from your energy base, too. Must have been trying."

"I never noticed. It all happened during my 'party, party, party' period, the one I told you I went through when my sculpting wasn't working. I was zonked ninety percent of the time, and when I wasn't, the only thing I was worried about was getting somewhere where I could *get* zonked. I married anyone who asked me, it seemed, and if they didn't get around to proposing, well, I'd usually go with them anyway. Not a real high self-esteem period when I look back on it now. There was a song that was popular a few years back, had a line that went something like 'I've been undressed by kings, and I've seen things that a lady shouldn't oughta see.' Remember it? Well, those lines in that song pretty much sum up my life for a few years there. I got busted for drugs a half-dozen different times, I muled stolen art objects for the Sicilian Mafia, I danced topless at the Cannes Film Festival, I got in a catfight with another woman over a Latin playboy on the Via Veneto, and on and on. And practically every episode made the papers—if not in Hatchaloo County, then for damn sure in one of those sleazy tabloids. My father's image was that of a sort of downscale Walt Disney, and I was 'The Toy Wizard's Wild Daughter.' I'm sure I brought him and Mother a great deal of pain and embarrassment, and for that I'll be eternally sorry. But you know something? As wild and immoral and naughty as I got during that period, I was never malicious or harmful to anybody—except maybe myself. I was never truly evil, you know? I think that was my power base, my midwestern upbringing sticking with me even through that. I don't think it would have let me sink too low. Even if Mother hadn't passed away when she did and caused me to come home to care for my father and reevaluate things, I think I would have gotten straightened out, gotten my shit together before much longer. I may have abandoned it, but my power base never abandoned me. Not completely."

I smiled gently. "Hard to imagine you without your shit together."

She drank some champagne. "How about you, Hannibal? You always had yours together?"

I nodded. "Mostly. Only trouble was, sometimes I couldn't lift it."

She laughed a little at that. Then: "So what's your story? How does somebody get to be a private eye?"

"Lot of different ways," I told her. "As many ways as there are ways. Except I don't know of anybody who ever *started out* to be one."

"You mean when your first-grade teacher went around the room asking each kid what he or she wanted to be when they grew up, you didn't stand and proclaim your aspiration to be the next Sam Spade?"

"Not hardly. I wanted to be the next Dick Tracy. My grandfather'd been a cop, I wanted to be a cop. Simple and straightforward. Made it, too. The Chicago P.D.—pretty big time for a farm boy from the boonies of Wisconsin. I put on a badge just in time to fight the hippie wars of the middle and late sixties. That bothered a lot of cops my age, standing in a barricade line against student protesters not much younger than us, moving on them while they were singing and chanting about peace and love and demonstrating against a war the whole country seemed to be losing faith in. But for me, it was never a problem. I saw things in a lot simpler terms then, almost always in black and white. The law was right, anybody who broke it was wrong. I married the girl I'd dated through most of high school and had taken to the senior prom. We set up housekeeping in a nice little duplex apartment with gingham curtains on the kitchen windows and a fireplace in the living room that we made love in front of for endless hours. I made detective in near record time. We started shopping around for a house, started planning a family. Hi-fiddledy-dee, it was a storybook life for me."

"So what happened?"

I took a long pull on my champagne. All of a sudden it tasted like vinegar again. I said, "I found out the princess in my storybook was a witch. Or maybe just a bitch. I stopped by the apartment unexpectedly one afternoon and found her in bed with a guy who'd been one of my prowl-car partners when I was in uniform. I stood in the doorway of the bedroom for I don't know how long, watching them fuck, and they didn't even know I was there. Not until they heard me cock the service revolver I'd drawn. When they looked up, I had it leveled on them, ready to shoot them where they lay, ready to kill them both. But I never did. Know why?" I didn't wait for an answer. Didn't need one. Already knew it all too well. "I didn't kill them," I went on, "because I was wearing my badge. I was aware of my reflection in the vanity mirror across the room, standing there with my gun aimed, my jacket hanging open, and I could see that damn badge pinned to my shirt and a voice somewhere inside my head kept saying 'You can't do this, you're a cop.' I wanted to kill them—had every right to kill them—but because I wore a badge, because being a cop meant something to me and I was supposed to be above that sort of thing, I *couldn't.* That's the day I quit wanting to be a cop. Matter of fact, I quit wanting to be about everything I'd ever wanted to be up to that point. I left the apartment, left the force, left the city. I drifted across the country, drinking too much, getting into fights, screwing anything that'd hold still long enough— preferably some other guy's wife. I couldn't kill the two people I wanted to kill, so I guess maybe I was trying to kill myself. I dunno. But like you said, you can only go so low. I hit bottom in Tucson, Arizona. I woke up there one morning in a roach-infested motel room just outside of town. There was a girl in the room with me. She was already awake, sitting Indian-style at the foot of the bed, watching Saturday morning cartoon shows on the TV and eating Froot Loops cereal dry out of the box. She couldn't have been more than fourteen. I had no recollection of how I'd met her, but it didn't take a genius to figure out why we were in that motel room together. Once again I looked at my reflection in the mirror, and I didn't like what I saw very much. I went into the bathroom and threw up. I puked for hours it seemed, puked out all the bad booze and greasy food as well as a lot of the hate and bitterness and disenchantment that had been festering inside me for so long. When I came out, I hugged the girl gently to me, kissed her hair and cried and told her how sorry I was, and she didn't have the faintest idea what the fuck I was talking about. I gave her twenty dollars—all the money I had on me—and she went away, smiling, still crunching on her dry cereal. I eventually made my way back to the Midwest, settled in Rockford. I didn't want to go back to Chicago and I didn't want to go back to Wisconsin. Rockford was a compromise; it was neither one, but it was close by, familiar. I knocked around, pumped some gas, punched a time clock in a factory for awhile—but investigative work was what I really knew, so before long I started doing some free-lancing, favor-type jobs for people I heard about who had problems I figured I could help with. The Rockford cops were cool, but they frowned on the free-lance aspect. It was just a matter of time before I got a license and went into business."

Courtney was watching me intently. "You've got a wonderful face," she said quietly. "Not handsome by any means, but fascinating and full of character—like Flo Odum's. I'd like to sculpt it sometime. Everything you've just told me is right there in it; not open wounds or visible scars, but in ways that are almost as plain."

"Uh-huh. Maybe the reason the scars aren't visible is because I don't make a habit of picking at the scabs. Like we've both been doing here for the past several minutes. How the hell did we get on this kick anyway? I think I liked the history lessons better."

"Sometimes the best way to heal a wound is to expose it to fresh air."

"Everybody's got wounds, lady. It would get real messy in the streets if we all walked around with them exposed."

She drained her glass, held it out for a refill. I obliged.

She drank some more, then gestured with the glass, pointing out across the river. "Look down there. Straight ahead. The big house with the porch lights on. See it?"

I nodded, told her I saw it. A ways to the right of the house she was indicating—to the west, that would be, about a mile or so—the lights of Cedarton winked and glimmered. Somewhere on the edge of those lights lay the silent, blackened remains of the Odum shack. For some reason I found myself wondering if Old Flo had ever had a porch light, or if the fire that took her life was the first time her yard had seen illumination after dark.

"That was our family home, where Clayton and I were raised," Courtney said, drawing my attention back to the house she had pointed to. "Father built the first three rooms with his own hands, back during the Depression. He had it added on to and modernized over the years. It was a wonderful, special place, a great house to be a child in. In his will, he left it to the county with the stipulation that it be turned into a museum showcasing his toy collection and various other memorabilia. Things haven't progressed very far, unfortunately, due to lack of funding and one thing and another. I suppose it will be up to me to finally lose my temper one day and take over the whole matter in order to ever get it done."

"Watch out, museum board," I said.

She gestured again with her glass. "My room was right there on the end, upstairs, with a window that faced this bluff. I used to lie on my bed Friday and Saturday nights all through high school and watch the headlights of the cars that came up here, and I never felt more lonely or miserable in my whole life. I was attractive, intelligent, I went out of my way not to come across as a snob—yet all the boys my own age were so intimidated by me, by my family's wealth and standing in the community, that I might as well have been a leper. This bluff became the symbol of my frustration. I used to hate it, hate what it stood for, hate the thought of what went on here. But every Friday and Saturday night, there I'd be, looking out that damned window, making myself more miserable, usually crying myself to sleep."

I said, "No matter what you might have heard, I expect a lot of frustration went uneased up here, too."

She shrugged. "I learned to deal with it. By my junior

year, I'd become an expert liar concerning members of the opposite sex. I simply made up boyfriends—wealthy friends of the family, distant cousins, college guys I'd met while visiting the city, like that. I gave them names, even wrote them letters in study hall. God, it would all seem so silly now, if it hadn't been so damned painful. And then—to really add insult to injury—there was Clayton. He's only a couple of years younger than I. When he got to high school and became interested in girls, everything was totally different for him. The family name, the wealth—all the things that scared guys away from me—made *him* fucking irresistible. He used to march up and down the halls with an *entourage,* for God's sake! It all seemed so cruel and unfair."

"So," I said, "as far as Hatchaloo County was concerned, you became an ice goddess."

"You make it sound like it was a conscious decision."

"Wasn't it?"

"It's their tag, not mine."

"Maybe not, but you're doing your damnedest to live up to it. The jerks around here had their chance once, they'll never get another. Right?"

"There you go practicing you pop psychology again."

I smiled, lots of teeth. "Yet here you are with me."

"This is business."

I shook my head, showed her some more teeth. "Maybe going to Clayton's party together was business. But not this."

"Why, of all the conceited . . . are you saying you believe I had you drive up here because—"

I reached for her, gripped her firmly by the shoulders, pulled her to me and kissed her on the mouth. For a long time. She didn't exactly melt into my arms but she didn't try to pull away either. When our lips parted, I said, "What got us here doesn't matter. Where we're at—and I don't mean geographically—is what we need to deal with now."

We kissed again. This time both of us participated. Like Bacall said, it's better that way.

The champagne bottle and the glasses rolled to the floor mat. Buttons popped, zippers hissed, we murmured each other's names. There was frenzied kicking and struggling to remove clothing—lustful gymnastics that, in retrospect, seem seriocomic at best, but in the heat of the moment seemed only terribly urgent and important—and then I was over in the passenger seat, her seat, with my pants down around my ankles and she, totally naked, was straddling me. Her body was a shapely silver column with her long hair snapping in the breeze like the flame of a torch. When she leaned and offered her breasts to me, her nipples were salty-sweet to my tongue and hard-soft, like pliant pencil erasers. She moaned and my mouth left wet trails across her.

The flesh of her hips was like warm velvet under my kneading hands. I felt her muscles working, flexing, and then tensing as I entered her. She lowered herself onto me and I braced my hips, letting her take the first thrust at her own pace. Then we moaned together as the wonderful rhythm began. Slowly, slowly, then faster, with the seat springs chirping in time and our sweat-slick thighs clapping at irregular intervals. She leaned into me again and we kissed hungrily. When she pulled away to catch her breath, arching her back, I craned my neck and continued to kiss her body. Her bouncing breasts were like moving targets.

I felt her start to shudder with a climax and I began to buck harder and faster, wanting to take her over the edge, wanting to join her. But suddenly her movement froze. She pressed restraining palms against my chest. "Wait," she said. "Please. Wait."

My movement ceased also, and I thought: what the fuck? Before I could protest, say anything, she brushed a quick kiss across my lips, then agilely swung her right leg over so that she sat sidesaddle on me for a moment, then swung her

left leg back the other way so that she ended up still astrad-
dle me but with her back to me now.

Tossing her hair and reaching down to guide my penis
back inside her, she said huskily, "Now, lover—Now."

The awkward pause was past in an eyeblink and our passion resumed with added intensity, as if we were trying to
regain the lost seconds. Courtney ground down onto me and
I slammed up into her, hard, deep. I reached around and
cupped her breasts as I nuzzled her back, kissing the nape of
her neck and the tiny bumps of her spine.

She pounded the dash when she came and when I spilled
inside her a short time after I was biting my lower lip so
hard it bled.

Afterward, she lay back against me, our bodies hot and
flushed, our breathing ragged. I wrapped my arms round
her and we stayed like that for a long time without speaking.

It was sometime during then that I realized a deeper in-
sight into part of what had just taken place . . .

Courtney had turned when she did in order to be looking
down at her bedroom window—the scene of so much long-
ago anguish for her—when she climaxed.

15

It was past eleven when I returned to my motel. I entered the pressed wood and plastic little box that was my room, snapped on some lights, dropped my keys into a chair. The room was stuffy from being shut up all day so I punched on the air conditioner and dialed it to medium. While it shuddered and groaned and started to do its thing, I shed my jacket then went into the bathroom and turned on the water at the sink.

My hands—and no doubt other parts of my anatomy—carried the musky scent of Courtney Cord's most intimate regions. I ran half a basin of lukewarm water, worked up a light lather with the sliver of perfumy soap, scooped a couple sudsy handfuls to my face and across the back of my neck. The water and the cooling breath of the air conditioner felt good, bracing.

I was tired. Not sleepy tired, but bone weary and achey, the way you get at the end of a long day when you've pushed past the yawns and the initial waves of grogginess and the aches start to become the main thing keeping you awake. All that tossing and turning I'd done on the lumpy motel mattress the night before hadn't helped any. Nor, much as I might hate to admit it, had my recent sexual calisthenics within the cramped confines of Courtney's car.

Not matter how willing the spirit, the old bod just wasn't as limber as it used to be.

I looked at my reflection in the mirror over the sink. For Christ's sake, I thought, pushing forty and still humping in parked cars like some hormone-inflamed teenager. What the hell's the matter with you anyway?

My reflection grinned lopsidedly back. Yeah, but the car was a 'Vette, man. And the lady was stunning and eager and delicious. Ain't that worth a stiff back and a charley horse or two?

I pulled the drain plug, dragged a towel off the rack, walked back out into the motel room proper, drying myself. I sat on the bed and lit a cigarette. After awhile, I stretched out, letting my feet dangle over the end of the mattress. I lay there on my back, running things through my mind as I watched the smoke spin to the ceiling and disperse into brief phantom shapes.

Intertwining thoughts of Courtney kept nudging aside anything else I tried to concentrate on. She was as fascinating and complex a woman as I'd encountered in a long time. Maybe too long. Maybe not long enough. And the fact that she was strikingly beautiful, of course, only made her that much more mesmerizing. My senses tingled with the recollection of how she'd felt, how she'd tasted. My mind's eye played and replayed images of her moonlit nakedness, of her cascading hair, of her face in the throes of passion. And then there was her face—the hurt on it, and the anger—when, after returning to her apartment and being informed via a thinly veiled hint I would be welcome to spend the night, I'd been forced to put her off with a feeble excuse about not wanting to do something that could cause her embarrassment later on and reminding her I really needed to get an early start in the morning anyway. . . .

Big noble gesture. Big fat lie.

Much as I would have preferred to dwell on the more pleasurable aspects of my interlude with Courtney. I finally forced myself to think beyond that. I considered my upcoming meeting with Junior Odum. I didn't have a hell of a lot to report to him, certainly not in the way of anything positive. I'd managed to get into a scuffle with his sister and her husband—make that *two* scrapes with the latter—and I'd managed to pretty much eliminate everybody's favorite suspect, Clayton Cord. That was about the extent of my achievements. I didn't figure my client was likely to be impressed. What's more, unless he had something new for me to go on or unless The Bug was able to turn up something in the morning, my remaining options were damn slim. Especially considering the forty-eight-hour time limit—which was nearly half gone already—that we'd agreed to.

I rolled over and stabbed out my butt in the bedside ashtray. I rolled back, emitting a long, shuddering yawn. The prone position had started to relax me, to unknot some of the aches. I checked my watch. Going on twelve now. Reba Dallas had said she'd be by to take me to Junior "around midnight." That could be in five minutes, could be forty-five minutes.

I was debating whether or not to allow myself the luxury of dozing until she showed up, when the knock came at the door.

Ain't promptness grand?

I heaved up off the bed, stifling another yawn as I walked over to the door and pulled it open.

The guy standing there was hardly Reba Dallas. He was tall and broad, with bloodshot eyes set close together in a fleshy, florid face and a thin-lipped mouth twisted into what looked like a permanent sneer. He wore green twill work pants and a matching shirt with the sleeves rolled up to reveal thick, shaggy forearms. He stank of cigarette smoke and stale sweat and raw booze.

"You the detective?" he wanted to know.

"I'm *a* detective," I answered. "You looking for any particular one?"

"I'm lookin' for the nosy sumbitch been askin' questions 'bout me all over town, causin' folks—even my own damn wife—to wonder maybe did I have somethin' to do with burnin' up that crazy old Odum broad."

I nodded. "You must be Tom Wykert."

"Bingo, motherfucker!" And he brought a basketball-sized fist up and around and bounced it off the side of my head.

The fact that I was standing in the doorway probably saved me from being decapitated. The close quarters cramped Wykert's swing, prevented him from getting full power into the roundhouse. Still, there was enough steam in the punch to jar me all the way down to my toenails. It would have taken me off my feet if the door frame hadn't been there to intervene once again. I fell against it, hard, the sharp wooden edge of the jamb biting into my arm and shoulder and sawing across the side of my face. I tasted blood in my mouth and felt the oily warmth of it trickle down inside my shirt collar.

I shoved away with an enraged roar, slipping the follow-up jab he threw, driving my shoulder high into his rib cage. A huge gust of air "whoofed!" out of him, but the big bastard held his ground. I hadn't had the chance to build much momentum, but I pack two hundred thirty-odd pounds and it's damn seldom I've thrown my weight against anything or anybody and not had them go down. My surprise cost me some valuable seconds, nullified whatever advantage the move might have gained me. Wykert wrapped his left arm around the back of my neck in a kind of reverse headlock and began pounding his right fist into my kidneys. I clutched his leg desperately, lacing my fingers behind the knee, then, when I had him hopping on one pin, braced my feet against the door frame and pistoned into him once more.

This time he went down. Both of us did. Tumbling and

rolling and skidding across the narrow sidewalk and out onto the crushed gravel of the parking lot.

I was a shade faster getting to my feet and when my visitor bobbed up I tagged him with a right-left-right combination that put him back down. I had the satisfaction of seeing blood blossom and spray from his nostrils.

He rolled animatedly away, indicating my punches had unbalanced him more than injured him. When he stopped rolling and bunched to rise again, I pressed in closer. Too close. He dropped back and lashed out with a low, sweeping kick that knocked my feet out from under me. I crashed down beside him, gravel chewing into the palms of my hands, which I threw out instinctively to catch myself.

Wykert scampered on all fours and pounced on me like a dog on a chew toy. We clinched together there on the sharp, dusty gravel, sweating, bleeding, grunting, cursing, kicking, gouging, pummeling. No finesse, no style, not a hell of a lot of skill. Just two primal brutes locked in combat as old as the dirt we were rolling in. And from some dark, shrouded corner of my brain came the realization that in a crazy kind of way I was enjoying this. The taste of the blood, the feel of the grit and the sweat, the sharp, clean pain of getting hit, the sensation of landing a good shot of your own—all these things, for a few insane seconds anyway, seemed a refreshing change from the duplicity and frustration and bullshit of the everyday world. Yeah. Everything right up front, basic and instinctive. After all, what's more basic than a thrown punch or more instinctive than a counterpunch? I'll take those over lawsuits and litigation every fucking day of the week.

Damn straight.

But when Wykert grabbed a double handful of hair and started trying to drill for oil with the back of my head, I decided I'd had about all the enjoyment I could stand for one night. I grabbed a double handful, too—of his balls. I yanked out and away. The rest of him went along, accompanied by a keening howl.

We rolled clear of each other. Again I was first on my feet. When Wykert made it most of the way up, cupping his crotch with one hand, I was waiting with a swooping uppercut. It put him down, but not out. Twice more he got up, twice more I knocked him back down. My fists were split and sore, my eyes stung from sweat, each gasping breath I took burned like fire. And I was getting the best of it. Only Wykert wouldn't quit. The fourth time I hammered him down, he fell heavily, sprawling with arms and legs thrown wide like he was going to make angels in the snow. I figured he *had* to be out.

But when I moved closer, I saw that his eyes were still open, swimming around, trying to focus, trying to establish his bearings. I swore under my breath I'd kill him as he pushed himself up on his elbows.

"Stay down," I panted, the words scraping the inside of my throat and mouth.

His eyes found me, narrowed blearily beneath scowling brows. His face, where it wasn't caked with dirt, glistened wetly from sweat and blood. "I never had nuthin' to do with burnin' up that old woman," he insisted in a low rasp.

I loomed over him. "Who did then?"

He looked genuinely bewildered. "How the fuck should I know? . . . She did it her own self . . . didn't she?"

I shook my head. "Lot of folks around here don't buy that. Count me as one of them."

He renewed his efforts to get back up. "Don't care what you buy, fucker," he grumbled. " 'Cept I'm gonna by God show you it wasn't *me* had anything to do with that fire."

"Stay down," I warned again.

But he wouldn't listen. He kept coming, grunting with each slow and creaky movement, breath chugging laboriously. Yet still too big and strong and mean to fuck around with. I stepped over beside him—my throbbing fists held down at my sides—waited until he was on his feet, squatting, starting to stand, then kicked him across the backs of his legs, about six inches above the heels, and spilled him onto his can. He landed with crunching impact, his shoulders slapping the gravel hard.

He rolled slowly onto his stomach, craning his neck turtlelike to glare up at me. A string of bloodied snot ran from the end of his nose to the ground between his hands. He began scraping the gravel with his fingers and feet, trying to raise himself to his hands and knees. "Gonna show you . . . damn you . . ." he panted. "Make you take back what you said . . . what you told everybody about me . . ."

I watched, swallowing some of my own blood, as he—incredibly—got his ass up and his knees under him and strained to lift his head and shoulders. None of it was much fun anymore.

"Stay down, you dumb fucker," I said huskily. This time it was more a plea than a warning.

"He won't do it. He won't quit 'less you put him away cold."

The new voice—not unfamiliar and not entirely unexpected—came from off to one side and slightly behind me. I turned to look at Reba Dallas standing there. She still wore her T-shirt, cutoff jeans, and cowboy boots. She stood with her arms folded loosely beneath her perky breasts, watching Wykert with an expression on her face as impassive as if she were watching a deodorant commercial on TV. Behind her, the row of motel units stood silent, their windows (all but mine) dark, their doors (again all but mine) shut, their occupants so far undisturbed by what had transpired between Wykert and me.

"How long have you been there?" I wanted to know.

She shrugged. "I been around. Saw Wykert's pickup turnin' in here when I was comin' down the road, so I laid my bike down in the ditch back there, quiet-like, and waited and watched to see what would happen."

"So you saw it all then?"

"The fight you mean? Uh-huh. You handle yourself pretty good. Kinda dumb, though, to let him nail you with that sucker punch like he done. Coulda been all over but the shoutin', right there."

We both looked back at Wykert, who continued struggling to try and get to his feet, making guttural noises.

"Speaking of getting this over with," I said to Reba. "You got any ideas?"

"Tire iron'd do the trick," she said decisively.

"I'm sure it would."

"It's somethin' he'd understand. Don't ever think he'd hesitate to use one on you in the same situation."

"Yeah, well that's the difference between him and me, okay? I don't pound a man into the ground after I've got him beat." I looked around, agitated. "You said he came here in a pickup. Which one—that one? All right, go put the tailgate down."

While Reba went to do my bidding, I walked over to Wykert, grabbed him by the scruff of the neck, pulled him up. He muttered something unintelligible and threw a couple of weak punches against my hip. I cuffed his hand away, then jerked him the rest of the way to his feet and shook him.

"Listen, asshole," I said with my face pushed close to his, "it's over, you understand? You lost the fight, but you convinced me you had nothing to do with the Odum fire. So we're even, got it? You go home, I go home, that's the end of it."

"Make you take back . . . what you said about me," he slobbered, spit bubbling at the corners of his battered mouth.

I walked him to the end of the pickup, where Reba stood beside the lowered tailgate. "You come after me again," I promised Wykert icily, "I'll put you in the hospital." I shoved him up onto the truck bed, where he flopped like a beached whale. Reba slammed the gate, drove home the lock pins. I leaned against the side of the truck for a minute or so, catching my breath, then turned to Reba and said, "Unless you think we should call somebody, he ought to be able to sleep it off there awhile, then drive himself home."

She looked puzzled. "Why the hell would I want to call somebody? For all I care, he can drive off the edge of a fuckin' cliff."

I grinned. "You're a pretty tough cookie, aren't you?"

"Maybe tough, maybe just practical."

"You'd really have used a tire iron on him?"

"Betcher ass. *That* woulda been practical. Speakin' of which, seems to me it'd also be practical to get you somewhere where we can clean up some of those cuts and scrapes. Or are *you* such a tough cookie you figure you can just stand around bleedin' all night?"

16

Picture a remote forested area, a rumpled green-black blanket beneath the night sky, rising and falling over jagged hills and furrowed into shadowy gorges. The higher, early-turning leaves, breeze-stirred, are painted shimmering silver by splashes of moonlight spraying down between skidding clouds. Rocky outcroppings and broad, deeply eroded cliff faces are tinted a ghastly bluish orange by the same process. You walk down one of the gorges—more of a gully, really, probably an ancient creek bed—after leaving your car back where the road ran out. Insects drone in the air around you, unseen creatures rustle through the underbrush on either side, night birds call out from indiscernible locations. You're gripped by a sense of surrealism. You've walked wooded trails at night before, but it's never felt quite like this. There is anticipation of . . . something. First, you smell it: wood-smoke and cooking fat odors, overriding a sour-sweet mix of animal and human scents. Then, ahead, you spot a soft glow of light. The gully grows shallower, its floor rockier, the ground harder packed. The snagging underbrush seems to be thinning, as if worn away. And then you see the light source: it spills from the mouth of a cave, a gaping slit in a mossy, root-ensnarled mound of rock. The opening is framed by rough-hewn logs, which have been notched into the bare rock and mortared there with dried mud. A heavy plank door has been fastened to this rugged framework. The latter is standing open, propped by a block of wood, and a wide section of the cave's interior is visible. A natural pocket of stone had been turned into a crackling fireplace with a metal grill wedged across it for cooking. Animal skins and quilts—once brightly colored perhaps, but dingy now in the smoke and gloom—adorn the walls. There is a smattering of rough furniture, including several stands upon which dripping tallow candles in upturned jar lids have been placed to augment the flickering light provided by the fireplace. It takes a minute or two for all of this to penetrate your slightly bewildered, urbanized, twentieth-century brain. But it finally sinks in. You are looking at a permanent dwelling, at someone's home.

It was here that Reba Dallas brought me.

It was here that Junior Odum waited. . . .

He sat on a bench at a wooden table just outside the entrance to the cave. Scratchings on the ground behind the table indicated that in inclement weather it was dragged inside. A steaming mug of coffee rested on the tabletop in front of Junior and beside that a burning candle, its jar-lid base doubling as an ashtray for the cigarette he was smoking. He took a hard drag on the butt, watching through squinted eyes as we crested the rocky slope that led up from the gully.

When we stood across the table from him, he nodded at me and said, by way of greeting, simply, "Hannibal."

I nodded back. "Quite a hideout you've found for yourself."

"Gets the job done," he allowed. He squinted some more, examining me. "No offense, hoss, but you look awful bad used. Heard you had a run-in with my sister and that damn Vern, but I didn't realize it got so rough."

I grinned with half my mouth, the half that hurt the least.

"Pearl got in a couple licks," I said, "but most of what you're looking at came from a more recent encounter."

"Tom Wykert," Reba put in, an excited edge to her voice. "They went head to head only just an hour or so ago, and damned if ol' Hannibal here didn't leave Wykert a-layin' in the dirt pure beat to shit."

Junior cocked an eyebrow. "That a fact?"

"Damn betcha," Reba went on. "Whipped him fair 'n square, too, right in the middle of the parkin' lot there at the motel. Not only whipped him, but did it *after* he let Wykert throw the first punch."

I smiled tolerantly at Reba's exuberance. It was a welcome change from the cynicism she'd been aiming at me prior to this, and I'd had no trouble adjusting to it during the trip here. Her new attitude had blossomed back at my motel room, where we'd gone to clean up my wounds after depositing Wykert in his truck; it was in full bloom by the time she'd finished administering to said injuries with a first aid kit from my car, a task at which she showed surprising gentleness and skill.

"Needless to say," I commented now, in response to her description of the fight, "the telling of it is considerably easier than the task itself was."

"I can believe that," Junior replied. "Tom Wykert's been kickin' ass around these parts for nigh onto thirty years. Nobody's left him layin' in the dirt since he was in his teens. I had my crack at him a few years back, when I was maybe a little scrawnier, maybe not so savvy to the ways of in-fightin'. Got my clock cleaned like everybody else and I ain't ashamed to say I never been in any hurry to try my luck again." He gestured toward the opposite side of the table, where I stood. "Set yourself down, Hannibal. You've damn sure earned the right."

I didn't have to be asked twice. I lowered my aching ass onto the rugged bench and no high-priced recliner ever felt more comfortable.

"Get you something to drink?" Junior asked.

"That coffee you've got there looks mighty tempting."

"I'll get it," Reba said, moving on around the table and into the cave.

"Bring out a jug of that moon, too, why don't you?" Junior called after her. Turning back to me, he said with conviction, "Good girl there." Then, after a minute, his mouth curved devilishly and he added, "Good girl, that is, far as cousins go. Gonna be a pure fire-breathin' hellcat for any crazy sumbitch tries to make a wife out of her, though."

"Yeah," I said agreeably, "she'll be a handful all right."

As we sat there making small talk, I gradually became more perceptive of our surroundings. I noted for the first time that off to one side of the cave mouth a sturdy pen had been erected under an overhang of gnarled roots and stunted branches growing out of the rock; in it, a handful of hogs lay snoring in the mud. On the other side, a latticework of chicken roosts had been put up and the grayish white shapes in them, I guessed, were laying hens. Once or twice, not far off, I thought I heard the mournful lowing of a cow.

While I was still digesting these discoveries, Reba emerged from the cave. I looked up reflexively and was somewhat startled to see another person moving through the cave behind her—a hulking, wild-haired shape snuffling purposefully across in front of the fireplace, carrying a steaming pot in one hand and gesturing animatedly, meaninglessly with the other.

Whatever my face showed, Junior said, calmly, without turning to look, "That's Mary. Treefoot Mary folks call her. Been livin' in these woods, in this cave, for long as anybody can remember. Some say she's a witch, some say she's only crazy. However they believe, most folks steer plenty clear of her. Her right foot is real bad deformed, the skin lumpy and rough like tree bark with toes that shoot out all twisty and curled like roots—that's how she got the name. Big as a plow horse, almost as strong. Legend has it she was the illegitimate child of a preacher's daughter who went a little insane with the shame and pain of givin' birth. When she saw the baby, huge and deformed like it was, she vowed it had to be some demon offspring and brung it out in these woods, where she left it to die. Only Mary lived. Somehow. And a few years later, the preacher's daughter, who stayed a little addled in the head and became what they called back then a woman of easy virtue, died a horrible death. Got bit by a rabid dog. They couldn't get any vaccine to her in time so they had to tie her to a porch post out front of Doc Swain's office, where she came to her end a-foamin' at the mouth and havin' fits and barkin' and snappin' at the towns-people who gathered to watch. They never caught the dog that bit her and nobody ever saw it again 'cept that one day. But word spread that some who *did* see it claimed it had a deformed right front paw. Wasn't long before a lot of folks were believin' the dog was Mary herself, her shape changed through the same sort of dark powers that allowed her to survive as an infant alone in the woods, come back to get her revenge on the mother what abandoned her. Been stories about her, been fear and mystery surroundin' her ever since."

By the time Junior was finished with this narrative, Reba had taken a seat at the table with us. She pushed a mug of coffee over in front of me and, at Junior's elbow, placed a plastic gallon milk jug three-quarters full of watery-looking liquid. The hulking figure inside the cave had disappeared again. I looked back and forth from one cousin's face to the other, trying to read something in their eyes, trying to decide if somebody was putting me on, attempting to rube the city slicker. If that's what they were up to, they were damn stone-faced good at it.

I cleared my throat and said to Junior, "But here you are, hiding out from the law, making yourself at home . . . Apparently you don't put much stock in those witch stories."

He shook his head. "No. No, you're wrong there, hoss. I

been in and around these hills too long, seen too many strange things, to be able to flat discount the stories and legends that come out of 'em. Oh, I ain't sayin' I'm able to swallow that Ol' Mary actually went and turned herself into a rabid dog and bit her ma; but on the other hand, I don't exactly *not* believe it either, you understand? Reason I'm able to come here without fear or concern goes back a lot of years, back to when I was a boy of nine or ten. It was winter, near Christmas, and Ma sent me out one evenin' to cut us a tree. The ol' man was passed out drunk somewhere, as usual, and Pearl was just a little bit of a thing, still peein' her pants. Anyway, I was down by Miller's Creek, pickin' through the pines there, when I seen Treefoot Mary a-comin' across the ice. At that age, I was scared shitless by only the mention of her name, let alone the sight of her. I just froze where I was, too scared even to run. Then, when she was most of the way across, near my side, the ice gave way under her. Miller's Creek never was very deep, but it was bitter cold that winter and you could see the water that wasn't froze through had built up quite a current. She was too far away from the bank to grab hold of anything to help herself, so there she was a-scratchin' and a-clawin' at the ice, tryin' to pull herself out with no luck at all. To this day I don't remember makin' any conscious decision about it, but all of a sudden I was crouched on the edge of the bank, shovin' out a long ol' branch to her and layin' my full weight across it, to anchor it, so's she could pull herself out. When she got on shore, she peeled off some of her outer clothes and I took off my coat and gave it to her. She was such a big ol' thing it looked like a napkin in her hands. But she used it to dry off her hands and face and hair some, then gave it back to me and just stood there for a long time, smilin' down at me. That's the only time I ever seen her smile. Far as I know, it's the only time anybody ever seen her smile. Then she turned and walked off in that shufflin' way of hers. Only that wasn't the end of it. Not as far as I'm concerned, anyway. It was Christmas a couple days later, and we was even poorer than usual that year. Ma had bartered to get me and Pearl each some little gift, I don't remember what, but Christmas dinner was set to be just Spam and beans. And where I say beans, that's what I mean: beans. Period. Not pork 'n beans, or beans with ketchup or tomato sauce or gravy—just fuckin' beans. Navy beans boiled in water. And I guess we felt lucky enough to have that. But when I went out to the shed to fetch some wood first thing that mornin', what do you suppose I found? The biggest, fattest ol' wild tom turkey you ever did see had somehow got hisself cornered in the woodshed. I didn't waste any time whackin' him over the head with a piece of kindling, then I went in and got the ol' man and he came back out with the axe and by the time we left for church an hour later, that bird was a-roastin' away in our oven. And if that wasn't enough, on the way back from church what did we find but a five-pound sack of brown sugar layin' alongside the road right at our driveway. The ol' man said it must have fallen off the back of somebody's truck. Do I have to tell you how much a brown sugar basting added to those fuckin' beans? Now consider this, Hannibal: hadn't been a wild turkey in these parts for years before that day, hasn't been any since. And folks damn sure never got in the habit of spillin' groceries off their trucks almost at our door. So what do you think? You think all that good fortune on that special Christmas day was just a quirk of fate? Or you think maybe the fates got a little nudge from somebody down here who figured they had a debt to repay?"

I drank some of my coffee, which was excellent, then gave a small shrug. "I don't know what to think," I said honestly. "That's quite a story. Have you ever asked her about it?"

"How's that?"

"Treefoot Mary. Have you ever asked her if she was the one who provided those things?"

He made a face. "Why, hell no, man. You never want to *ask* about a thing like that. That'd go and spoil it for everybody."

I wasn't sure I understood the reasoning there, but I let it go. "At any rate," I said, "would I be wrong to guess that this isn't the first time since then you've come here to hide out?"

"No, you wouldn't be wrong at all. I started comin' here when I was barely in my teens, back when I'd get in too much trouble to go home but not enough to run far away. I showed up here one day when I was feelin' desperate and Mary was a-standin' there at the mouth of the cave like she was expectin' me. Neither one of us said a word. She looked down at me, nodded once, slow, like she understood everything about everything, then motioned me on in. She's been motionin' me on in like that whenever I've showed up ever since. She don't ask questions, she don't preach, she's just there for me when I need her."

"Like you were there for her," Reba said softly.

"Maybe. But that was only one time. Been dozens the other way around." Junior sighed. "In other words, I've tooken advantage of her like I done practically everybody else who ever showed me any kindness in my life."

He reached for the jug, unscrewed the cap, cradled it across the crook of his arm, and then raised the arm and took a long swig.

Not wanting him to get maudlin on me, I said, "Haven't the cops ever come out here after you?"

"Wouldn't do 'em any good," he said, lowering the jug, wiping his mouth with the back of his hand. "They know they'd never be able to corner me here, leastways not without surroundin' the whole damn forest—and they ain't enough soldier boys in the Illinois National Guard for that. Nobody can get within a mile of this place without Treefoot Mary knowin' they're comin', knowin' right down to what blades of grass they're gonna step on."

I glanced over at the cave. "How can that be?" I wondered.

Junior Odum smiled. "It's like they say, hoss; if you gotta ask, you'd probably never understand."

"Look," I said, "I'm getting a little tired of this mumbo jumbo talk, okay? If the Good Witch of the Wildwood in there is such hot stuff, why not ask *her* who killed your mother? Because the sad, sorry fact of the matter is this: I've just put in a real ballbreaker of a day—I've been pounded on, cussed at, thrown out of places, threatened, and most likely lied to—and I don't have shit to show for it except one big ache from my ass both ways and about eight dollars' worth of fresh bandages that I'm now sporting as part of my wardrobe."

Junior's smile faded during the outburst and by the time I was finished there was a kind of tension swirling in the air between us. Reba shifted uncomfortably on her seat. A gust of wind rolled up out of the gully, pushing ahead of it a rattling handful of fallen leaves. The fire inside the cave flared, its burning logs popping ominously and coughing bright geysers of sparks.

After several beats, a careful, measured smile returned to Junior's mouth. "You'd best try to calm down some, hoss," he suggested easily, " 'fore you bust a gut. Here"—he pushed the jug over in front of me—"try some of this. Guaranteed good for what ails you."

I waved the jug away. "What ails me," I said, "is this cockamamie damn case I let you rope me into."

He shook his head. "I know your kind. You don't stay roped very long into anything you don't want to be a part of. 'Sides, I can tell by your tone—you don't believe my ma burned her own self up, either. Do you?"

I let the question hang around my neck for a minute, wishing I could just shrug it off. But I couldn't. Junior's eyes wanted an answer. Finally, I said, "No, I guess I don't. But that's just a hunch, a feeling. It's not based on anything solid. It doesn't do a damn thing toward *proving* she was murdered."

Junior spread his hands. "One step at a time, hoss. You convinced yourself, now all you got to do is convince a few others. Get enough noses sniffin' for a killer instead of breathin' easy 'cause they don't figure there's one out there, you watch how fast the sumbitch gets treed."

"And everybody knows," Reba put in, "who to stand down wind from. One way or another, that fuckin' Clayton Cord is the one behind it. I don't see why we don't just lay for the fucker some night and—"

"No!" Junior's fist came down hard on the tabletop, causing the candle to flicker wildly and the contents in the plastic jug to slosh back and forth. "Goddammit, I said I want this done right. For Ma's sake. I want her killer brought to justice all legal as shit—no goin' off half-cocked, no midnight ambushin', none of the kind of wild things I used to woulda done. Is that clear?"

"What if there ain't no other way?" Reba demanded. "What if Hannibal here *can't* convince anybody she was killed, *can't* get a lead on who done it? You just gonna leave it go?"

Junior glared at her hotly, and Reba returned as good as she got. The shifting light made shadows dance across their faces, heightening the respective determination and defiance that showed there.

"If that's what it comes down to," Junior said at length, his voice low and huskier than it had been, "yeah, that's what I'll have to do. If we can't do this right, we don't do it. Otherwise it wouldn't mean none of the things it's supposed to mean. Can't you see that, girl?"

She shook her head. "No, I can't. All I see is that one of the finest persons I ever knew is dead—killed—and nobody seems to be doin' anything about it. And now you're settin' there tellin' me maybe we ain't gonna be *able* to do anything about it, and you want me to understand. Well, I don't."

"It'll get tooken care of," Junior said, almost softly now, "one way or another. Don't you remember what it was Ma always said?"

Reba's expression melted into puzzlement. "What do you mean?"

" 'God will sort the souls.' Remember how she'd always say that when folks was bad-mouthin' somebody, allowin' as to how it looked like they maybe was gettin' away with somethin' and it just didn't seem right."

"Yeah, I remember," Reba said sullenly. For a moment it looked like she might give in, but suddenly her defiance flared anew. "So if that's the case and the law can't nail Cord's ass, then I just might have to see to it that his soul goes into the sortin' bin a little sooner than anybody figured on."

So saying, she got up from the table and stalked off into the deep shadows at the edge of the light. After a few seconds, we saw the flash of a match being struck and then the glowing red dot of a lighted cigarette.

"God damn a bull-headed woman!" Junior declared, shaking fists balled in frustration. He looked at me. "You ever see the like of her?"

I shrugged. "Like I said before, seems like she can be a handful."

He grunted. "A damn pain-in-the-ass handful. Worst part is, she reminds me exactly of me . . . up until not too long ago."

He reached for the jug again, swung it high, took another long hit.

"Just what is that stuff anyway?" I wanted to know.

He lowered the jug, frowned deeply at me. "Come on, hoss, if you don't know what this is you're a real disappointment for a detective. I guess moonshine is the popular name. Some call it just plain moon, some just plain 'shine. Also knowed as white lightnin', mountain dew, everclear, who-hit-John, panther piss . . . and on and on. Whatever you call it, it's the stuff dreams are made of."

"And a few nightmares, I'd bet."

"The next mornin' sometimes, yeah. I seen my share of snakes." He pushed the jug over in front of me again, grinning. "But don't take my word for it."

This time I tried some. I took a couple tentative sniffs, lived through that, then hoisted the plastic container the way I'd seen him do and took a brave swallow. And another. It stung the cuts inside my mouth but otherwise went down with surprising smoothness. "Not bad," I said, lowering the brew.

Junior's grin broadened. "Watch out, though, it'll sneak up on you like a hungry brother-in-law and knock you sillier'n a lodge member at a convention."

"They make it around here?" I asked.

"Oh sure, all over in these woods and hills. No real big operations like they got down through Kentucky and other places, but a lot of little backyarders lookin' to make some Saturday night spendin' cash. Never seemed worth the bother to me. One of the few illegal activities I guess I never got tangled up in. I remember the ol' man tryin' his luck a few times, but he'd usually get plastered and pass out about halfway through the process and then his batch'd be spoiled by the time he woke back up to tend to it. And Pearl's husband, Vern, now, he's about the best moon runner in these parts. Prick ain't good for much else, but he knows his shit behind the wheel of that souped-up car of his. On a clear night, in the wee hours of the morning, you can sometimes hear his windin' down out of the hills on his way with a load to Saint Louis or maybe up to Springfield. He makes more of a production out of it than he needs to, really. The sheriff he don't pay much never mind to none of it, 'less somebody puts out a bad batch and folks start turnin' up sick or dead. And the revenuers hardly come around any more on account of, like I said, there ain't no big operations usually in these parts. But, to give the devil his due, on the times they *have* laid for him, ol' Vern flat blew away from 'em without no sweat."

I dumped the last quarter-inch of cold coffee from the cup Reba had brought out to me, replaced it with a couple fingers from the jug. It tasted just as smooth that way. "Getting back to your mother's death," I said to Junior. "While it's true I haven't been able to accomplish much in the way of proving it was no accident, I do think I've managed to weed out some suspects."

His interest sharpened. "Go on," he said with a nod.

Quickly, underplaying Courtney's part in it, I told him of my meetings with Clayton Cord and what came out of them. "In other words," I summed up, "despite Reba's strong feelings about him and despite his obviousness as a prime suspect, I don't think he's our man. He's not without some guilt, and he knows it; he put a lot of pressure on your ma and he encouraged others to do so as well. But as far as having anything to do with the fire—or *any* action that might have directly resulted in her death—I'd say he's clean. It'd be a lot easier if he wasn't, but that's the way it shakes out."

Junior had poured some of the 'shine into his coffee cup, too. As I talked, he'd rolled the cup slowly back and forth between his palms. He continued to do so. "What about Wykert?" he said, his voice sounding far away.

I made a gesture with one hand. "Reba was there, she saw and heard most of it. His weren't the actions of a murderer, either. He didn't come after me to try to put me out of commission or to scare me off. He was . . . well, offended by the questions I'd been asking about him. Made him look bad to his friends and to his wife. He meant to get an apology out of my hide. Again, he's not without guilt; he bad-mouthed your mother pretty fiercely and stirred up a lot of harsh feelings toward her. But as far as directly causing her harm—I can't see it."

Junior stopped rolling the cup but kept it gripped in both hands. Like he wished it was somebody's throat. "So what are you saying, Hannibal?" he wanted to know.

I picked my words carefully, feeling the pressure of his stare. "I guess what I'm saying is that if we're right, if the fire that killed your mother was intentional rather than accidental, then the person responsible for it might turn out to be the hardest kind of killer there is to nail."

"And what kind is that?"

"The gray, quietly desperate little fucker with motives so obscure it's damn near impossible to uncover them with standard investigative procedure." I explained to him, as I had to Courtney, how his mother's refusal to sell her land—no matter how impressive it might seem on a certain level—could be viewed as a very real and very personal threat by a lot of people in Hatchaloo County. "So you see the possibilities. All it would take would be one disturbo, maybe a wimp who never harmed a fly before in his life, feeling desperate, egged on by the rhetoric of Cord and Wykert . . . somebody like that could have twisted things all around and sold themselves on the idea they were doing a kind of community service."

Nobody said anything for a while. The wind was picking up, breaths of it gusting more and more frequently up out of the gully. Dry, fallen leaves rattled around our feet.

Absently, Junior leaned over and plucked one up. He'd set aside his coffee cup and now it was the leaf he held in both hands, examining as if he'd never taken a really good look at one before. "They're turnin' early this year," he observed.

I nodded. "Yeah. I've noticed."

Ma used to call the fall of the year 'the burning season.' When I was a little kid, she'd stand in the backyard with me and point out across the meadows and the stands of timber with their leaves all orange and gold and fiery red and she'd say, 'Looka there, Juney—' "

He paused, eyed me uncertainly above a sheepish grin. "Juney, that's short for Junior," he said. "No fault of mine, but that's what everybody called me as a kid."

I nodded understandingly. "Me, I was 'Joey' until I was about fifteen."

"Anyway," he went on, "she'd say, 'Looka there, Juney, they're on fire.' And then, a few days or a few weeks later, when folks started rakin' their lawns and the air of an evenin' would be filled with the smell of burnin' leaves, she'd look at me with a twinkle in her eye and say, 'See, didn't I tell you they was on fire?'"

He was holding the leaf cupped almost reverently in his palms. He looked up from it. "Crazy, ain't it, how a body thinks of things like that at the oddest times?"

I shook my head. "No, it's not crazy at all. Having things like that to think back on may be what keeps the rest of us from turning into desperate little gray fuckers too close to the edge ourselves."

He looked back down at his leaf. "I never bothered comin' back for the ol' man's funeral, you know. They got word to me and all, but I was already on the run and . . . well, it didn't seem worth the risk. I ain't particularly proud to say that, but that's what it came down to. I woulda walked over hot coals for Ma, but me and the ol' man . . . there never was much between us. I can't say he mistreated me none. Never gave me but a few lickin's or anything, and none I didn't have comin'. Mostly he was too drunk to pay much attention to what I was doin', good or bad. I guess I was kinda ashamed of him. And there's another odd thing. I was ashamed of him and yet—'cept for the bad drinkin'—I turned out so damned much like him." He paused, blew out a long, ragged sigh. "And now I'm settin' here thinkin' that if I *woulda* come back for his funeral, maybe Ma woulda shared with me her idea not to sell the land. Maybe I woulda picked up on the ugly mood that was waitin' for her out there. Maybe I coulda done . . . hell, I don't know.

Somethin'. Somethin' besides settin' here feelin' sorry about all the damn things I *didn't* do." Abruptly, savagely, he crumpled the leaf in his hands and flung the shredded pieces away from him. "Fuck it all anyway!"

I gave him a while to settle down, then said, "Hey. One step at a time, remember? You can't go back and undo what's already done, you can't go back and redo what wasn't done. All you can do is move forward from this point. You're on the right track, you're trying to see to it that your mother's killer is caught and punished in the proper way. Stay with it."

"How about you, Hannibal? You going to stay with it?"

"I promised you forty-eight hours. You'll get all of that."

"And then what? You haul me away and just leave it unfinished? Knowin' there's a killer runnin' loose somewhere down here."

"I don't know that for a fact. I *feel* it, but I don't *know* it."

"And you can live with that?"

"You do what you can, you live with what's left."

"But my ma can't say that, can she?"

"Look, the opera isn't over until the fat lady sings. I've still got a few things to check out, a few angles to play. Our best hope is to get the sheriff convinced that fire was no accident. If we can do that much, get him to reopen his investigation, then it won't matter whether I'm on the scene or not. If the killer *is* an obscure little nobody like I suspect, then it's going to take time—a slip of the tongue, a wrong reaction at an unguarded moment—for him to show his hand. That's where an open police investigation shines. A month from now, a year from now, somebody sees or hears or remembers something and all that machinery is just waiting to swing into action."

Junior considered this. "Yeah, I reckon nobody knows that better'n me. The law don't forget shit. It not only has a long arm, it has a powerful long memory."

I nodded. "That's the way it works." I rubbed my grainy eyes with the heels of both hands, then pulled the palms down over my face, trying to drag away some of the exhaustion. I stood up. "Unless you've got something else, it's time I headed back. I need to catch some z's and I want to get an early start in the morning." I purposely hadn't mentioned the scheduled "arson investigation" by The Bug. No need to get anybody's hopes up, and no need to let all of my tricks out of the bag.

Junior stood also. "You're welcome to sack out here for awhile if you want."

"Thanks anyway. Be easier if I just went back to the motel."

Junior turned and hollered at the darkness. "Reba June, quit your sulkin' and get over here. Time to take Hannibal on back."

There was no response, but he seemed to take for granted that she was coming. He turned back to me, brow furrowed with concern over something else. "Listen, hoss, about some of those things I said . . . I know you're givin' it your best shot. I can't ask no more than that. I just want you to know I ain't thinkin' of turnin' rabbit on you. When it's time for you to take me in, no matter how things stand, I'll be ready. I wouldn't do you dirt after all you've done to help us."

I nodded. "I'm counting on that."

Reba materialized out of the shadows. She walked silently past us and started down into the gully. Over her shoulder, she said, "You comin', Hannibal, or are you two gonna hug 'n kiss good-bye?"

17

*R*eba remained sullen and silent during most of the drive back to Cedarton. As we neared the motel, she finally decided to speak. "I heard what you told Junior back there . . . about Clayton Cord and all."

"And?"

"I don't buy it."

I shrugged. "That's your prerogative I guess."

"Clayton Cord is a spoiled, greedy, snot-nosed sonofabitch."

"Maybe. Hell, probably. But that doesn't make him a killer."

"How can you decide he ain't no killer just by talkin' to him?"

"It's what you call a hunch. A feeling I got, from the way he acted, the things he said. In my line of work it's a sense you develop and learn to trust."

"What about the *proof* you're always talkin' about?"

"Okay, I don't have any proof that Cord isn't the killer. But *you* don't have any proof that your aunt was even killed. Yet you believe so with all your might, don't you? That's based on a feeling of yours, a hunch—isn't it the same thing?"

"Don't go puttin' words in my mouth!"

I started to say something further, but bit it off and emitted an exasperated sigh instead. I braked as we came abreast of the Lincolnway, nosed the Plymouth into the parking lot. My headlight beams swept across an empty slot where Tom Wykert's pickup had been.

"How about Wykert?" I said. "I reached the same conclusion concerning him based on the things he said and did. You were here, you saw how he kept getting back up because he wanted me to take back what I'd implied about him. Would that be the concern of somebody who'd committed murder?"

Reba snorted derisively. "I never figured Wykert had nuthin' to do with it nohow. He's a loudmouth and a bully. If he ever worked up enough gumption to kill anybody, he'd blow about it all over the county. The way they burned up Aunt Flo was the work of a lowdown, snake-fuckin' sneak—like Clayton Cord."

I pulled up in front of my unit, cut the engine. Reba's door popped open and she started to get out. I reached across and grabbed her by the wrist, stopping her.

"Wait a minute," I said. "I want you to hear me out."

She glared at me but didn't try to pull away.

I said, "I don't much give a damn what you believe, and I'm too tired to argue with you anymore even if I did. But I don't want you to queer this for your cousin, you hear? Let him play out his hand with me before you do anything stupid. It's important for him to see this thing through, no matter how it turns out. After I take him away—and I *will* take him away, make no mistake about that—you can knock yourself out playing vigilante or whatever it is you feel you have to do. But not before. Got it?"

She continued to glare at me and I countered with a flat, patient gaze. When she tried to jerk free, I held tight.

"I'm waiting for an answer," I told her.

"Fuck you! How's that for an answer?"

I shook my head. "No, Junior's the one who'll end up

getting fucked. For the first time in his life he's trying to set his priorities straight, trying to get his shit together. It could be a turning point. But you go and do something dumb and blow it all out of the water, he'll likely figure it's not worth the trouble to try again. He'll spend the rest of his life living in caves and jail cells."

Some of the heat left her eyes. "All right," she said, "you've made your point."

"Have I?"

"I said you did, goddammit, now let go of my arm. You're hurting me."

I released my grip and she bounced hurriedly out of the car. I got out, too, and stood leaning on the open door, watching her stride angrily across the parking lot toward where she'd left her bike.

At twenty paces, she stopped, spun around, and pointed an unwavering finger dead at me. "You got twenty-four more hours, Hannibal. This time tomorrow, your time's up. After that, don't you or Junior or nobody else try to stand in my way."

18

If you've ever read the comic strip *Peanuts,* then you're probably familiar with the character called Pigpen, the smudged little guy who's so messy he's followed around by a perpetual cloud of dust and debris. I think of Pigpen whenever I see Frankie The Firebug. Not because Frankie's dirty, but because, due to his reputation, my imagination always conjures up a cloud of smoke and soot hovering nearby.

It was like that when I spotted him standing outside the bus stop in Marieville. It was past five-thirty when I pulled up and he was leaning against the side of the building with both hands jammed in the pockets of his long topcoat, looking not very happy. The Marieville bus stop amounted to a couple folding chairs and a theater lobby ashtray arranged in one corner of a twenty-four-hour gas station/convenience mart. The canned goods on the shelves had dingy, peeling labels and the fat, dozing clerk behind the counter had sweat stains under her arms as big as Cadillac hubcaps. I could see why The Bug was cooling his heels outside.

"Been waiting long?" I said through the open window.

He pushed off the wall. "Five seconds in this stinking mud puddle of a town is too damn long."

He came around the end of the car, pulled open the passenger door, got in. He took a good look at me and said,

"Jesus Christ, Hannibal, you look worse than this piece of shit you're driving."

I smiled. "Gee, it's good to have you aboard. I needed a morale booster."

Actually, regardless of The Bug's disparaging remark, I felt pretty good. After Reba Dallas had spurted away from the motel on her motorbike, I'd gone inside and taken a long, hot-as-I-could-stand-it then cold-as-I-could-stand-it shower. Emerging from that, I'd applied fresh bandages, then washed down a handful of aspirin with three cups of black coffee made from hot tap water and some packets of instant crystals that I keep in the glove compartment. That left room for an hour of hard, fast sleep. By the time my wristwatch alarm went off at four-thirty, the caffeine had started to kick in and I awoke feeling more or less refreshed.

As The Bug and I rolled back toward Cedarton now, the new day, such as it would be, was dawning. The wind had died down during the night and a cloud cover had rolled in. It looked like the morning was going to be gray and dismal.

Dismal indeed.

After listening to The Bug gripe and grumble every mile of the way, we arrived at the burnt-out shell of the Odum house around six, and by half past, in spite of all the hopes I'd pinned on him, he turned to me and announced with calm conviction: "I don't know what you expected me to find, man, but there aren't any signs of arson here."

All my aches and pains and weariness returned with crashing impact. I suddenly felt like one of the charred timbers, ready to crumble and drop. If that wasn't enough, a misting rain had started to fall.

"Fuck!" I said. "Are you sure?"

His narrow, pale face took on a slightly offended expression. He spread his hands. "What do you want me to say? I can't state beyond a shadow of doubt that the place *wasn't* torched, no. All I'm saying is that there are no overt signs of it. But hell, that's not surprising, really. What'd they have here, just an old wood house, right?"

"A clapboard shack," I said, quoting Junior Odum, "with newspaper insulation and tar paper patches on the outside."

The Bug rolled his eyes. "Jesus Christ, a torch's wet dream. Drop a match in any corner and the whole fucking thing is gone"—he snapped his fingers—"just like that."

"A woman died here, Frankie," I reminded him, trying to drive home the importance of what this was all about. "The official verdict, without benefit of a proper arson investigation, is that she fell asleep in bed with a lit cigarette and her death was an accident. But there's reason to believe she could have been murdered."

He shook his head. "Sorry, Joe, but that doesn't change anything. I can tell you that the fire started over there—" he pointed to a section of blackened rubble which, when mentally compared with the photographs I'd seen at Courtney's, was exactly where Flo's bedroom had been "—and if that's where she was supposed to've nodded off, well, it could easily have been a dropped cigarette. There's no sign of any kind of ignition device or fuel or accelerator having been used, nothing to be suspicious about."

I stood there, letting his words and the rain soak into me, silently cursing both.

We made the return trip to Marieville. I popped for breakfast at an edge-of-town diner whose fare was passable, though nowhere as good as what I'd experienced in Cedarton the previous morning. If The Bug found it lacking, he didn't say so. As a matter of fact, he seemed to have abandoned his griping ways entirely. I guess he was smart enough to recognize I was no longer in any mood to listen.

I dropped him off at the bus stop fifteen minutes ahead of the next scheduled bus out. The sweat-stain queen had been replaced behind the counter by a wizened old bat who was evidently a graduate of the Tammy Faye Bakker school of cosmetology.

When I thanked The Bug for coming down, he gave me an "as if I had any fucking choice in the matter" look, but said nothing. I reimbursed him the price of the bus tickets, padded the amount fairly, told him I'd see him around. Then I climbed back in the Plymouth and pointed it once again toward Cedarton.

Breakfast lay heavy in my gut, disappointment and doubt weighted down the rest of me. The aspirin and caffeine I'd loaded up on were starting to wear off. I didn't know what my next move should be. My brain seemed to be functioning with all the clarity of a ball of lint. I thought about what I'd told Junior Odum last night and wondered if there was a fat lady singing her ass off somewhere and we were just being too stubborn to pay attention.

As I drove, I backhanded away a series of yawns. I rolled down the side window several inches and let some of the cool mist blow in on my face. I decided I'd return to my motel, sleep until noon, see if things looked less bleak when I awoke with my batteries recharged.

19

Gus Wilt was waiting for me back at the motel. He was parked directly in front of my unit, cruiser engine idling, windshield wipers making slow, lazy swipes at the rain.

I pulled in beside him, my mind jerked suddenly into alertness, ticking off possibilities, trying to guess what had brought him here. It came down to, I concluded, Clayton Cord either having purposely gone back on his word to call off the sheriff or having simply failed to get in touch with him as of yet. Either way, what the hell; the prospect of getting run out of town at this juncture wasn't without a certain amount of appeal.

Wilt and I cut our engines and got out of our vehicles.

"Morning, Sheriff," I said across the flasher bar.

He nodded. "Hannibal. Like to have a few words with you."

"Right," I said. "Didn't figure you were here checking the sani-wraps on the toilet seats."

I unlocked the door and he followed me inside. I'd left the air conditioner running and now, after the cooling effect of the rain, the air in the room had an uncomfortable bite to it.

I walked over, switched off the AC. Turning back, I tapped out a cigarette and got it going.

The sheriff and I regarded one another through exhaled smoke.

His eyes flicked, indicating the unmade bed. He said, "Surprised to see you landed here long enough to even muss the blankets."

"Why does that surprise you?"

"Had some of my boys on the lookout for you last night. You seemed to be making yourself mighty scarce."

I shrugged. "You know how it is. New in town—I was seeing the sights. What was it your boys were wanting to see me about?"

"Come on, Hannibal, let's not try to be cute with each other. You know damn well Clayton Cord pitched a bitch after you showed up at his office yesterday afternoon. I warned you about stepping on the wrong toes around here. It was obvious you needed a reminder."

"Is that what this is?"

He sighed with exaggerated weariness. "You also know damn well that Clayton Cord got in touch with me a second time and allowed as to how he'd changed his mind about you and now figured it might be best to let you go ahead and poke around in order to 'clear the air' once and for all concerning the death of Flo Odum."

"How about that?"

"Uh-huh. Under different circumstances I'd be real curious to know more about that change of heart; ain't exactly what you'd call in character for young Cord. But as of this morning I suddenly got a more pressing matter to worry about—murder. I guess you can understand how that sorta weighs on my mind heavier'n most anything else?"

I experienced a rush of sucker's hope. "You mean you're finally admitting Flo's death wasn't an accident?"

He shook his head. "I ain't admitting no such thing. The murder I'm talking about don't need somebody like you going around beating the bushes trying to sell other folks on the notion it *was* a murder. I got the mortal remains of a woman named Meg Ainsley laying on a slab over at Huppert's Funeral Home, been beat and strangled plumb to death."

I took a long drag on my cigarette, curious as to why he was telling me all this. Then, abruptly, something about the name clicked and I spewed a mouthful of smoky words. "Meg Ainsley—dark hair, big boobs, hangs out at a bar called Murphy's?"

"Used to hang out at Murphy's—that's the one."

"Jesus."

"Yeah. Jesus. I don't like people getting killed in my county, Hannibal. I don't like it worth shit."

"I don't suppose Meg Ainsley was real crazy about the idea, either," I said pointedly. "Or Flo Odum."

"Will you goddamn *forget* that Odum business for five seconds!"

"It's my job to see it isn't forgotten."

"Well you're doing pain-in-the-ass terrific at that, let me tell you. From what I've heard, though, in the course of doing your duty you managed to squeeze in a fair amount of time with the Ainsley woman yesterday afternoon. Is that right?"

"I spent awhile with her, yeah. There at Murphy's. Bought her a drink or two, talked about . . . things. I guess we even got around to flirting with each other some."

"Uh-huh. But then it ended on a pretty sour note, didn't it?"

"When Vern Stroud showed up, you mean. Now there's a fellow who could strike a sour note to just about any proceeding."

"No argument on that. Only the way I heard it, the blowup between you and Meg came after Vern had already left."

"Come on, I'd hardly describe the circumstances under which Meg Ainsley and I parted company as a 'blowup.'

What are you building up to, Sheriff—labeling me your prime suspect?"

"You know the routine. You follow all leads. Like a dance drill. You were seen talking at length with the victim only hours before she was killed; there reportedly were some heated words exchanged. Maybe that don't make you a full-fledged suspect, but it sure puts you in the running."

"Awful damn slim."

"Oh, that's rich. Here you are chasing all over hell's half acre trying to dig up a murder where there ain't no murder, and *I'm* the one picking at slim leads?"

"Slim is slim. One thing has nothing to do with the other. Sure, Meg got a little sore at me; I guess she felt I'd been stringing her along just to pump information out of her. Hell, maybe I was. Or maybe she just read too much into the flirtation bit. Whatever—she got huffy and I split and that was that."

"You didn't see her again after you left Murphy's?"

"Nope."

"Not while you were out seeing the sights, painting the town last night? Maybe at a different bar? Maybe you tried to smooth things over by offering to buy her another drink?"

"Now you're really reaching."

He thoughtfully stroked his mustache with the ball of his thumb. "Maybe. The thing is, though, Meg got batted around pretty good before she was strangled. Did I mention that?"

"You know damn well you did!"

"Uhmm. Well, I can't help but notice you seem to've taken on a powerful number of lumps and cuts and bruises since we talked just yesterday."

"Meg Ainsley looked to be a real healthy gal, Sheriff, but do you believe for one minute she was capable of inflicting this much damage to me if there'd been any kind of struggle between us?"

"Terror, panic, adrenaline rush—those things are able to

produce some mighty amazing results when a body's life is on the line."

"Yeah. And a cop's brain is able to produce some mighty amazing ideas when his investigation is going nowhere. You're no longer reaching . . . you're groping."

"Call it what you want. Who *did* do the pounding on you then?"

"Another one of your more charming locals—a fella by the name of Tom Wykert. His name initially came up as someone who'd made some pretty unpleasant remarks concerning Flo Odum, so I was asking around about him. It turned out he took exception to my interest."

"Sounds like something Tom'd take exception to. And he's plumb single-minded when it comes to showing his displeasure over a thing. When did all this take place?"

"About midnight, maybe a little before. He came here to the motel right after I got in. We held most of our, ah, discussion out in the parking lot."

"I don't recall anything on the docket this morning about a disturbance being phoned in."

I shrugged. "Then I guess we didn't disturb anybody. Like I said, it was midnight; the other rooms were dark, we didn't do a lot of shouting or furniture-breaking. Unless somebody happened to look out their window, they'd have had no way of knowing we were out there. Apparently nobody looked."

"My boys patrol this end of town every hour on the half hour during that stretch of night and early morning. Plus, like I said before, they were especially on the lookout for you. Why didn't they see anything when they made their twelve-thirty pass through?"

"How the fuck should I know? Ask them."

"I'm asking you."

"All right, I guess Wykert and I were finished with each other by then. Neither of us were having such a swell time we saw fit to prolong our business together. By twelve-thirty

I'd say Wykert was sleeping it off in the back of his pickup and I'd gone . . . elsewhere."

"Elsewhere? You came back here just long enough to duke it out with Tom Wykert, then you left again?"

"That's the way it went."

"Where might 'elsewhere' be?"

"It *might* be just about anyplace," I growled. For the first time he was pressing into an area where I felt uncomfortable, uncertain as to how to answer him. I sure as hell didn't want to get pinned down for a murder rap, but wasn't ready to hand over my association with Junior Odum, either. Not yet anyway. I said, "Look, Sheriff, let's quit dicking around here and get to the bottom line. You've got a time of death established for the Ainsley woman, right? Why not just come right out and ask me if I can account for my whereabouts then?"

His smile was tight and brittle-looking. "Really appreciate your helping out with such sound advice, Hannibal, 'stead of leaving me continue to 'grope' around. All right. Where were you between the hours of two and three o'clock this morning?"

Shit, Meg. You couldn't have picked a worse time to get yourself done in.

I reached over and stabbed out what was left of my cigarette in the bedside ashtray. As I looked back up from the task, the lie tripped easily off my tongue. "I was with a young lady."

"Good for you," Wilt said dryly. "She have a name?"

"Of course she had a name." I could have used another cigarette, but I didn't want to do anything to make him think he had me sweating. My mental machinery hummed, trying to weigh all the risks of venturing out onto the limb I was about to choose. I said, "But I've got a problem with that."

"You've got a problem with the young lady's name? A problem remembering it, you mean?"

"No. I remember it very well. The problem is whether or not I'm prepared to tell it to you."

"Whether or not you're pre . . . Goddammit, man, this is a murder investigation coming down here!"

"Come on, Sheriff, if you *really* thought there was a chance I had anything to do with killing Meg Ainsley, we'd be having this conversation in an interrogation room somewhere."

"That can be arranged, bub."

"Where I come from, a guy doesn't spend the night with a girl and then blab about it to the first person who asks, not even a cop."

"Well, that's real noble. If you also had a rule about not getting yourself in the position of being a suspect in a killing, then you wouldn't have a problem, would you? Dammit, man, I was pulling for you, I really was. You came to town, you seemed to have the right attitude, you seemed to have your head screwed on straight. There were a few things about Old Flo's death niggled at me, too, so even though I couldn't justify keeping an official investigation open, to tell the truth I was kinda glad to have you poking around. Just in case there *was* something more to be nudged loose. But now, in just a little over one day, look at you: you're crowding hard up against a fresh murder, you've managed to get the most important man in the county pissed off at you, you've been swung on by Tom Wykert and Vern Stroud and God knows who else . . . the word *discretion* don't crop up a lot when folks are talking about you, does it?"

"Maybe not. But if it's any consolation, it figures prominently in my ad in the Yellow Pages."

"Then you ought to try reading the Yellow Pages more often. Meanwhile, where was it you wanted to tell me the name of that girl . . . here or down at the county building?"

20

"*B*oy, you have got some damn nerve, you know that? Last night you had all kinds of reasons why you had to split, but now—now that you need an alibi—you expect me to tell the whole fucking county we spent the night together!"

I had the feeling that Courtney Cord was pretending to be somewhat angrier than she really was; yet she was plenty steamed all the same. The canvas-draped shapes that cluttered her studio loomed around us like heavily cloaked sentries, ready to attack if she gave the word.

"Hey," I said, "don't you think I *wanted* to stay with you? I've explained about the meeting that was set up with Junior Odum." I'd told her all of it: about Junior's fugitive status, about the crazy deal I'd struck to investigate his mother's death, about why I wasn't prepared to tell Gus Wilt where I really was at the time of Meg Ainsley's murder. I even threw in a brief recap of my bout with Wykert.

"Why couldn't you have leveled with me last night?" Courtney wanted to know. "Told me what you were actually up to, instead of making those pitiful excuses and leaving me to think . . ." She let it trail off.

"Old habits die hard," I tried to explain. "Nothing personal, but in my line of work you tend to keep as much as possible to yourself."

"Your line of work gets to be a real bite in the ass, Hanni-bal."

"Maybe. But if the truth about Flo's death is ever uncov-ered, it's going to be because of what I am and what I do."

She scowled. "Well, if I go along with this cock-and-bull story of yours, that'll be the reason why—because of Flo, not because I give a damn how much hot water you've got-ten yourself into."

"Naturally the use of your name cut me quite a bit of slack. The sheriff even allowed me to come here like this and be the one to tell you that I had to involve you. I promised him you'd be in by noon to corroborate my story. He as-sured me your statement would be handled with as much discretion as possible."

"Awfully damn sure of yourself, weren't you?"

I showed her a cautious smile. "Not really. I'm still not. I haven't heard you say yet you're going to back my play."

She scowled at me some more. After about a minute, her expression shifted and she said, "Come over here. I want to show you something."

I followed her to the opposite end of the studio, down near her desk and darkroom again. She was wearing a man's faded blue work shirt with the sleeves rolled past her elbows and a pair of bright red gym shorts with white stripes run-ning up both sides. Her legs and feet were bare. From be-hind, the shirt's long tail hid any trace of the shorts and it wasn't hard to imagine she had on nothing at all down there. I found the thought stimulating.

She walked to a kind of pedestal upon which sat a large mound of greenish-gray clay. The latter had been roughly formed into the shape of a human head and shoulders. On an easel beside it rested a two-by-three-foot blowup of that memorable close-up photo of Flo Odum.

"I started this last night," Courtney said. "You made me so mad, the way you took off, that I couldn't sleep. So I came down here and released some energy creatively. I've been casting about for precisely the right way to present the statement I wanted to make with a sculpture of Flo. I'd rejected any number of ideas, and then it hit me—the very words I said to you when we were going through that pile of photographs. Everything I wanted to say was right there on Flo's face in that one close-up. If I can capture it in a simple, carefully detailed bust, I will have done what I set out to do. I plan to call it 'Spirited Woman.' "

"That's uh, real interesting," I said, not at all clear as to what any of this had to do with why I'd come here.

"I also," Courtney announced, "came up with the idea for another piece I want to do sometime. I'd like to do a sculpture based on you, Hannibal."

"Sure you would. You're kidding, right?"

"No, I'm not. You may be a jerk at times but you're also a fascinatingly complex blend of images. Soldier of fortune, gladiator, gunslinger . . . you do carry a gun sometimes, don't you?"

"Every day of my life."

She frowned. "But last night in the car, you didn't . . . ?"

I looked around, spotted a wooden packing crate a couple steps away. I planted my right foot atop it and then hiked my pants leg up to reveal the two-shot .22 Magnum derringer clipped inside the rim of my boot. I said, "This is what directs my feet to the sunny side of the street. So happens it was with us every step of the way last night."

Her frown stayed in place. "But isn't it . . . well, it's such a puny little gun."

I grinned. "Haven't you ever heard that it isn't the size that counts?"

"Sure. But I didn't know you guys made that claim outside the bedroom, too."

"We get a good line, we try to stick with it."

"Be serious."

"You want serious? All right, this 'puny little gun' has

'saved my butt more times that I care to go into. Basically, that's what it is, an emergency weapon, a comfortable, inconspicuous, everyday carry-around piece. When I recognize in advance that a situation could turn hairy, then I'll break out some heavier artillery—like this." I opened my jacket and displayed the .45 nestled under my arm. All right, as gestures go it was maybe a bit showy. But give me a break; guys have been showing off for gals since before Samson demonstrated to Delilah how many Philistines he could coldcock with one chunk of bone. The lady wanted to see an *un*puny gun; I showed her one.

"Jesus," she said, "that certainly wasn't there before."

"With people turning up dead and other people turning up at regular intervals intent on popping me in the nose, I decided to shore up my defenses a little."

"But if you had the derringer when you fought Wykert, why didn't you use it then?"

"Situation wasn't right."

"Wasn't right! You mean it was better to get all banged up and bruised and bloodied like you did, when you could have stopped it at any time by simply drawing your gun?"

"There are times when it's okay to bring a gun into a thing, times when it isn't."

"Oh, I get it—some kind of macho bullcrap code, right?"

"No, you don't get it. Any time a woman doesn't understand why a man behaves the way he does, she labels it 'macho bullcrap.' Far as I'm concerned, that only amounts to feminist bullcrap."

"Well, you're right about one thing—I sure don't understand why men behave like they do. But going back to what you said about shoring up your defenses because people are turning up dead, you don't think Meg Ainsley getting killed had anything to do with your investigation of Flo's death, do you?"

"It doesn't seem likely. But on the other hand—at least

until a motive and/or killer are established—it isn't outside the realm of possibility."

She studied me for a long moment. "You look at almost everything with a certain amount of suspicion and distrust, don't you?"

"It's my form of health insurance. It'll keep me alive longer."

"Do you trust me?"

"If I didn't trust you, I wouldn't have counted on you to help get the sheriff off my back."

"I consider that a compliment."

"Does that mean you're going to corroborate my story to Wilt?"

"On one condition."

"And that is?"

"I want you to pose for some photographs so I can do that sculpture of you."

"Come on. Get serious."

"I'm dead serious, Have you ever seen any of the ancient Greek or Roman sculptures, the heroic poses of Achilles or Hercules or the like? They're invariably wearing very little in the way of clothing, usually a fig leaf or a brief loin wrap of some sort, and armed with a sword or a bow. I see you in a modern variation on that—jockey shorts instead of fig leaf, shoulder-holstered .45 instead of sword. I'd call it 'Urban Gladiator' or something like that. What do you think?"

"What do *I* think? I think either you're just plain nuts or you've smoked too many of those funny little brown cigarettes. Jesus Christ, Courtney, look at me. Even when I'm not battered and bandaged, I'm hardly a Greek god or one of the beefcake boys. I've got a junk food paunch, a car window suntan on one arm only, snarly old black hairs growing all over my back and shoulders. And my face looks like it's already been sculpted—by a sackful of marbles. You make a statue of me, lady, and not even the pigeons are going to pay attention."

"I'm the successful artist, I'd say that makes me a better judge of a viable concept than you. I'm also a woman. The beefcake boys, as you call them, have a certain amount of appeal, it's true. But there are other traits a woman can find exciting. That's what you have, Hannibal—a kind of excitement about you."

"Yeah, well, I might be exciting as shit, but if you think I'm going to prance around here in my skivvies and shoulder holster and let you take pictures of me, you've got another think coming."

She made a disdainful gesture with one hand. "Fine. That will just save me a trip to the sheriff's office, that's all."

Can you believe the hoops a woman will try to put you through—and at the damnedest times?

"For crying out loud, Courtney," I said. "You can't be serious about this."

"We already covered that. I *am* serious. You pose for me, I lie for you. That's the deal."

I awoke to the sound of music, a distant, driving disco beat that sounded vaguely familiar. But then, that's how all disco music sounds, doesn't it? Not memorable—only vaguely familiar.

My slumber had been the deep, exhaustive kind that seems to release its grip on your brain one molecule at a time. I sat up feeling disoriented. Strange bed, strange room, music playing—where the hell was I?

I shoved down the covers in a kind of mild panic. But by the time I'd swung my bare feet to the floor and stood up, most of it was starting to come back to me. I was in Courtney Cord's bedroom. After finally agreeing to see the sheriff on my behalf, she had insisted I stay here and get some rest because "you look like hell and you're going to drop over if you don't." The deal was, though, that she was supposed to have awakened me in a couple hours. My watch indicated it was going on two, which meant she had reneged on that promise by a substantial amount.

I spotted my clothes draped across a chair. Padding in that direction, I caught sight of myself in a dressing table mirror and one more thing popped free from the sleep fuzz still clogging my head—the recollection of what I'd had to do in order to get Courtney to pay that visit to Sheriff Wilt. I've put myself in some sorry situations before, but I never felt like more of a horse's ass than I did while parading about in my underdrawers with Courtney snapping shots from a variety of angles and distances. It was enough to make Sam Spade roll over in his grave.

I pulled on my clothes, shrugged into the shoulder holster, clipped the derringer inside my boot. The transformation from groggy bewilderment to square-jawed, steely-eyed P.I. was as complete as it could be with the humiliating experience still fresh in my mind.

The music I'd noted upon waking was still playing. It came from below, somewhere down in the studio. I could feel the throb of it in my feet as I walked through the apartment.

I made my way down the spiral staircase and followed the disco noise to its source in a far corner of the studio. An area had been cleared there, no crates, no easels, no pedestals. A simple turntable with twin speakers was arranged on a low stand against one wall; on the floor were a handful of brightly colored mats and a scattering of gleaming chrome dumbbells. Trained observer that I am, I had no trouble recognizing the setup as an exercise area. If there'd been any lingering doubt, it would have been removed by the routine —aerobics or dancercise or whatever the hell they're calling it these days—Courtney was doing to the music. She was clad in a skin-tight outfit of diagonal purple and pink stripes, with a matching headband and cumbersome-looking —yet somehow sexy—leg warmers. A patina of sweat shone on her face and shoulders as she whirled and gyrated to the beat.

I lit a cigarette, leaned against the wall to watch and wait. It wasn't hard duty.

When the record ended, Courtney reached for a towel to pat away some of the perspiration. Turning to me, she said somewhat breathlessly, "Hi there."

"Hi yourself," I returned. "You move nice, but you sure tell time lousy."

"So sue me. Like I said, you needed the rest."

"Not that much."

"Four hours hardly puts you in a league with Rip Van Winkle."

"I've got things to do."

"So you'll do them quicker and more efficiently now that you're better rested. I figured the music would eventually wake you. If it hadn't, I'd have left you sleep even longer."

This was obviously going nowhere, so I decided to change the subject. "How did things go with the sheriff?" I asked.

"No problem. Except I think maybe I embarrassed the old fart when I offered to go into detail on *exactly* how we spent our time together."

"If word gets out, your Hatchaloo County ice goddess facade will be shattered once and for all."

"Discretion—remember?"

"Uhmm. I also remember the thoroughness of small-town grapevines. And believe me, Cedarton is no slouch in that department."

"Well, if it comes to that, I'm sure I can live with it. After all, my reputation has withstood worse. But what about yours?"

"What do you mean?"

"Think about it. Joe Hannibal—hard-boiled private eye/ part-time beefcake model. What would that do for business if word got back to Rockford?"

"Oh, very funny. Very fucking funny."

She laughed and swatted me with the towel. "Look, I need to grab a shower and change. You could probably stand some coffee and something to eat, right? There's a fresh-brewed pot up on the stove, you can help yourself. When I get dressed, I'll make us some lunch. Then you can go do . . . whatever it is you're in such a hurry to go do."

I followed her up the winding stairs. The close-up view of her spandex-encased rump was almost as good as what my imagination had been able to conjure up when she was wearing that long shirt.

She steered me into the kitchen and left me there to light a fire under the coffee pot and rummage for a cup while she went on back to the bathroom. In a few minutes, I heard the shower come on. A cup of coffee had sounded great when she first mentioned it, but as I sat at the kitchen table waiting for it to heat up, my desire for same seemed to decrease rapidly and in direct proportion to an increasing desire along other lines.

The shower stall was a roomy rectangle behind chrome-framed pebbled glass. I dropped my clothes in a pile beside her exercise outfit, then slid back the door and entered purposefully. If Courtney was at all startled by my appearance she hid it well. She merely smiled and nonchalantly continued to lather up a large orange washcloth with a bar of pink soap.

I held out my hand. "After all you've done to help me with my investigation, and especially with the sheriff this morning," I said, "I decided the least I could do to show my appreciation would be to offer to scrub those hard-to-reach places for you."

"Why, how very kind and generous of you, Mr. Hannibal."

She handed me the washcloth and impudently turned her back to me. I ran a trail of suds across her shoulders and then began working my way down her spine, making slow, widening circles. As I began to lather her buttocks, she leaned back against me and I nibbled her ear and kissed the side of her face. The water from the shower spray cascaded down between her glistening breasts.

It wasn't long before she turned to face me again. "What is it that keeps poking me in the hip?" she demanded teasingly. "Did you bring one of your guns in here with you?"

"No gun," I told her, grinning. "I guess I'm just happy to be here."

She looked down. "Oh, my goodness, you appear to be *very* happy to be here."

We kissed then, long and hard and steamy. When our lips parted, Courtney placed her palms on my chest and began slowly lowering herself to her knees. Her body glided down mine on a slick layer of suds.

"I bet," she said huskily, looking up at me, "I can make you even happier. . . ."

21

It was past four when I returned to the Lincolnway. The rain had stopped and the overcast sky was starting to break up. Slices of blue peeked through here and there.

I'd climbed out of the Plymouth and was just inserting my key in the door to my unit when I heard someone call my name.

I turned to see a lanky youth trotting in my direction from the office. It had been he who'd signed me in when I initially registered. I couldn't remember his name, but I guessed him to be the manager's son.

"Mr. Hannibal," he said as he reached me. "Some woman's been calling for you all day. She finally left her name and number. Said you should get in touch with her as soon as you get in, it's real urgent."

I took the slip of paper he held out to me. On it was written the name "Donna," followed by a phone number with the local prefix. I scoured my mind but couldn't remember having encountered anyone named Donna since my arrival here.

"Did she indicate what this is about?" I asked.

The lad shook his head. "No, sir, just that it was important and you should get back to her right away."

I nodded. "Okay, I'll do that. Thanks, son."

He turned and trotted away before I thought to give him a tip. I considered calling after him, but decided he hadn't been expecting one anyway. Wouldn't want to contribute a jolt of culture shock to the young fellow's life.

Inside my room, I spread the slip of paper out beside the telephone and let it lay there while I stripped down and changed into fresh underwear, socks, and shirt. As I did this, I ran the name Donna through my mind several more times but kept coming up blank. Urgent, the kid had said.

When I was dressed again, I lit a cigarette, then went over and dialed the number on the paper.

The third ring was interrupted midway through and a twangy female voice said, "Golden Cedar Rest Home."

That caught me a little by surprise. "Donna?" I stammered. "Uh, may I speak with Donna please?"

"One moment."

I was put on hold, and treated to an earful of Muzak. Muzak in Hatchaloo County, who would have guessed. My turn for a bit of culture shock.

"Hello." Another female voice, coarse and rather unpleasant.

"Donna?"

"Who's this?"

"My name is Joe Hannibal."

"The detective?"

"That's right. I received a message to call you at this number."

"I want to talk to you. I got some information I think you'll find useful."

"Oh? Information about what?"

"I don't want to go into it on the phone. I been saving my break. You come here, we'll talk."

After asking directions of the lanky youth at the motel office, I found the Golden Cedar Rest Home with no trouble. It was located near the river, a single-storied tan brick building of recent vintage, curved around a smoothly paved crescent drive with broad expanses of emerald lawn and tall shade trees that were not golden but were at least cedar.

As I made the short drive over there, I reflected upon how welcome the call from this mysterious Donna was. For, despite my ragging at Courtney about having "things do to," my options as far as the Odum investigation went were actually pretty much exhausted. Especially with time running out. I warned myself not to get my hopes up, but at the same time I could feel my pulse quickening with anticipation; this could be the break I so desperately needed.

"Donna" turned out to be Donna Trebelow, one of the attendants at the home. She was a tall, heavyset woman with facial features as coarse and unpleasant as her voice. If you dreaded the possibility of growing old and spending your final years in a care facility, the head nurse of your nightmares would probably look something like Donna Trebelow.

She led the way down a long, broad corridor, her spongy-soled nurse's shoes silent on the shiny tiles, my boot heels cracking ominously. We passed a number of elderly folks, both men and women, who seemed completely mobile and bright and alert. But in the central lounge area I'd noted several others, placed in wheelchairs and rolled out for display—or so it seemed, anyway—who looked hauntingly vacant and lost somewhere inside themselves. Glancing into some of the rooms we passed, I saw still others lying shrunken and motionless, many in fetal positions. Returning to the womb. But with agonizing slowness.

Golden years my ass. It was enough to make you consider eating a .45 slug for breakfast the morning you turned sixty-five, just to make fucking sure you didn't end up like that.

I followed the Trebelow woman through a door marked STAFF LOUNGE. This placed us in a square, low-ceilinged room with modest but comfortable-looking couches lining two of the walls, a row of lockers and a bank of vending machines occupying the other two. In the middle there was a pair of long, formica-topped tables surrounded by folding chairs. The room was windowless but a top-notch ventilation system was doing a good job of keeping the air fresh, with only the faintest overlay of stale smoke and food odors.

"Like I told you," Donna Trebelow said, "I held my afternoon break. The others have all taken theirs, so we should have a decent amount of privacy. You want something to drink? Coffee? A Coke?"

"Nothing, thanks."

She walked over to one of the vending machines, fed it some coins, punched out a can of Coca-Cola Classic. She went through the same procedure to get a bag of potato chips from another machine. We then seated ourselves facing each other across one of the tables.

"I know why you're in town," Donna said, "and I know about the fix you're in. This information I got, I figure it could help you out quite a bit."

By "the fix you're in," I assumed she was alluding to the fact that my investigation was nearly dead-ended. I said, "Any help would be greatly appreciated."

She shoved a handful of potato chips into her mouth and began chewing them with crunching thoroughness. Each time her teeth came together, the pouch of pale flesh under her chin undulated. The whole time she eyed me with a kind of expectant glint in her eye, as if seeking approval for the way she chewed her food. After she'd swallowed and after her tongue had flicked out in a practiced maneuver to whisk away any stray granules of salt or crumbs from her lips, she said, "On the TV, you private eye guys are always slipping money to people who provide you with valuable information. Ever work that way in real life?"

I grinned a little at her bluntness. "I've been known to pay snitches, yeah."

"I figure what I got ought to be worth something."

"Okay. Tell me what you've got, I'll pay you what it's worth."

She shook her head. "I already decided what it's worth. I want fifty dollars."

I took out my wallet, withdrew a ten and a pair of twenties. These I folded and slid halfway under the napkin holder that rested on the table top between us. "I won't pay for a pig in a poke," I said. "There's the fifty. If what you got is worth anything, it's yours. If what you got is crap, the bills go back out the door in my pocket."

She shoveled in some more chips and went to work on them in the same manner as before. This time her eyes stayed on the folded money.

After she'd gone through the lip-licking routine once again, she said, "What it amounts to is I heard her being killed. I didn't realize at the time that's what was going on, of course, or I would've tried to do something. But thinking back on it now, that's what it was—I heard her get killed. And I know almost for certain who done it."

If my pulse had quickened before at the mere possibility of a breakthrough, it was thundering inside me now. With slow, deliberate calmness, I pulled over an ashtray, tapped out a cigarette and lit it. Through the ensuing smoke, I said, "Let me get this straight. You were *there* when Flo's house was being burned, you *heard* it happening. Where exactly were you? What did you see?"

Donna Trebelow drew back her head and frowned mightily. "House burned? Flo? What in hell are you talking about, mister?"

This dragged a frown out of me as well. "What are *you* talking about, lady? I'm referring to the death of Flo Odum, that's the matter I've been investigating. You called me here, said you had some information for me."

She began shaking her head even before I was finished. "The death I'm talking about is the murder of Meg Ainsley. I heard how the sheriff was zeroing in on you on account of you being seen with Meg yesterday and arguing with her and all. You being a stranger in town, things could stack up against you in a hurry. I wanted to try and help and to set the record straight by telling what I know about what really happened."

"Why didn't you just go to the sheriff then? Why all this?"

"Because the sheriff's office has too damn many big ears and big mouths, that's why. How do you think word spread about their interest in you? All I'd need is for Vern Stroud to catch wind I was the one fingering him and then come after me before they got the cuffs on him. Yeah, I'd really need that. Besides, fat chance in hell I'd have of ever getting fifty dollars out of Gus Wilt."

This conversation was taking more unpredictable bounces than a boulder rolling down a hill. Yet something she'd just said made me want to grab hold and go along for the ride, regardless.

"You're saying you believe Vern Stroud is the one who killed Meg Ainsley?" I asked.

Her eyes turned shrewd. "I thought your interest was only in the death of the old woman?"

"That's where my primary interest lies, it's true; but not my only one. As you just pointed out, circumstances have forced me to take an interest in Meg Ainsley's death as well —strictly from the standpoint of covering my butt." Apparently the Cedarton grapevine hadn't yet caught up with the fact that Courtney had alibied me for the Ainsley matter, and if it gave my would-be informant impetus to think she was dealing with a desperate man, well, I wouldn't spoil her fun.

Donna Trebelow's gaze flicked hungrily to the folded bills, then back to me. "But are you interested enough in Meg's murder to still be willing to pay for information about it?"

Sighing heavily, I snatched the money out from under the napkin box and sent it skidding across the table to her. "There's the goddamn fifty. Now talk to me, Donna. Earn it."

22

I sat for a long time in my car parked outside the Golden Cedar, mentally reviewing and expanding upon the things Donna Trebelow had just told me. The implications of her testimony—unless I was jumping to conclusions a mile off the mark—were numbing. If I was right, then it would be a classic example of having not seen the forest for the trees and I probably deserved to have my ass kicked the length of the state for failing to spot it sooner.

Damn.

When I'd done enough mulling and administered enough self-reproach, I began to form a rough action plan, one designed to test my suspicions without leaving me wide open for too much backlash in case I *was* way the hell off beam.

Step one was to put the Plymouth in motion and drive to the nearest pay phone. It took me three calls to catch up with Gus Wilt at his home.

"Sheriff. Joe Hannibal here."

"What's on your mind, Hannibal? Make it quick, I'm about to set down to supper."

"How are things going on the Ainsley case?"

"Could be worse, could be better. Not that it's any concern of yours whichever way. That all you called for?"

"Not exactly. I've got a couple things, I'll try to make them brief."

"You will. One way or another. When my wife calls me to cut the roast, this conversation is finished."

"Okay. It probably won't disappoint you to hear that I'm thinking about pulling the plug on the Odum thing. I'm getting nowhere and I've nearly run out of directions to turn. What I want to know is, am I in the clear about the Ainsley murder or would you object if I decided to leave town?"

There was a moment of silence as he thought about it. Then: "No, I got no problem with that. You never were all that strong in the running, and then you came up with a pretty high-toned alibi to boot. First chance I get, by the way, I'm going to set down and have a real long think on what a classy gal like Miss Courtney could possibly see in a hardhead like you."

"You must be forgetting my boyish charm. Not to mention my sparkling wit, my soulful eyes, my—"

"You said a couple things. What else?"

Now came the meat of it, the real reason I'd called him. I said, "Look, uh, I'm not very good at being a snitch or a fink, but, getting back to the Ainsley business, there's something I want to make sure you know about."

"And that is?"

"When Vern Stroud showed up at Murphy's yesterday and he and I had our little clash . . . well, there was also some heat exchanged between him and Meg. It looked to me like there'd been something between them at one time or other, and maybe Vern still felt there was. He said some pretty threatening things to her, as well as to me."

There was another stretch of silence before Wilt said, "That's it? That's the thing you wanted to make sure I knew about?"

"Yeah. I never thought of it at the motel this morning. You were keeping me too busy covering my ass. I figure

Reggie, the bartender, must have been the one who told you about Meg and me and the events at Murphy's; I wanted to be sure he gave you *all* the details."

Wilt actually chuckled. "Well you can rest easy, Reggie *did* give me all the details. Hell, Hannibal, everybody in Hatchaloo County—everybody except maybe Pearl Stroud, that is—knew Vern and Meg Ainsley had been sniffing around each other for years. Damnedest love-hate relationship you ever saw. One time you'd see them hanging on one another, all smoochy and feely-feely; next you'd see them apart, maybe scuffed up a bit, bad-mouthing the very existence of each other to blue blazes and back. Then, before long, you'd see them together again and it would start all over. Surprised folks that they never got married in one of their fits of passion. That would have been a match made in heaven. Surprised folks even more when Vern up and married Pearl."

"Things cool down between him and Meg after that?"

"Not for very long. They tried to hide it some is all. Unless they were both drunk, which was at least half the time they were together."

"Jesus, Sheriff, you realize you're listing some textbook ingredients for murder, don't you? Passion, jealousy, alcohol, adultery . . ."

"Yeah, yeah, of course I realize that. And don't think I didn't take one hard damn look at Vern for Meg's killing. Trouble is, he went straight home after the incident at Murphy's, cussed you and Meg and Reggie all three up one side and down the other in front of his wife and kids, then staggered into the bedroom and passed out across the bed, where he stayed until my boys rousted him early this morning."

"That's his story?"

"Pearl backs it up right down the line."

My grip tightened on the phone receiver and through clenched teeth I said, "Yeah, she would."

"What's that?"

"Nothing. Never mind."

"Here comes my wife with the roast, Hannibal. You got anything else to say, you'll be talking to yourself 'cause I'm gone."

I pulled up in front of Handee's Auto Salvage just as a burly guy in a sweat-and-grease-stained T-shirt was flipping over the cardboard sign on the door so that it read CLOSED instead of OPEN. He glowered out at me through the smeared glass, as if daring me to try and get some service this late in the day.

I didn't accept his challenge. I wasn't here for auto parts. I cut the Plymouth's engine, lit a cigarette, and leaned back to wait.

On the way to our rendezvous with Junior the previous night, Reba and I had passed by Handee's and she had pointed it out as the place where she worked, inventorying parts and making deliveries. I'd driven over here now in the hope of catching her before she left for home. Judging by the fact that her motorbike was propped against one end of the squat, white-brick building, it appeared I was in luck. Inasmuch as the place had ceased doing business for the day, I figured she ought to be coming out shortly.

Half a cigarette later, she did. The side door of the building opened and Reba and the burly guy and two other grease-monkey types emerged. Reba walked over to her motorbike and the others moved in the direction of some vehicles nosed up against the high, rust-stained, galvanized sheet fence that ran along the backside of the building and encircled the salvage yard behind.

Reba reached her bike, turned, and looked sullenly in my direction.

I got out of the car, came around to the front end, leaned back against the grill with my arms folded across my chest.

In a voice as sullen as her expression, Reba said, "What do you want?"

"I came to see you."

"Be still my heart. You know, you only got about a half-dozen hours left before your time's up, Mr. Detective. A body'd think you'd have better ways to spend it than comin' round to bother me. I got nuthin' more to say to you."

"I need your help, Reba."

"What? To clear Clayton Cord some more? No fuckin' thanks."

"I know who killed your aunt and burned her house."

"So do I."

I shook my head. "No you don't. You only *think* you do —based mostly on some cockeyed, longstanding have-not versus have prejudice."

"Take your twenty-five-dollar words and shove 'em up your ass."

"I know who killed your aunt, Reba. And with a little help from you, I can prove it."

The burly guy picked that moment to wheel around in a gleaming Jeep Cherokee and pull up beside us, studded tires crunching to a stop on the gravel. He poked his fat face out the cab window and said to Reba, "This fella givin' you any trouble?"

"Nuthin' I can't handle, Virgil."

He swiveled his head and glowered at me again. He was an ugly fucker, with a thick, pugged nose and piggy little bloodshot eyes which he kept fixed on me while he addressed Reba again. "Wouldn't be no trouble to run him off. I plumb don't like assholes who park right up front with piece-of-shit cars any fool can see belong in the junk pile out back."

I smiled and said, "You're wrong, Virgil. It would be a *lot* of trouble for you to try and run me off."

Air whistled out of him and I could see the reddish hairs in his nostrils quiver. "You think so, do you?"

"Damn," I said. "Good-looking and fast with a witty rejoinder to boot. I want to party with you sometime, pal. But right now me and Reba here have what's known as pressing business. So why don't you run along and join your buddies at the nearest bar before they beat you to all the pickled pig's knuckles. Watch out you don't eat one of your ancestors, though."

His nostrils flared anew and this time the air wheezed out of him louder than a factory whistle at high noon. "You smart-mouthed sumbitch!" he exploded. He wanted to get out and get his hands on me so bad that he banged clumsily against the inside of the door with his shoulder and then his chest before his clawing fingers ever found the latch. When the door finally did pop open, it threw him off balance.

Reba stepped over and slapped her palms against the outside of the door, shoving it back against him. "Goddamn you, Virgil!" she shouted. "I said I could handle this."

"Lemme at that smart-mouthed sumbitch," Virgil fumed.

"You back off. This is a family matter."

"He ain't family."

"Maybe he ain't, maybe he ain't even a friend. But it's still a family matter what brung him here. We take care of our own—problems and otherwise. You know that."

"What about what he said to me?"

"That's yours to deal with. Another time, another place."

Their faces were only inches apart, framed by the open vehicle window, their bodies pressed against the door from opposite sides. When he could no longer match Reba's stare, Virgil turned his gaze to me and wheezed another noseful of air in my direction. Then, glancing at Reba again, he seemed to shrink back inside the cab of the Cherokee. The door relatched with a soft metallic sound.

Virgil gunned the powerful engine to life and jabbed a sausagelike forefinger out the window at me. "I'll see *you* around, you smart-mouthed sumbitch!"

I waggled my fingers at him. "I'll be counting the seconds, Virg."

He left in a spray of gravel and dust.

When the pebbles had quit pinging around us, Reba stood facing me with her fists planted on her hips. "Now what in hell was the sense of that—baitin' him the way you done?" she demanded.

I shrugged. "He started it."

"It didn't take a helluva lot of proddin' to get you to jump aboard."

"All right," I admitted. "I'm in a mood to belt somebody in the mouth; he seemed like a good candidate."

"That's gonna solve my aunt's murder, you goin' around beltin' people in the mouth?"

I pushed myself away from the Plymouth's grill and stood up straight. "What's going to solve your aunt's murder," I said, "is me getting a little cooperation out of you. Now, are you ready to climb down off your high horse and help me or not?"

With Reba following on her motorbike, I drove to the wayside park where I'd first encountered Courtney. I picked the spot for no particular reason other than I wanted some place out of the way and private where we could talk, and it was the first location that came to mind. We sat at the same table where Courtney and I had sat, the same breeze licked at us from across the river. The emotions running through me, however, were far different.

"The first thing I want from you," I told Reba, "is a promise that you'll try to hold your temper in check and not go off half-cocked when I tell you the things I'm about to tell you."

She regarded me over the glowing tip of the cigarette she'd bummed off me. "I can promise," she said somewhat begrudgingly, "but you know I have a little trouble with that—holding my temper, I mean."

"So I've noticed. But this is damned important, Reba. We're talking about nailing a killer. If I'm right, not only the killer of your aunt but of another woman as well."

"All right already—who *are* we talking about? Who is it you figure done Aunt Flo that way?"

I hesitated, not for dramatic effect, but because *thinking* someone is a murderer and stating it out loud are two very different things. But I was right, damn it. I *knew* I was right. I said, "Her own son-in-law."

Reba did some things with her eyebrows. "Vern? You mean Vern Stroud?"

"That's the way it shapes up."

"Jesus. I dunno, Hannibal. I mean, Vern's a grade-A asshole, everybody knows that. But a killer? . . . I wouldn't give him credit for having the balls. Besides, Aunt Flo was one of the few people who treated him decent."

"So did the other woman he killed. It has nothing to do with how he was treated. It has to do with plain old greed. We were all so busy looking at who stood to lose if Flo *didn't* sell her land, that we forgot to look at who stood to gain if she *did.*"

"Who's this other woman you keep mentionin'—the other one you think Vern killed?"

"Her name was Meg Ainsley. Did you know her?"

"Knew *about* her. Kind of a whorey ol' barfly, the way I heard tell. Almost anybody with the inclination and the price of a few drinks could replace the bar stool that was usually between her legs."

Her bluntness rankled momentarily, but then my own thoughtless appraisal of the dead woman ("dark hair, big boobs, hangs out at a bar called Murphy's"—as stated to Sheriff Wilt) echoed hauntingly through my mind and I decided I had no room to criticize. Flushing with a twinge of shame, I said, "Did you also know that Vern Stroud and the Ainsley woman had a thing going before he married Pearl? And that they kept it going even after the marriage?"

"I heard talk of that, yeah. Don't surprise me none. Vern's the kind of lowlife peckerwood who's willin' to quench his crotch fire in any tank he can find. And Meg Ainsley sure as hell wasn't the type to care if a man happened to be attached to another woman."

"Their relationship was described to me as a love-hate one."

"I don't know about that. I don't even rightly know what it means."

"Never mind. What about Pearl? It seems just about everybody in Hatchaloo County knew what was going on between Vern and Meg—didn't she? Or did she just choose to look the other way?"

"Can't say for sure. You got to remember Pearl ain't awful smart. And she's really been shit on by men. Four different ones knocked her up and then dumped her. When Vern came along and was willin' to marry her . . . well, I reckon she decided she was goin' to stick it out no matter what. Maybe she even loves the asshole. Bad as he treats her, I guess she must figure it's better than how she got treated before."

"Would she lie to protect him?"

"I 'spect so. But not about killin' her mama. I won't believe that. I'm still havin' trouble buyin' Vern as a murderer, ain't no way Pearl coulda been part of it."

"Since Flo's death was never accepted as murder and there was never an official investigation into it, there was also never a need for anyone to establish an alibi. But Meg Ainsley's murder was clearly that—murder. Pearl swore to sheriff's deputies this morning that Vern was home in bed all night last night, during the time Meg was killed. I have reason to suspect he wasn't."

"What makes you think so?"

"A little while ago I had a long talk with a friend and a neighbor of Meg's—a woman who had cause to tell me some things she wouldn't tell the police. She and Meg lived right across the hall from each other in an old house that's been divided into apartments. At around three o'clock this morning—the time that's been established for Meg's death—this woman was wakened by noises and loud voices coming from Meg's apartment. It wasn't unusual for Meg to get into arguments with the men she brought home from the bars, so when this one quieted down only a few minutes after the neighbor was disturbed, she rolled over to go back to sleep and thought little of it. It had been a man's voice arguing with Meg, one the neighbor woman hadn't been able to recognize. What she did recognize, though, just before she dozed back off, was the sound of a car engine starting up and driving away; a rather distinctive car engine, one she'd heard many times before leaving in the middle of the night—that of Vern Stroud's souped-up GTO."

Frowning, Reba rubbed out her cigarette on the edge of the table. "All right," she said, "it sounds kinda bad for Vern as far as the Ainsley woman goes. But what's any of this got to do with Aunt Flo?"

"Plenty, when you start adding in all the other bits and pieces. First you need to ask why—why, after all this time, after all the passion and bickering and deceit that marked their stormy relationship, did Vern suddenly, brutally murder Meg Ainsley?"

"You tell me. Why?"

"Because he saw her—what she knew, or what he was afraid she *might* know—as too much of a threat to him. You see, things had been especially hot and heavy between the two of them lately, up until a few days ago. There'd been a blowup then, the neighbor woman wasn't sure what about, but prior to that it had been pretty intense. Meg confided in her, and according to what she said there was even talk of Vern leaving Pearl and finally making a real commitment to Meg. But first Vern wanted to make—and these were his words—a 'big score.'"

Reba snorted derisively. "Biggest score Vern Stroud ever

made was when he ran moon two nights in a row for Cotton Mayfair and had maybe a hunnert dollars in his pocket all at once for the first time in his life. Shit. What was this big fuckin' score supposed to be anyway?"

I fixed her with a solemn gaze. "The neighbor woman didn't know. It's my guess, though, that Vern figured on getting his hands on the money Pearl would receive once Flo was out of the way and her land was sold to Cord Toys."

I watched the color climb in Reba's face as the inevitable anger—now that she was finally beginning to accept that her aunt might have been killed by Stroud—started to course through her. Her eyes narrowed. "You mean that sonofabitch killed and burned up Aunt Flo like that just so's he could get the land money and run off with some ol' whore?"

"I'm not sure about the running-off part. That may have just been a line he was feeding Meg. But he wanted that money, yeah. Badly enough to kill for it. And then kill again to cover up the first killing. He knew why I was in town, that I was digging into Flo's death. That explains his immediate belligerence toward me. Then when he saw Meg and me together at Murphy's, he must have panicked. I don't know how much he'd actually let slip to her, maybe he wasn't sure himself. But he knew that they were now on the outs and he knew she'd been talking to me. That was enough to send him to her house last night. Whether he went there to try and patch things up or he'd already made up his mind he had to kill her, only he can say. But I know how it ended up. And now I know why."

Reba stood up, her fists clenched into tight, sharp-knuckled little balls. "Let's go get the fucker!"

I lifted my hands in a palms-out gesture. "Whoa up, there," I said. "It's not quite that simple. Ninety percent of what I've just outlined is pure conjecture. The strongest part is the neighbor woman's testimony, and even she can't swear beyond a doubt that the car she heard pulling away was Vern's—only that it *sounded* like it. What we need is some kind of proof."

"You and your goddamn *proof* are startin' to chap my ass, Hannibal."

"That's the way the game is played, kid."

"How about we hang Vern Stroud's balls on a barbecue spit and roast 'em 'til he admits to everything we want to know—would that be enough fuckin' proof to suit you?"

"It'd suit me right down to the ground. I'm afraid a judge and jury might have some trouble with it, though. Remember, Junior wants this handled properly. I think a better way would be to break Stroud's alibi for last night; then the rest of it would start to crumble out from under him. But that means somebody's going to have to get to Pearl."

She considered this a long moment. Then: " 'Somebody' meanin' me, right?"

I nodded. "That's what I had in mind when I came to see you. She damn sure won't have anything to do with me. You and her get along okay, don't you?"

"Yeah . . . as long as that fuckhead Vern ain't around."

"That's definitely a prerequisite for this particular conversation with Pearl. I get the impression Stroud isn't the type to sit home evenings watching *The Cosby Show* with his wife and kiddies gathered around him on the couch anyway. Plus he's likely to be edgy. If we're in luck, that means he'll be on the prowl tonight, out doing something to keep his mind busy with other thoughts. And Pearl will be home alone, where you can get to her."

"What should I do—come right out and ask her about last night?"

"You know her a lot better than I do; that places you in a position to better judge how you should handle it. If you put her on her guard before you get a straight answer out of her, though, then she'll probably clam up on you. My inclination would be to try and be clever with it; make small talk, work your way up to it gradually, then drop something casual, like you thought you saw Vern's car go by such-and-such a place at such-and-such a time last night. See what kind of reaction you get."

Reba cocked a single eyebrow. "Are all detectives as sneaky as you?"

"Comes from dealing with sneaky people," I said. I stood up. "Let's go do some of that right now."

23

*D*usk had thickened into darkness by the time I pulled off onto the shoulder of the road a hundred yards down from the entrance to the Shady Willow trailer park. I switched off the Plymouth's engine as Reba putted to a stop alongside me on her motorbike.

Through the open window, I said to her, "Well, this is it, kid."

She looked over at me, her eyes bright and determined in the moonlight.

"Remember," I cautioned, "if Stroud's in there, don't go in. Just roll on by. We'll wait for him to leave or we'll distract him out if we have to. But don't try anything with him there. He's killed twice. He's big, he's mean, he's dangerous."

"I ain't about to do nuthin' dumb," she assured me.

"Another thing," I said. "Don't take Pearl entirely for granted. We're assuming she's an innocent in this, except for her blind loyalty to her husband. We *could* be wrong. She may be as big a toad in the puddle as Stroud. I know you don't want to consider that, but believe me, anything's possible. Which would mean your questions, no matter how cleverly brought up, could trigger some kind of violent reaction from her. So be on your guard."

Reba shook her head stubbornly. "I ain't worried about Pearl. She might be a little slow upstairs, but she wouldn't have nuthin' to do with killin' her mama. I know it. I don't even think she'd cover for Vern if she suspected he had anything to do with killin' that Ainsley woman. Somehow he smooth-talked her, convinced her wherever he went last night was plumb innocent. As far as lyin' to the cops . . . well, that ain't something comes hard to anybody of Odum stock."

"I hope you're right," I said sincerely. "I hope her devotion to Stroud isn't so desperate she can't break free of it. Because if we can make her see the light, if we can get her in our corner, then we'll be able to bring that sonofabitch down for sure."

"We'll bring him down," Reba said grimly. "One way or another."

She went on in then, while I sat and waited. The hardest duty of all.

I lit a cigarette and tried to get comfortable. My mind churned with a thousand thoughts stirred by a thousand questions. Did I really have this thing figured out correctly? Should I have brought Sheriff Wilt in on it? Or Junior? Was there any angle I could be overlooking, failing to take into consideration?

When five minutes had gone by and Reba hadn't returned, it seemed evident she must have found Pearl home alone.

I lit a fresh cigarette from the smoldering stub of the first one. I thought about the threatening messages Flo had received and the phone call Clayton Cord had gotten in the middle of the night, and wondered if Stroud was behind them as well. I decided not; I didn't give him credit for that much imagination. He'd be the type to concentrate everything he had on one plan. Those other incidents were exactly what we had perceived them to be: indications that the deadlock over the Odum land had a *lot* of people on edge.

I watched lightning bugs blink on and off in the high weeds of the ditch that ran beside the road. What the hell do lightning bugs do anyway?

Now and then a mosquito would invade the interior of the Plymouth, its high-pitched whine as irritating and ominous as a miniature dental drill.

I worried at the cuts inside my mouth with the tip of my tongue.

I thought about Courtney and ended up with a surprisingly aggressive hard-on that only made it more difficult to sit comfortably.

At the twenty-minute mark, I flipped my third spent butt out the window, then followed it out and walked around to the rear of the car to take a leak. I hadn't initially driven into the trailer park for fear that, in case Vern was at home, he might spot me and recognize my car. Inasmuch as it now seemed clear he wasn't around, I decided as soon as I finished relieving myself I'd cruise through and look things over at a little closer range. At least it would give me something to do.

I'd just rezipped my fly and was starting back around the end of the car when Vern Stroud's GTO came snarling out of the trailer park drive. It swung onto the road, skidding in a wild turn, shot away with a piercing screech of tires.

My first instinct was to give chase. But then an intervening thought made me wince: what about Reba?

God*damn*it, I'd told her not to go in if Stroud was at home!

I threw myself into the Plymouth, twisted the ignition key, slewed onto the road and went tearing into the trailer park as recklessly as Stroud had departed. Seconds later, I braked to a gravel-flinging halt in front of trailer number twenty-seven. I leaped out and went pounding across the patch of dusty lawn and up the tinny steps with my heart thundering in my throat and my drawn .45 clenched tightly in my fist.

I slapped open the door and they were there on the living room floor. Reba lying face down in a loose, motionless sprawl beside an overturned coffee table; Pearl kneeling nearby with hands cupped to her face, body shuddering with uncontrollable sobs.

Kids wailed hauntingly in one of the other rooms.

Swallowing hard, I reholstered the big automatic, walked slowly over, and knelt next to the two women. The upturned left side of Reba's face was marred by a massive, steadily darkening bruise that covered almost the entire temple and cheekbone area. The flesh of her arm was alarmingly cool to the touch but when my trembling fingertips found her pulse it was good and strong. Her breathing sounded regular. When I gently peeled back her eyelid and the pupil responded to the light, I was able to breathe a sigh of relief. She was out cold, but apparently not too severely concussed.

I turned my attention to Pearl, who continued to blurt wracking sobs into the hands she held clawlike over her face. "Pearl?" I said, placing my own hand on her arm.

She recoiled violently from my touch and tipped back against the edge of the couch, her sobs intensifying.

When I said her name a second time, I said it much more sharply. "Pearl!" I gripped her by her shoulders and gave a gentle but insistent shake. "You've got to pull yourself together," I said. "I need to know what happened here."

The sobs continued. I finally had to resort to pulling her hands down and away. Her face was blotchy red, her eyes wild and frightened and tear-streaked. A smeary mixture of snot and tears dripped from her nose and chin.

"What happened here?" I said again.

She managed to get some words out between the hiccuppy, short gasps that were starting to replace the sobs. "He . . . he . . . killed my mama," she groaned.

"Who? Vern?" I demanded, wanting to be sure.

"Y-yes . . . He admitted everything . . . Said he held a pillow over her face, then . . . then . . . then dropped a lit cig-cigarette on her blankets . . . and b-burned her up . . . like . . . like a stubborn old sow in a roaster oven, he said!" She went into a long, keening moan.

I shook her again to bring her out of it. "When did he tell you all this?" I wanted to know.

"Af-after he fought with Reba . . . after he . . . after he came rantin' out of the bedroom when he heard her talkin' to me . . . askin' me things . . . She swore at him and accused him of stuff . . . and . . . and he hit her an awful lick!"

I would later learn that Stroud had been doing some mechanical work on his car that afternoon and had left it parked in an empty lot a few trailers down, a spot he frequently used because it offered more room to work with jacks and ramps and so forth. When Reba arrived, he had been taking a nap in the back bedroom before going out for the evening. All of which explained why Reba had assumed he was not at home and had gone in and begun the routine with Pearl.

As I said, these were details that would eventually come out. At the moment, however, there were hotter questions burning inside me. "Where did he go?" I wanted to know. "Where is Vern running to?"

Pearl clutched my arm, her nails biting into me so fiercely they nearly drew blood through my jacket and shirt-sleeves. "No!" she hissed. "No, you can't go after him!"

"Why the hell not?"

"He took one of the kids—my little Tabitha. . . . Said if anybody came after him, he . . . he'd kill her, too! . . . Said if he gets away clean, then he'll send word where to pick her up safe and sound."

The shrieks of the children in the other room suddenly seemed like a disembodied cry for the abducted girl.

I shook my head. "You can't trust him, Pearl. He's already killed twice. Vern is sick. He's crazy and he's desperate."

"But my baby—"

"Her best chance is for someone to rescue her from him—save her and capture Vern. He needs to be punished for the things he's done, to be put away so he can't do them to anyone else."

Pearl began trembling, threatening to slip back into uncontrolled sobs. "My baby . . . my mama . . ."

I gripped her roughly by the shoulders again, fighting an urge to slap her. "Goddammit, Pearl, don't fold on me," I growled. "Think! You must have some idea where he's headed, where he'd take the child."

I felt her tense against my rough handling. It was enough to snap her out of her slide into self-pity, at least for the moment.

"Think, Pearl," I implored, softer now.

She held her eyes shut hard and fought to get her breathing leveled off. The veins and muscles in her throat stood out like cables on smooth sand. After several beats, without opening her eyes, in a tight, barely controlled voice, she said, "He . . . Vern has kinfolk down in Arkansas."

"Arkansas," I repeated, prodding gently. "You think he might be headed there?"

"Only he ain't got hardly no money . . . leastways not enough to get that far. He was supposed to run a load of 'shine over to Saint Louie for somebody later on tonight. I don't see nuthin' for him but to stick around long enough to do that . . . in order to get paid so's he has somethin' to light out on."

"Where and when was he supposed to pick up this load of moonshine?"

She choked out a single sob. "I don't know. Honest I don't. . . . He usually does his moon runnin' after midnight, but he hauls for a half-dozen different blockaders back in those hills. . . . I ain't got no idea where he'd be makin' the pickup tonight."

Shit! So near and yet so far.

I racked my brain to try and come up with something further I could say or do to coax more out of her. Unfortunately, I was convinced she had nothing more to give. How else, then, to get a line on the run of illegal whiskey that was scheduled to go down? I considered Gus Wilt. Junior Odum had said the sheriff didn't pay much attention to moonshining activities in the area, but that didn't mean he didn't have sources he could call upon in case he *did* decide he wanted to get on their trail. But bringing Wilt into it would mean having to hand everything—including control of how it got handled the rest of the way—over to him. And that, in turn, would almost certainly mean calling out some deputies, possibly some state troopers, possibly even more feds if there were any handy. Cops like to work in packs. No, I told myself. No good; not in this case. That would be too many fingers in the pie—too many bodies in motion, all zeroing in on Vern Stroud, each one representing an added risk of somehow showing our hand, spooking him prematurely and causing tragedy for little Tabitha. No, my gut feeling was that this was something best handled by one man, maybe two . . .

A wild notion seized me and all of a sudden I had an idea how I might be able to get a handle on where Stroud was going to make his pickup. It was a long shot. It was so long it was crazy. Hell, it was fucking insane. But I'd been tainted by a kind of craziness ever since getting caught up in this mess. Why should it stop me now?

24

I found the spot where we'd left the car, and then I found the gully.

It felt right, the eerieness, the sounds and smells, the snagging underbrush and the rugged footing. I plunged into it and tonight these elements seemed welcome things, even though, in my haste, I managed to stumble and fall twice before I'd gone five hundred yards. I forced myself to slow down, fighting to hold back the adrenaline rush that fueled me. I worked my breathing and my footfalls into a kind of rhythm, then switched my forward momentum onto auto pilot and let my mind whirl down various other paths.

Don't get lost, don't fall and break your leg, don't fuck this up, I told myself. Somewhere out there is a frightened little girl—maybe in darkness even blacker, even more all-consuming than this—who is dependent on you to get her out. After all, in a roundabout way you're the one who put her there.

And there's another girl—a near-woman, actually—in another kind of darkness, the blackness of unconsciousness. You damn sure played a part in putting *her* there. Do you think the paramedics you phoned for have arrived yet? What if they find her head injuries to be more serious than you figured? What the hell did you send her into, man?

And there's yet another out there somewhere—one you *want* to thrust into darkness, into the permanent blackness of death. You wish he were between your hands right now, don't you? But what of Junior Odum's wishes, of his desire to see "the right thing" done? What *is* the right thing when it comes to a cold-blooded bastard like Stroud?

My meandering thoughts crashed suddenly to earth along with the rest of me as I stumbled and fell for a third time. The impact was great enough and I was exhausted enough so that I played it for all it was worth and just lay there for a time, catching my breath.

How far had I come anyway? Had Reba and I traveled this far last night? It hadn't seemed like it. At the very least I ought to be smelling the smoke or the animals by now. Jesus, *had* I somehow gotten myself lost?

When I looked up, Treefoot Mary was standing there.

She had appeared as soundlessly as one of the intermittent shafts of moonlight that sprayed down through the trees, streaking the darkness. She loomed over me now in continuing ghostly silence, her face an unreadable grayish blur, her eyes black and glistening, like two shiny buttons.

I swatted a mosquito away from my face and stood up. She still loomed over me. "You probably don't hear this very often," I said, craning my neck to peer up at her, "but am I ever glad to see you."

Junior Odum, his expression taut and grim, heard me out without comment. We sat in Treefoot Mary's cave, hunched over mugs of strong black coffee, with firelight flickering across our faces and curls of smoke and an occasional spark drifting through the air around us. The old woman had led me here with wordless gestures, then had evaporated like one of the wisps of smoke, leaving the two of us alone to talk.

"So that's the long and the short of it," I summed up. "I pinned down our killer, but then I let him slip away. What's worse, I let him injure Reba and take the little girl hostage in the bargain."

Junior shook his head. "You didn't *let* him do nuthin', hoss. It's greed and desperation pullin' Vern's strings, and they can yank a man in ways nobody can be ready for. What galls me is that I had the fucker right under my nose the whole damn time and I never once gave him a thought."

"What's done is done," I said. "Where we're at now is him getting ready to make a break for it and us running out of time if we're going to try and stop him. You're the one who bought my ticket to this dance, so I'm willing to let you call the tune. Top priority has to be that no harm befalls the child. After that comes consideration for your desire to see your mother's killer brought to proper justice. The two may not be compatible. If we go in after her, the only way to guarantee Tabitha's safety might be to take Stroud out cold. Do you understand what I'm saying?"

Junior's mouth was a hard, tight line, his eyes narrow and far away. "I understand," he bit out through clenched teeth. "But it really ain't no contest, is it? We got to go after the girl, that's all there is. And whatever we got to do to keep her safe . . . well, how can that *not* be the proper thing?"

I nodded. "I was hoping you'd feel that way. Now—last but not least—there's still the problem of determining where Vern is going to make his pickup."

The narrowed eyes shifted, regarded me. "I think I already know what you got in mind along those lines. Mary, right?"

I made a gesture with one hand. "You're the one who told me she has a way of . . . knowing things. Things that are going on back in these woods."

"You kinda scoffed at the notion as I recall."

"Yeah, well I'm not scoffing now, all right? I need that handle, Junior. Bad. I don't care if it comes from voodoo or Hindu or doggie-doo. Just get it for me."

He stood up. "She's out tendin' the animals. Wait here."

I don't know exactly what transpired between the two of them. I don't think I care to; I must not, because I never asked. There are any number of perfectly logical explanations for how the strange old woman could have known where Stroud would be taking on his load. Then there are the other possibilities. Believe what you want. All I know is that Junior was back in less than a minute, his eyes wide now, alive, burning. From the mouth of the cave, he said, "Okay, let's do it."

25

*T*he place had once been a small farm, but all that remained now were a few ragged sections of foundation wall, a pile of brick rubble and splintered lumber, and the silo—a domeless, weather-scarred old concrete cylinder standing tall and proud in its role of sole survivor. It lay at the end of a long, winding, weed-choked lane, in the center of a shallow depression between two gradually sloping ridges.

Junior Odum and I crouched in dense underbrush about a third of the way down from the crest of one of the ridges. We'd left the Plymouth concealed in a grove of fruit trees some distance back, on down the far side of the ridge and across a broad cornfield, just off a section of nameless gravel road.

"The still's inside the silo," Junior was explaining in a cautious whisper. "They must have a water line runnin' down from somewhere up on that north hogback. Looks like a good setup, one that's probably been used before. A good blockader'll do that—move his still around. When enough time has passed, then he'll go on back to a spot and work it again."

I shifted my weight, rubbing at the knot of muscles in my right thigh that kept threatening to cramp on me. I wished I could light up a cigarette.

"The fat one standin' talkin' to Vern," Junior went on, pointing out some of the players in the scene that was unfolding below, "that's Cotton Mayfair, probably the biggest blockader left in these parts. The tall, stringy one just now turnin' around there, that's his half-wit son Lester. I don't know who the nigger fella is."

The moon-bathed activity taking place down in the former barnyard was indeed centered around the silo. Vern Stroud's GTO was parked about thirty feet from the structure, trunk lid raised high, like a hungrily gaping mouth. Stroud and a round-bellied, bib-overall-clad man stood beside it, jawing, making occasional hand gestures. Stringbean Lester and the husky, anonymous black were trudging back and forth between the silo and the car, carrying plastic gallon milk jugs filled (presumably) with moonshine from the former and loading them into the latter. A rusting, battered old pickup truck sat off to one side with a pair of spotted hounds tied to its back bumper. And in the front seat of the Pontiac, if you looked real close just above the bottom sill of the passenger side window, you could see a cap of thick blond curls. Every now and then, as the men deposited their loads, she'd raise up a little in the seat, turning to look back at them, and you'd catch a glimpse of wide, frightened eyes.

"So there's the whole ball of wax," Junior said. "Including Vern and little Tabitha, the two things we came for. Now what? What's our plan?"

"Distraction," I told him. "We need to get Stroud and the others away from that cart so we can snatch out the girl. Once she's in the clear, we can try for Stroud."

"Sounds reasonable," he agreed.

"How much trouble can we expect out of Mayfair and his boys?"

"Not much, I wouldn't think. Blockaders are funny that way; they'll go to every kind of bother you can think of to hide their stills and so on and so forth, but once they're nabbed they hardly ever put up a squawk. I guess they just sorta accept it as part of the game. And if things start comin' down here tonight, that's what they're gonna figure —that we're some kind of law hittin' the still."

"Any chance they could know about the trouble Vern's in?"

"No way. Cotton Mayfair's a real upright fella, a family man and a churchgoer. He just don't see nuthin' wrong in brewin' his own whiskey is all. But if he had any idea what Vern's up to, I can guarantee he wouldn't be havin' no truck with him."

"How about Stroud himself? He likely to be armed?"

"Not normally, no. Fella'd have to be a plumb fool to carry a gun on a moon run. In case you did get nabbed, that could be a bigger charge against you than the whiskey. But Vern knows how to handle a gun, I've hunted with him. And this here tonight ain't exactly a normal run. All things considered, I'd say yeah, we'd best figure on him bein' armed."

"Swell," I muttered.

I rubbed at my leg, trying to work out the kink, while I mentally worked the kinks out of a hastily formed strategy for our two-man raiding party. "Okay," I said at length, "here's how we'll work it. See where that chunk of foundation juts out down there, comes within ten or twelve feet of Stroud's car? Think you can work you way down and along and get close without being spotted?"

"Betcher ass," Junior replied.

"All right. You get in position there then. I'll come in from the other side, over by the pickup. I'll do something—I don't know what yet—to cause a commotion. If I succeed in drawing Stroud away from the car, you get the girl the hell out of there."

"Got it. Then what?"

"How the fuck do I know? Then we start making it up as it goes."

"Good plan. I never did like havin' no leeway in a thing."

My objective was a fat clump of bushes growing stubbornly in and around a rock pile about a dozen yards from where the old truck sat. Picking my way unseen and unheard down the slope, however, took longer than I'd anticipated. I began to fear the car would be loaded and gone before I got into position. I was dripping sweat—as much from apprehension as exertion—when I finally slipped in behind a leafy branch and settled one knee onto a securely lodged stone.

Sleeving away perspiration, I scanned the situation from my new vantage point. Lester and the black were still lugging jugs of 'shine. Stroud and Cotton Mayfair were still jawing. The dogs at the rear of the truck appeared to be asleep, heads resting on forepaws, folds of skin dripping down over their closed eyes, ears splayed out like airplane wings. I couldn't see hide nor hair of Tabitha from this angle and only a sliver of the foundation wall where Junior should be. I had to assume he was in place; his route had been shorter and more direct than mine.

I continued studying the scene. My move. A commotion. A distraction. I considered skirting around and getting into the silo, doing some damage there, making some noise. But I quickly discarded that idea. For one thing, I'd be leaving myself trapped. For another, while I didn't know a hell of a lot about stills, I did know there was heat and steam and pressure involved somewhere along the line; I might upset the wrong thing and blow my fool head off.

What, then?

My gaze returned to the two spotted hounds. Barking dogs, agitated dogs—who doesn't grow curious when a dog starts carrying on about something? Yeah, that was it. Stir the dogs up and the men were bound to come over and see what was going on.

I grabbed a double handful of the bush and shook it. The leaves rattled nicely but the dogs paid no attention. I shook harder. The beasts went on snoring.

I pursed my lips together and made smacking noises, continuing to shake the bush. Still no response. I had a couple of either very weary or very stupid canines here.

I scraped up a handful of pebbles and tossed them in the air, letting them rain down on the larger rocks of the pile. It sounded like corn popping. Only nobody but me showed the slightest interest—not the dogs, not the men over by the silo. Jesus Christ, and here I'd been so cautious working my way down that slope; judging by this, I could have driven down in my fucking Plymouth without attracting any attention.

Swearing under my breath, I stood up and heaved a damned rock straight at the two mutts. It kicked dust about an inch from one's nose and finally—finally—got a reaction. The hound raised his head, looked sleepily about, spread his jaws in a huge, slobberingly long yawn. Completing that, he looked sleepily around some more—never once focusing on my bush, I might add—then abruptly hiked his hind leg, stretched his neck down, and began licking his balls. He went about this so energetically that he succeeded in rousing the second animal.

I rattled my bush anew and made more smacking noises and at last got the desired results. The second dog emitted a series of guttural barks and lunged in my direction, its leash pulling taut from underneath the hound involved in self-gratification, sending him rolling and yipping in surprise. In a matter of seconds they were more or less untangled from each other and both straining at the ends of their chains, barking and slavering and pawing dirt in the direction of my hiding place.

I eased the .45 out of the shoulder rig and turned my attention to the men. Come to papa.

All four were craning their necks to see what was wrong with the dogs. Stroud and Mayfair had stopped talking, Lester and the black had paused in their tracks on a return trip to the silo. I rattled the bush a little more and added to the animals' frenzy.

I heard Cotton Mayfair call out to his son, something in regard to "what in tarnation's ailin' those fool dogs."

Why don't you come find out for yourself, lard-ass? I thought. Bring a friend.

The dogs continued to bark and bay and carry on very satisfactorily. They'd been a little slow on the uptake, but now seemed to be caught in the spirit of the thing and really rolling with it.

Lester and the black moved tentatively toward the pickup, eyes sweeping ahead, scanning the general area (including my bush) where the dogs seemed to be pointing. Both men had worked up a sweat with their work and the perspiration sheen on the black's face and bare shoulders, in the moonlight, reflecting silver-blue in contrast to his dark skin, created a St. Elmo's Fire-like effect.

Cotton Mayfair watched the progress of his men. As they drew abreast of the pickup, his curiosity finally got the better of him and he began to drift in our direction as well. Vern Stroud made a gesture with his hands, said something I couldn't hear, then slammed his fists frustratedly onto his hips as Mayfair kept moving away from him. It was obvious Stroud wanted to finish getting loaded so he could get out of there. It was just as obvious he was going to have to wait awhile. Unless he did the loading himself.

Which, somewhat surprisingly, is exactly what he started to do. Making a castaway at Mayfair's receding back—as if to say "Who needs you anyway"—he turned and started purposefully toward the silo.

I felt my pulse quicken and my grip tighten on the .45. This should be it.

Right on cue, Junior Odum skimmed over the foundation wall and covered the distance to the Pontiac in long, silent strides. In a matter of seconds he had Tabitha swept up in his arms and the two of them were disappearing back behind the crumbling concrete. Beautiful. Rambo couldn't have pulled it off any slicker, and he would have needed air support and a couple bazookas.

Now the ball was back in my court. Lester had the passengerside door of the old truck open and was rummaging around inside. Above the din of the hounds, I'd caught the word "flashlight" tossed back and forth between him and the black. I couldn't see much percentage in waiting until they had a beam of light to blind me with.

I stood up and stepped out from my concealment. I had the .45 leveled in my right hand and in my left, held high, I had my wallet, flipped open to my P.I. ticket. "Hold it right there," I said in a strong, bold voice. "My name's Eliot Ness and you're all under arrest for violation of the Volstead Act."

Lester jerked back out of the truck cab and straightened up so fast he banged his head on the top ledge of the door. The black obligingly raised his hands. Lester, wincing in pain, raised only one of his; the other he used to rub his bashed noggin. Cotton Mayfair had come to a halt and stood frowning without raising either of his. We all stood glaring at each other.

"You, Fatty," I said, waggling my gun at Mayfair, "get your hands up and get over here with the others."

He did as he was told, but the frown turned into a scowl. "There must be some mistake, Officer Ness," he protested. "We don't know nuthin' about no Bumstead Act. We're just some good ol' boys runnin' a little 'shine. Why—"

That's when Stroud came out of the silo. He spotted me immediately, dropped the jugs of moonshine he was carrying, whipped a revolver from his waistband without hesitation and began banging away. Bullets sparked off the rocks in the pile, slashed through the leaves at my elbow. I went into a diving roll, vaguely aware of Mayfair and his boys scattering and of the dog cacophony increasing in volume.

I rolled to a stop on my belly, back arched, arm extended, .45 raised. I fired blindly toward the silo, striking some sparks of my own.

But Stroud was no longer there. He was making for the GTO at a dead run. I swung my gun barrel to the right and squeezed off two more quick ones. I heard both slugs punch into the open trunk.

Stroud entered the car via a Dukes of Hazzard dive through the open window. An instant later, the engine roared to life and the Goat leaped away in a spray of dust and shredded grass, trunk lid whapping up and down like mocking applause.

On my feet, running, I snapped off two more hurried rounds. I skidded into a crouch and would have fired again —taking more careful aim, trying for the tires—if Junior hadn't picked that moment to vault over the foundation wall and make a run at the fleeing car as it tore by him. He got his head and arms through the passenger side window and hung on, one foot kicking the air, the other dragging in the dirt. I gritted my teeth, expecting any second to hear the report of Stroud's revolver and see Junior's head fly back in a spray of blood. But before it could come to that, he simply lost his grip and fell away tumbling.

I straightened up, paused long enough to make sure he was clambering to his feet okay, then turned and ran back toward the old truck.

"Keys!" I demanded of Cotton Mayfair, wagging the .45 at him once more.

He sat on the grass in pasty-faced befuddlement. Raising a trembling finger, he pointed. "Th-they're in it."

I sprinted past him. The black guy was peeking around

the edge of the tailgate as I yanked open the door and threw a leg into the cab. "Better loose your dogs," I called to him, "unless you want them dragged to hell and gone."

I heard the rattle of chains being unsnapped as I twisted the key in the ignition. By the time the engine caught, I could see, in the rearview mirror, the black and Lester each leading away one of the still-barking hounds.

With much gnashing of gear teeth, I finally rammed the floor shift into a slot that produced a lurching forward motion. The motor revved with an ungodly clamor of rods and lifters. I fought the wheel until I got the tank swung around and aimed in the direction Stroud had sped. I had about as much chance of catching his souped-up mill with this bucket of bolts as I did of sticking a feather in my ear and flying to the moon. But I was damned if I was going to just stand by and let him run without at least making an effort.

I found the headlight switch and snapped on twin yellow-ish beams that poked feebly through the clouds of dust hanging in the air from the GTO's ground-chewing departure. There was a sudden thump and I felt the cab tip as Junior landed on the running board. A moment later, he'd wrestled open the passenger door and was sliding into the seat beside me.

"You ought to try boarding a vehicle sometime when it isn't already moving," I suggested wryly.

"Tell me about it," he grunted. "I'm gettin' too old for this shit."

I ground the shift lever into the next gear and we bounced on in pursuit. Above the howl of the engine, I called, "What about the girl?"

"I told her to stick close to Cotton," he answered. "Like I said before, Cotton ain't' a bad ol' boy. Besides, he got a good look at me—he knows better than to let any harm come to a niece of mine."

We were into the lane now—the twisting, deeply-rutted, weed-clogged and tree-crowded avenue that eventually wound its way out to the county truck. If Stroud beat us there, we didn't have a prayer of catching him. Our only chance was if he spun out on a turn or busted an axle or suffered some similar form of bad luck.

A couple times I had to hit the brakes because the dust got so thick I couldn't see. That involved downshifting and then trying to coax the ancient truck back up to speed, no easy task considering the luck I was having hitting the gears and the crate's overall lack of pep to begin with.

"Cumbersome piece of shit!" I swore, pounding the steering wheel after one such episode.

"Could be worse," Junior observed offhandedly. "We could be tryin' to catch him in that rust-bucket Plymouth of yours."

I shot him a dirty look as I missed yet another gear. When I got it on the next try, I popped the clutch and jerked him back in his seat.

I lost all perception of how far we'd gone. The choking dust and the limited visibility created a kind of combination vertigo/claustrophobia. More than once I fought a panicky urge to stand on the brakes and just say fuck it to this futile, blind chase.

From somewhere not far ahead came a dull, booming sound. Then another. A moment later, in a brief gap between dust clouds, we spotted a horizon's-edge slice of the night sky starting to fill with a bright glow. Seconds after that, there came a third boom—this one a jarringly loud blast.

Junior and I exchanged uncertain frowns. I slowed the truck to crawl.

The dust began thinning.

Seconds and minutes dragged into what seemed like hours as we continued to roll cautiously forward. At last, just ahead, I saw where the lane sloped sharply upward and came to an end, T-ing onto the county blacktop.

And then I saw the rest of it.

Reba Dallas stood up in the middle of the county road, feet planted shoulders' width apart, arms hanging at her sides, smoking shotgun gripped loosely in her hands. The side of her face and head was swathed in bandages.

Fifty feet in front of her—to her left, our right—off the edge of where the lane began its incline, wedged against the side of a massive corrugated steel culvert that cut under the road, the twisted wreckage of Vern Stroud's Pontiac burned with brilliant fury. Blue alcohol flames mingled with yellow and gold tongues of blazing rubber and upholstery. A thick column of black smoke was pouring into the sky, smudging the stars.

I brought the truck to a halt and cut the engine. Junior got out and ran up the slope toward his cousin. I followed, but more slowly, trying to piece together in my mind what had happened here. It wasn't that hard, really. The gutsy little shit must have been waiting at the end of the lane, and when Stroud came at her she had pumped shotgun blasts into him (the first dull booms we'd heard), causing him to veer off and strike the culvert. A spark had ignited either the gas tank or the moonshine and the rest, as they say, was history.

I made my way up the slope, buffeted by the intense heat of the seething, sizzling, hissing inferno, the odor of charred meat assailing my nostrils. The burning season, I thought grimly; what sad yet satisfying irony that after what he'd done to Flo Odum, Stroud should meet his own end like this.

EPILOGUE

*D*isplaying typical pluck and stubbornness, Reba Dallas had refused to be taken to the hospital by the rescue squad I'd had sent to the trailer. Instead, after they'd patched her up and fed her some painkillers, she'd sent them packing and then made Pearl tell her everything she told me. Inasmuch as Cotton Mayfair had been in Handee's that afternoon talking freely about the latest batch of 'shine he was getting ready to ship, she had known immediately where Stroud would be making his pickup. Armed with angry resolve and with the same ancient twelve gauge she'd held on me that first night in the cemetery, she had ridden out on her motorbike to participate in bringing down the man responsible for her aunt's murder. Luckily—and again displaying typical pluck—she had chosen to come in the front rather than skulk around a back way, as Junior and I had done. She'd arrived just in time to hear the shooting and the distinctive sound of Stroud's GTO winding out and had correctly guessed that he was getting away from us. So she stood her ground at the mouth of the lane and from there it had gone down pretty much as I'd calculated.

Afterward, up on the road, wrapped in Junior's embrace, she'd had a terrifying moment. "Tabitha!" she suddenly shrieked, jerking away, looking wildly about, apparently realizing for the first time that the child might still have been with Stroud.

Junior and I were both quick to assure her that all was well in that department, that the girl was safe. And then Reba had wept. I never asked, but I was willing to bet you could count on one hand the number of times she'd shed tears before in her life.

In a little while, she asked sniffingly of Junior: "Are you mad at me?"

He held her at arms' length and frowned deeply. "Good God amighty, girl, why would I be mad at you?"

"Well, you been sayin' how you wanted Aunt Flo's killer to stand trial and all. . . . I know how much that meant to you . . . and now . . . I . . . well, because of me it didn't end up that way nohow. . . . He kept on comin', and I started shootin'. . . . I was tryin' for his radiator or his tires, just to stop him . . . but then the car . . . it . . . it . . . he . . ."

Junior shook his head soothingly. "It ended up the way it was supposed to end up. Don't ever think I'm mad at you, little darlin' . . . No, what I am is just plumb bustin' proud!"

They'd embraced again and this time Junior wept, too.

It took a day and a half of answering questions and giving statements and then answering more questions and giving more statements and, just for variety, giving statements and then answering questions, before Gus Wilt decided I was free to return to Rockford and to take my prisoner with me.

In the interim, I at least got caught up on my sleep and I had the opportunity to say good-bye to Courtney. We said the usual crap about don't forget how to dial a phone and be sure to stop in if you're ever in the area and so on and so forth, but we both knew even while we were saying it that neither of us were likely to ever do so.

When it was time to go, I paused on my walk to the car, turned back and said, "One last thing."

"What's that?"

"If you ever get around to doing a sculpture from those pictures you took . . . be sure to put a really big bulge in the shorts, you hear?"

She smiled smugly from where she stood leaning in the doorway of her studio, and replied, "That shouldn't be any problem . . . I've been putting a big bulge in your shorts ever since you laid eyes on me, cowboy."

Five hundred feet across the Hatchaloo County line, I pulled off onto the shoulder of the road.

"What's the matter?" Junior Odum wanted to know.

"Get out," I told him, switching off the ignition key.

We quit the Plymouth. We stood on the edge of a broad, rolling pasture fenced by a thin electrified wire. There were some cattle grazing in the distance, but no buildings in sight and no sign of any other cars on the road. The sky was cloudless and as blue as a jazz trumpeter's longest, lowest note.

Motioning for my prisoner to follow me, I walked over, stooped, slipped under the wire, and stepped into the pasture. Junior hesitated, frowning, then came after me.

When we were both standing inside the fence, I hauled off and belted him right on the point of the chin. He fell down, rolled over once.

After a little bit, he propped himself up on his right elbow. Cupping his chin with his left hand, he said, "What the fuck was that for?"

"That," I said, pointing a finger at him, "is for being such a likable sonofabitch."

He continued rubbing his chin and looked doubtful. "Well, I'm gettin' real fond of you, too, hoss. But I can think of a hell of a lot better ways of showin' it."

"The way I see it," I told him, "I didn't hold up my end

of the bargain. The deal was, I was supposed to turn your mother's murderer over to the law and see that proper justice was meted out. Well, it didn't go down that way."

"So what are you sayin'?"

"I'm saying look around you, you dumb ass. This isn't Hatchaloo County and it isn't Rockford. You aren't a wanted man here." I stopped. "Are you?"

He shook his head. "Not that I know of."

"All right then. Don't you think it's about time you grew up? Started playing by the rules for a change? Get an honest job . . . maybe a woman . . . settle down somewhere and raise some kids and tell them about that special grandmother they'll never know otherwise. Start leading the kind of life that doesn't have ornery bloodhounds like me stomping through it. Does that sound like too much of a stinking chore?"

"What it sounds like is an order."

"Maybe it is."

"Sounds like a pretty tall one."

"There's an even taller judge sitting on a bench up in Rockford waiting for somebody to haul your sorry ass in front of him."

"He don't scare me. I've danced to his kind of music before. But that other, the stuff you're talkin' about . . . *that's* scary."

"You tried to jump into a speeding car with an armed killer behind the wheel—you telling me you're gutless?"

"I'm tellin' you I'm goin' back to Rockford. With or without you. I got unfinished business there. Until I take care of that, what gives me any right to even *think* about the other?"

I looked down at him. "You once told me you didn't think you could handle another hitch in the joint."

He clenched and unclenched his jaw muscles several times before answering. "I figure I can handle that," he said, squinting up at me, "better'n you can handle livin' with yourself if you don't take me back the way you're supposed to."

Neither of us said anything for a long time.

After a while, I reached my hand out to him.

FREE FROM DELL

with purchase plus postage and handling

Congratulations! You have just purchased one or more
titles featured in Dell's Mystery 1990 Promotion. Our goal
is to provide you with quality reading and entertainment, so
we are pleased to extend to you a limited offer to receive a
selected Dell mystery title(s) *free* (plus $1.00 postage and
handling per title) for each mystery title purchased. Please
read and follow all instructions carefully to avoid delays in
your order.

1) Fill in your name and address on the coupon printed below. No facsimiles or
copies of the coupon allowed.

2) The Dell Mystery books are the only books featured in Dell's Mystery 1990
Promotion. No other Dell titles are eligible for this offer.

3) Enclose your original cash register receipt with the price of the book(s)
circled plus **$1.00 per book** for postage and handling, payable in check or
money order to: Dell Mystery 1990 Offer. Please do not send cash in the
mail.
Canadian customers: Enclose your original cash register receipt with the
price of the book(s) circled plus $1.00 **per book** for postage and handling in
U.S. funds.

4) This offer is only in effect until April 29, 1991. Free Dell Mystery requests
postmarked after April 22, 1991 will not be honored, but your check for
postage and handling will be returned.

5) Please allow 6-8 weeks for processing. Void where taxed or prohibited.

Mail to: Dell Mystery 1990 Offer
 P.O. Box 2081
 Young America, MN 55399-2081

NAME_____

ADDRESS_____

CITY_____STATE_____ZIP_____

BOOKS PURCHASED AT_____

AGE_____

(Continued)

Book(s) purchased:_____

_____

_____

I understand I may choose one free book for each Dell Mystery book purchased (plus applicable postage and handling). Please send me the following:

(Write the number of copies of each title selected next to that title.)

☐ **BLOOD SHOT**
Sara Paretsky
V.I. Warshawski is back—this time a missing person assignment turns into a murder investigation that puts her more than knee-deep in a deadly mixture of big business corruption and chemical waste.

☐ **FIRE LAKE**
Jonathan Valin
In this Harry Stoner mystery, the Cincinnati private eye enters the seamy and dangerous world of drugs when a figure from his past involves him in a plot that forces him to come to terms with himself.

☐ **THE HIT MAN COMETH**
Robert J. Ray
When a professional hit man who has his sights set on a TV evangelist wounds Detective Branko's partner instead, Newport Beach's hottest detective finds himself with a list of suspects that is as bizarre as it is long.

☐ **THE NANTUCKET DIET MURDERS**
Virginia Rich
A handsome new diet doctor has won over Nantucket's richest widows with his weight-loss secrets—and very personal attention. But when murder becomes part of the menu, Mrs. Potter stirs the pot to come up with a clever culinary killer.

☐ **A NOVENA FOR MURDER**
Sister Carol Anne O'Marie
"Move over, Miss Marple, here comes supersleuth Sister Mary Helen, a nun with an unusual habit of solving murders."
—San Francisco Sunday Examiner & Chronicle

☐ **SHATTERED MOON**
Kate Green
When a young woman gets involved with the L.A.P.D. and a missing person case, her most precious gift—her healing vision—becomes her most dangerous enemy, filling every moment with mounting menace. . . and turning the secrets of her past murderously against her.

☐ **TOO CLOSE TO THE EDGE**
Susan Dunlap
Jill Smith, a street-smart, savvy detective, finds herself trapped within a murder victim's intricate network of perilous connections.

☐ **A NICE CLASS OF CORPSE**
Simon Brett
When the sixty-seven-year-old Mrs. Pargeter checks into a seaside hotel for some peace and quiet, what she finds instead is a corpse in the lobby and a murder to snoop into on the dark side of the upper crust.

☐ **POLITICAL SUICIDE**
Robert Barnard
A member of Parliament meets an untimely—and suspicious—demise.

☐ **THE OLD FOX DECEIV'D**
Martha Grimes
When the body of a mysterious woman is found murdered, Inspector Richard Jury of Scotland Yard finds himself tracking a very foxy killer.

☐ **DEATH OF A PERFECT MOTHER**
Robert Barnard
Everyone had a motive to kill her. . . so Chief Inspector Dominic McHale finds himself stumped on his very first homicide case—puzzled by a lengthy list of suspects and a very clever killer.

☐ **THE DIRTY DUCK**
Martha Grimes
In addition to the murders being staged nightly at the Royal Shakespeare Theatre, a real one has been committed not too far away, and the killer has left a fragment of Elizabethan verse behind as a clue.

TOTAL NUMBER OF FREE BOOKS SELECTED ____ X $1.00
= $_____ (Amount Enclosed)

Dell has other great books in print by these authors. If you enjoy them, check your local book outlets for other titles.